EX L

VINTAGE **CLASSICS**

THE GENTLEMAN IN THE PARLOUR

William Somerset Maugham was born in 1874 and lived in Paris until he was ten. He was educated at King's School, Canterbury, and at Heidelberg University. He spent some time at St. Thomas' Hospital with the idea of practising medicine, but the success of his first novel, *Liza of Lambeth*, published in 1897, won him over to letters. *Of Human Bondage*, the first of his masterpieces, came out in 1915, and with the publication in 1919 of *The Moon and Sixpence* his reputation as a novelist was established. At the same time his fame as a successful playwright and short story writer was being consolidated with acclaimed productions of various plays and the publication of *The Trembling of a Leaf*, subtitled *Little Stories of the South Sea Islands*, in 1921, which was followed by seven more collections. His other works include travel books, essays, criticism and the autobiographical *The Summing Up* and *A Writer's Notebook*.

In 1927 Somerset Maugham settled in the South of France and lived there until his death in 1965.

OTHER WORKS BY W. SOMERSET MAUGHAM

Novels

The Moon and Sixpence
Of Human Bondage
The Narrow Corner
The Razor's Edge
Cakes and Ale
The Merry-Go-Round
The Painted Veil
Catalina
Up at the Villa
Mrs Craddock
The Casuarina Tree
Christmas Holiday
Liza of Lambeth
The Magician
Theatre
Then and Now

Collected Short Stories

Collected Short Stories Vol. 1
Collected Short Stories Vol. 2
Collected Short Stories Vol. 3
Collected Short Stories Vol. 4
Ashenden
Short Stories
Far Eastern Tales
More Far Eastern Tales

Travel Writing

On a Chinese Screen
Don Fernando

Literary Criticism

Ten Novels and their Authors
Points of View
The Vagrant Mood

Autobiography

The Summing Up
A Writer's Notebook

W. SOMERSET MAUGHAM

The Gentleman in the Parlour

WITH AN INTRODUCTION BY
Paul Theroux

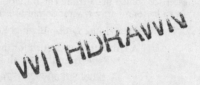

VINTAGE BOOKS
London

Published by Vintage 2001

15

Copyright © the Royal Literary Fund

W. Somerset Maugham has asserted his right under the Copyright,
Designs and Patents Act 1988 to be identified as the author of this work

First published in Great Britain by William Heinemann in 1930

Vintage
Random House, 20 Vauxhall Bridge Road,
London SW1V 2SA

www.vintage-classics.info

Addresses for companies within The Random House Group Limited
can be found at: www.randomhouse.co.uk/offices.htm

The Random House Group Limited Reg. No. 954009

A CIP catalogue record for this book
is available from the British Library

ISBN 9780099286776

Penguin Random House is committed to a sustainable future for
our business, our readers and our planet. This book is made from
Forest Stewardship Council® certified paper.

Printed and bound in Great Britain by Clays Ltd, Elcograf S.p.A.

Introduction

In 1922, when William Somerset Maugham was hugely successful as a playwright, short story writer and novelist, and even something of a socialite, he dropped off the map to take the long and occasionally rigorous journey recorded in this book. He had gone by ship from Britain to Ceylon where he met a man who told him of the joys of Keng Tung in the Shan States of remote northeastern Burma. This provoked him to travel via Rangoon to Mandalay, where he embarked by mule for this supposedly enchanted place. Twenty-six days later he arrived. He recorded its virtues in his notebook and then plodded on to the Thai frontier, where a Ford car awaited, to take him to Bangkok. After that, a ship to Cambodia, a trek to Angkor, another river trip to Saigon and a coastal jaunt via Hue to Hanoi. The book finishes there, though in fact, he traveled onward to Hong Kong, crossed the Pacific, crossed the United States, crossed the Atlantic and, back in London, resumed his writing career and his socializing. But he did not get around to writing this book until seven years later, and I think this fact needs to be taken into account when evaluating this oblique and selective travel narrative.

He wrote a great deal in the interval after the trip, *The*

Painted Veil (1925), and after another voyage to Singapore and Malaya the powerful stories in *The Casuarina Tree* (1926), *Ashenden* and its stories of espionage (1928), and at least two full-length stage plays. In this time he made at least one more visit to the United States, and in 1927 bought the grand house on the Riviera he named the Villa Mauresque. Here, in luxury, he finished his novel *Cakes and Ale* and at last wrote *The Gentleman in the Parlour*. Both these books were published in the same year, 1930, at what one of his biographers called the peak of his career. *The Gentleman in the Parlour* received the mixed, not to say envious, reviews that Maugham habitually got from critics who, well-aware that Maugham was wealthy, successful as a writer, socially connected, something of a snob, and living in style, saw little reason to praise him.

Maugham was given no credit for enduring difficult travel, yet parts of the trip were arduous. He toured the extensive complex of temples at Pagan in Burma, necessitating a trip down the Irrawaddy, and spent almost a month on the mule on the trip to Keng Tung. In Cambodia he sailed up the Tonle Sap River and crossed the wide lake to view the then remote precincts of Angkor, at the time just a fantastic set of uninhabited ruins in the jungle.

But the delay between the trip and the book interests me. Invariably a person who wishes to write a travel book goes on a journey and writes the book immediately afterwards. The notable exception is Patrick Leigh Fermor who walked across Europe from Holland to Constantinople in 1933-34, but did not write his account of the trip until many decades later – *A Time of Gifts* (1977) and *Between the Woods and the Water* (1986). These books are so fresh and full of detail you'd hardly know that such a long period of time had elapsed.

In Maugham's case, the hiatus made a difference, both for good and ill. I don't think it would have been the same book if he'd written it on his return home. The book's tone and structure is the result of this passage of time. The book is less detailed but more reflective, more deliberate, more artful and even contrived as a result; it summarizes, it avoids divulging much about the traveler's true personality and predilections. The high points are the mule ride through upper Burma, the period of time in Bangkok, and the description of Angkor.

In the course of the book, Maugham analyzes the wish to travel and the nature of a traveler. These observations are telling for the way they apply to Maugham himself: 'When [the traveler] sets out on his travels the one person he must leave behind is himself.' The text does not bear this out. And as for the nature of the travel book, 'if you like language for its own sake, if it amuses you to string words together in the order that most pleases you, so as to produce an effect of beauty, the essay or the book of travel gives you an opportunity.' This assertion also seems to me questionable. A travel book ought to be the opposite of an exercise in style, but rather a personal way of seeing the world as it is.

'Though I have traveled much I am a bad traveler,' Maugham says in another place. 'The good traveler has the gift of surprise.' Maugham adds that he lacks this: he takes customs as he finds them. He views travel as liberating, a refreshment: 'I travel because I like to move from place to pace, I enjoy the sense of freedom it gives me,' and he goes on in this vein, ending, 'I am often tired of myself and I have a notion that by travel I can add to my personality and so change myself a little. I do not bring back from a journey quite the same self that I took.'

These statements are wonderfully direct, and seem candid, but we know that in this travel book Maugham took extensive liberties; and that in his life and his work he was a master of concealment and indirection.

In great part, *The Gentleman in the Parlour* is a book of stories – travelers' tales, mostly; not Maugham's but those of the people he meets. This book is filled with distinct and well-told stories: the Mandalay tale of the marriage of George and Mabel, in Thazi the irregular alliance between Masterson and his Burmese mistress, in Mong Pying the story of the priest's isolation, in Lop Buri the story of Constantine Faulkon, the Bangkok fable about Princess September, various tales from shipboard, including how the French governor found his wife, and at least two more, one involving the old friend Grosely, the other about the American Elfenbein.

The stories appear to have been related to him by people he met, or in the case of 'Princess September' imagined in a sort of delirium during a serious bout of malaria in Bangkok. But some of these stories had been written prior to the trip – in some cases many years before. 'Princess September' he wrote for one of the tiny volumes in the library of Queen Mary's Doll House in 1922. The tale purportedly told to him on the ship to Hong Kong was the short story 'A Marriage of Convenience', which had been written in 1906, and was published in the *Illustrated London News* in that year. The Englishman Masterson, who may or may not have related the story of his liaison with a Burmese woman who bore him three children, in the Burmese town of Thazi, appeared as a short story, 'On the Road to Mandalay', in the December 1929 issue of the *International Magazine*, It was later published in his *Collected Stories* under the title 'Masterson'.

Except for 'Princess September', which does go on a bit (and seems anything but a malarial inspiration), the stories are arresting character studies and add the local color (dissipated colonial, lots of drink, love affair without benefit of clergy) that gave the Maugham short story, especially the far-flung subject, its tang. They also serve to prove Maugham's assertion in the short story 'Masterson' (and in Chapter X), 'I was a stray acquaintance whom he had never seen before and would never see again...I have in this way learned more about men in a night (sitting over a siphon or two and bottle of whisky, the hostile, inexplicable world outside the radius of an acetylene lamp) than I could have if I had known them for ten years.'

But Maugham did not do a lot of sitting alone over whisky with a stranger. Maugham was by nature reticent – because of his stammer, not much of a raconteur; because of his homosexuality, unforthcoming about his personal life and his loves. One of the important facts he withholds in this book is that he was not alone on the trip. He traveled with his lover and companion Gerald Haxton, who was eighteen years younger and although a drunkard and something of a rogue, was helpful in ice-breaking and meeting locals, as well as making arrangements en route, in many respects Maugham's common law husband. In *The Summing Up*, Maugham explained. 'I am shy of making acquaintance with strangers, but I was fortunate enough to have on my journeys a companion [Haxton] who had an estimable social gift. He had an amiability of disposition that enabled him in a very short time to make friends with people in ships, clubs, bar-rooms, and hotels, so that through him I was able to get into easy contact with an immense number of persons whom otherwise I should have known only at a distance.'

But you get the impression in this book that Maugham was alone, encouraging strangers in their disclosures, battling the uncertainties, struggling against the difficulties, solving the problems of transport and tickets, and all the rest of the hassles that make travel at times such a colorless bore. The first time I read this book I admired Maugham's stamina and capacity to deal with solitude. And then I read a few biographies and I realized that Maugham was not alone and was often traveling in style.

The revelation that the traveler presented in his or her book as a solitary wanderer is not that unusual. Bruce Chatwin never said that he invariably traveled with a friend, V. S. Naipaul did not reveal that he was never alone in his travels, but always (as his biographer showed) with his wife or his long-time mistress Margaret; Graham Greene was very nearly helpless without a constant companion, since he was unable to drive a car or use a typewriter, and the same can be said for Wilfred Thesiger, who never traveled alone. There are many other examples of the gregarious traveler presenting himself, of herself, as a solitary wanderer. There is no shame in this, though it makes the actual solitary wanderers, such as Doughty on camel back in the Empty Quarter of Arabia Deserta, seem almost heroic.

So Maugham was traveling with his friend and lover. And he said that he dictated the larger part of the book to him en route. He omitted the last part of the trip (Hong Kong to London). He included previously written material. And some of what he wrote appeared as non-fiction in this book and fiction elsewhere. And yet, for this manipulation, the book is perhaps his most satisfying narrative of travel.

In the Preface to the collected edition of *On a Chinese Screen* Maugham wrote that *The Gentleman in the Parlour* was not, like *On a Chinese Screen*, the result of an accident ... 'I wanted to try my hand again at the same sort of subject, but on a more elaborate scale and in a form on which I could impose a definite pattern. It was an exercise in style.' This 'style' is not discernible; structurally. It is a conventional travel book though the itinerary is Maugham's own, and even if they have been manipulated, the stories of the expatriates are wonderful.

Although he seems to be writing about himself the whole time, he discloses little about himself. He loses his temper at one point (his room wasn't ready), but he soon deflates himself. He talks a little about his drinking habits; he reveals that he once took opium. Like many writers who insist that they are not very interesting, he is highly observant. His description of Angkor is one of the best I have ever read, and his account of the Thai court is subtle – an insider's glimpse at Asiatic royalty; and (though he claims to be unimpressed) he does justice to the French-looking city of Hanoi. Maugham the narrator has no passion, though passion throbs in the people he encounters and in their tumultuous lives. Maugham's voice is that of the man who narrates his fiction, the watchful writer, humorless but reliable. There is hardly any difference between the man telling this story and the third-person narration of his fiction. Only now and then there is the flicker of a bias, as with the hosiery salesman Elfenbein, about whom he writes, 'He was the kind of Jew who made you understand the pogrom,' which is vicious. But Elfenbein was the occasion for a Maugham first, perhaps one of the earliest recorded instance of the expression 'a chip on his shoulder', as when he says of Elfenbein, 'He was a man with a chip on his shoulder. Everyone seemed in a conspiracy to slight or injure him.'

Maugham himself had a chip – perhaps more than one. But in general, he was stoical, even intrepid, in his travels. His traveling off the beaten track makes this book not just unusual but (to me the greatest attribute of the travel narrative) a valuable historical document.

In this curious, active, even hearty period of his life, traveling in the Far East and the Pacific, eavesdropping, note-taking, he was at his best, and was perhaps his happiest. A person only sets out on such a trip if he is confident, hopeful that he will discover something new. Maugham, a lonely man, was sensitive to the loneliness of others and keenly aware of his own limitations. Travel was a way of isolating himself, and after traveling became too much trouble, he found relief if not happiness himself in his own splendid isolation at the Villa Mauresque, where he wrote this book, recalling his happier moments, on the road.

Paul Theroux, 2009

Preface

I think it is very well for a novelist to give himself a rest now and then from writing fiction. It is a dreary business, to write a novel once a year, as many authors must do, to earn their year's keep or for fear that if they remain silent they will be forgotten. It is unlikely, however fertile their imagination, that they will always have in mind a theme that so urgently demands expression that they cannot help but write; it is unlikely too that they can create characters, fresh and vivid, that they have not themselves used before. If they have the story-teller's gift and know their craft, they will probably turn out an acceptable piece of fiction, but it is only by good luck that it will be anything more. Every work an author produces should be the record of a spiritual adventure of his own. This is a counsel of perfection. The professional author cannot hope always to follow it, he must often content himself with the smaller merit of producing a workmanlike piece; but it is one that it is well for him to bear in mind. Though the variety of human nature is infinite, so that it might seem that the writer need never want for models on which to create his characters, he can only deal with that part of it which is in accordance with his own temperament. He puts himself into the shoes of his characters; but there are shoes he cannot get into. There are people so alien to him that he can get no hold on them. When he describes them he will describe them from the outside, and observation divorced from sympathy can seldom create a living being. That is why the writers of fiction tend to reproduce the same types; they astutely change the sex, the station, the age, the appearance of their characters; but if you look at them closely you will find that they are the same persons reappearing in different guise. No doubt the greater the novelist the larger the number of persons he is capable of creating, but even with the greatest, the number is determined by his own limitations. There is only one way in which he can cope to some extent with the difficult situation: he can change himself. Here time is the prime agent. The writer is fortunate who can wait till this has effected such a change in him that he can see what is before him with fresh and different eyes. He is the variable, and the changing quantity gives an altered value to the symbols with which he is equated. But change of scene also, on one condition, can do much. I have known writers who made adventurous journeys, but took along with them their house in London, their circle of friends, their English interests and their reputation; and were surprised on getting home to find that they were exactly as when they went. Not thus can a writer profit by a journey. When he sets out on his travels the one person he must leave behind is himself.

This book is not like *On a Chinese Screen*, the result of an accident. I took the journey it describes because I wanted to; but I had from the beginning the intention of writing a book about it. I had enjoyed writing *On a Chinese Screen*. I wanted to try my hand again on the same sort of subject, but on a more elaborate scale and in a form on which I could impose a definite pattern. It was an excercise in style. In a novel the style is necessarily influenced by the matter and a homogenous manner of writing is hardly practical. The description of a state of mind demands a different mode of expression from the recital of incident; and dialogue, which should at least give a reasonable impression of current speech, cannot but preclude a uniformity of effect. A tragic passage needs a different manner again from a comic one. Sometimes your narration needs a conversational mode, with free use of slang and even of language that is deliberately careless; at other times it asks for periods as stately as you can make them. The result must be a hodge-podge. There are writers who attach so much importance to beauty of language, by which, alas, they generally mean the florid vocabulary and the purple patch, that they force their material, regardless of its nature, into a uniform mould. Sometimes they go so far as to make even their dialogue conform to it and ask you to read conversations in which the speakers address one another in balanced and carefully composed sentences. So life eludes them. There is no air and you gasp for breath. It is of course out of the question to be funny in this way, but this disturbs them little, for they seldom possess a sense of humour. It is a trait, indeed, that they regard with impatience. The better plan in a novel is to let the matter dictate the manner. The style of a novel is best when like the clothes of a well-dressed man it is unnoticed. But if you like language for its own sake, if it amuses you to string words together in the order that most pleases you, so as to produce an effect of beauty, the essay or the book of travel gives you an opportunity. Here prose may be cultivated for its own sake. You can manipulate your material so that the harmony you seek is plausible. Your style can flow like a broad, placid river and the reader is borne along on its bosom with security; he need fear no shoals, no adverse currents, rapids, or rock-strewn gorges. The danger, of course, is that he will be lulled to sleep and so not observe the pleasant sights along the bank with which you have sought to divert him. The reader must judge for himself whether in this book I have avoided it. I beg him only to remember that there is no language more difficult to write than English. No one ever learns all that there is to be known about it. In the long history of our literature it would be difficult to find more than six persons who have written it faultlessly.

1935.

I

I have never been able to feel for Charles Lamb the
affection that he inspires in most of his readers. There
is a cross grain in my nature that makes me resent the
transports of others and gush will dry up in me (against
my will, for heaven knows I have no wish to chill by my
coldness the enthusiasm of my neighbours) the capacity
of admiration. Too many critics have written of Charles
Lamb with insipidity for me ever to have been able to
read him without uneasiness. He is like one of those
persons of overflowing heart who seem to lie in wait for
disaster to befall you so that they may envelop you with
their sympathy. Their arms are so quickly outstretched
to raise you when you fall that you cannot help asking
yourself, as you rub your barked shin, whether by any
chance they did not put in your path the stone that
tripped you up. I am afraid of people with too much
charm. They devour you. In the end you are made a
sacrifice to the exercise of their fascinating gift and their
insincerity. Nor do I much care for writers whose charm
is their chief asset. It is not enough. I want something
to get my teeth into, and when I ask for roast beef and
Yorkshire pudding I am dissatisfied to be given bread and
milk. I am put out of countenance by the sensibility of
the Gentle Elia. For a generation Rousseau had pinned
every writer's heart to his sleeve and it was in his day
still the fashion to write with a lump in the throat,
but Lamb's emotion, to my mind, too often suggests
the facile lachrymosity of the alcoholic. I cannot but
think his tenderness would have been advantageously
tempered by abstinence, a blue pill and a black draught.
Of course when you read the references made to him by

his contemporaries, you discover that the Gentle Elia is an invention of the sentimentalists. He was a more robust, irascible and intemperate fellow than they have made him out, and he would have laughed (and with justice) at the portrait they have painted of him. If you had met him one evening at Benjamin Haydon's, you would have seen a grubby little person, somewhat the worse for liquor, who could be very dull, and if he made a joke it might as easily have been a bad as a good one. In fact, you would have met Charles Lamb and not the Gentle Elia. And if you had read that morning one of his essays in *The London Magazine* you would have thought it an agreeable trifle. It would never have occurred to you that this pleasant piece would serve one day as a pretext for the lucubrations of the learned. You would have read it in the right spirit; for to you it would have been a living thing. It is one of the misfortunes to which the writer is subject that he is too little praised when he is alive and too much when he is dead. The critics force us to read the classics as Machiavelli wrote, in Court dress; whereas we should do much better to read them, as though they were our contemporaries, in a dressing-gown.

And because I had read Lamb in deference to common opinion rather than from inclination I had forborne to read Hazlitt at all. What with the innumerable books it urgently imported me to read, I came to the conclusion that I could afford to neglect a writer who had but done mediocrely (I understood) what another had done with excellence. And the Gentle Elia bored me. It was seldom I had read anything about Lamb without coming across a fling and a sneer at Hazlitt. I knew that FitzGerald had once intended to write a life of him, but had given up the project in disgust of his character. He was a mean, savage, nasty little man and an unworthy hanger-on of the circle in which Lamb, Keats, Shelley, Coleridge and Wordsworth shone with so bright a lustre. There seemed no need to waste any time on a writer of so little talent

2

and of so unpleasant a nature. But one day, about to start on a long journey, I was wandering round Bumpus's looking for books to take with me when I came across a selection of Hazlitt's Essays. It was an agreeable little volume in a green cover, and nicely printed, cheap in price and light to hold, and out of curiosity to know the truth about an author of whom I had read so much ill, I put it on the pile that I had already collected.

II

When I had settled down on the boat that was taking me up the Irrawaddy to Pagan I got the little green volume out of my bag to read on the way. The boat was crowded with natives. They lay about on their beds surrounded by a great many small pieces of luggage and ate and gossiped all day long. There were among them a number of monks in yellow robes, their heads shaven, and they smoked cheroots in silence. Occasionally one passed a raft of teak-logs, with a little thatched house on it, going down-stream to Rangoon, and caught a brief glimpse of the family that lived on it busy with the preparations of a meal or cosily eating it. It looked a placid life that they led, with long hours of repose and ample leisure for the exercise of an idle curiosity. The river was broad and muddy, and its banks were flat. Now and then one saw a pagoda, sometimes spick and span and white, but more often crumbling to pieces; and now and then one came to a riverside village nestling amiably among great green trees. On the landing-stage was a dense throng of noisy, gesticulating people in bright dresses and they looked like flowers on a stall in a market-place; there was a turmoil and a confusion, shouting, a hurry and scurry as a mass of little people, laden with their belongings, got off, and another mass of little people, laden too, got on.

River travelling is monotonous and soothing. In whatever part of the world you are it is the same. No responsibility rests on your shoulders. Life is easy. The long day is divided into neat parts by the meals and you very soon acquire a sense that you have no longer an individuality; you are a passenger occupying a certain berth and the statistics of the company show that you have occupied that berth at this season for a certain number of years and will continue to do so long enough to make the company's shares a sound investment.

I began to read my Hazlitt. I was astonished. I found a solid writer, without pretentiousness, courageous to speak his mind, sensible and plain, with a passion for the arts that was neither gushing nor forced, various, interested in the life about him, ingenious, sufficiently profound for his purposes, but with no affectation of profundity, humorous, sensitive. And I liked his English. It was natural and racy, eloquent when eloquence was needed, easy to read, clear and succinct, neither below the weight of his matter nor with fine phrases trying to give it a specious importance. If art is nature seen through the medium of a personality, Hazlitt is a great artist.

I was enraptured. I could not forgive myself that I had lived so long without reading him and I raged against the idolaters of Elia whose foolishness had deprived me till now of so vivid an experience. Here certainly was no charm, but what a robust mind, sane, clear-cut and vivacious, and what vigour! Presently I came across the rich essay which is entitled *On Going A Journey* and I reached the passage that runs: 'Oh! it is great to shake off the trammels of the world and of public opinion – to lose our importunate, tormenting, everlasting personal identity in the elements of nature, and become the creature of the moment, clear of all ties – to hold to the universe only by a dish of sweet-breads, and to owe nothing but the score of the evening – and no longer seeking for applause and meeting with contempt, to be known by no other title than *The Gentleman in the Parlour!'* I could wish that Hazlitt had used fewer dashes in this passage. There is in the dash something rough, ready and haphazard that goes against my grain. I have seldom read a sentence in which it could not be well replaced by the elegant semi-colon or the discreet bracket. But I had no sooner read these words than it occurred to me that here was an admirable name for a book of travel and I made up my mind to write it.

III

I let the book fall to my knees and looked at the river flowing silently. The immense volume of slow moving water gave an exquisite sensation of inviolate peace. The night fell softly as a green leaf in summer falls softly to the ground. But trying for a moment to fight against the pleasant idleness of spirit that stole over me, I sorted in my memory the impressions that Rangoon had left on me.

It was a gay and sunny morning when the ship that I had taken at Colombo steamed up the Irrawaddy. They pointed out to me the tall chimneys of the Burmah Oil Company and the air was grey and misty with their smoke. But behind the smoke rose the golden spire of the Shwe Dagon. And now I found that my recollections were entirely pleasing, but nebulous; a cordial welcome, a drive in an American car through busy streets of business houses, concrete and iron like the streets, good heavens! of Honolulu, Shanghai, Singapore or Alexandria, and then a spacious, shady house in a garden; an agreeable life, luncheon at this club or that, drives along trim, wide roads, bridge after dark at that club or this, gin *pahits*, a great many men in white drill or pongee silk, laughter, pleasant conversation; and then back through the night to dress for dinner and out again to dine with this hospitable host or the other, cocktails, a substantial meal, dancing to a gramophone, or a game of billiards and then back once more to the large cool silent house. It was very attractive, easy, comfortable and gay; but was this Rangoon? Down by the harbour and along the river were narrow streets, a rabbit warren of intersecting alleys; and here, multitudinous, lived the Chinese, and there the Burmans: I looked with curious eyes as I passed in my motor car and wondered what strange things I should discover and what secrets they had to tell me if I could plunge into that enigmatic life and lose myself in it as a cup of water thrown overboard is lost in the Irrawaddy. Rangoon. And now I found that in my recollections, so vague and uncertain, that Shwe Dagon rose superb as on that first morning it had risen, glistening with its gold, like a sudden hope in the dark night of the soul of which the mystics write, glistening against the fog and smoke of the thriving city.

A Burmese gentleman having asked me to dine with him, I went to his office whither I was bidden. It was gaily decorated with streamers of paper flowers. A large round table stood in the middle. I was introduced to a number of his friends and we sat down. There were a great many courses, most of which were rather cold, and the food, served in little bowls, swam in copious sauces. Round the centre of the table were bowls of Chinese tea, but champagne flowed freely, too freely, and after dinner liqueurs of all kinds were passed round. We were all very jolly. Then the table was taken away and the chairs were put against the wall. My amiable host asked for permission to bring in his wife, and she came with a friend, two pretty little women with large, smiling eyes, and sat down shyly; but they soon found the position on European chairs uncomfortable and so sat with their legs under them as though they were sitting on the floor. An entertainment had been provided for my diversion and the performers made their entrance. Two clowns, an orchestra and half a dozen dancers. One of them, they told me, was an artist celebrated through all Burmah. The dancers wore silk shirts and tight jackets, and they had flowers in their dark hair. They sang in a loud, forced voice so that the veins of their necks swelled with the effort, and they danced not together, but in turn, and their gestures were like the gestures of marionettes. Meanwhile the clowns uttered their merry quips; back and forth went the dialogue between them and the dancers, and it was evidently of a facetious character, for my host and his guests laughed loudly.

For some time I had been watching the star. She certainly had an air. She stood with her companions but with an effect of being apart from them, and on her face she wore a good-humoured, but faintly supercilious smile, as though she belonged to another sphere. When the clowns attacked her with their gibes she answered them with a smiling detachment; she was playing her part in a rite as became her, but she proposed to give nothing of herself. She had the aloofness of complete self-confidence. Then her moment came. She stepped forward. She forgot that she was a star and became an actress.

But I had been expressing regret to my neighbours that I must leave Rangoon without seeing the Shwe Dagon; for the Burmese had made certain regulations, which the Buddhist faith did not demand, but to comply with which was humiliating to the occidental; and to humiliate the occidental was the object of the regulations. No Europeans any longer went into the wat-houses. But it is a stately pile and the most venerable place of worship in the country. It enshrines eight hairs from the head of the Buddha. My Burmese friends offered now to take me and I put my Western pride in my pocket. It was midnight. Arriving at the temple we went up a long stairway on each side of which were booths; but the people who lived in them, to sell the devout what they might require, had

7

finished their work and some were sitting about, half naked, chatting in undertones, smoking or eating a final meal, while many in all attitudes of abandonment were asleep, some on low native beds and some on the bare stones. Here and there, left over from the day before, were masses of dying flowers, lotus and jasmine and marigold; they scented the air heavily with a perfume in which was already an acrid decay. At last we reached the great terrace. All about shrines and pagodas were jumbled pell-mell with the confusion with which trees grow in the jungle. They had been built without design or symmetry, but in the darkness, their gold and marble faintly gleaming, they had a fantastic richness. And then, emerging from among them like a great ship surrounded by lighters, rose dim, severe and splendid, the Shwe Dagon. Lamps illuminated with a sober glow the gilt with which it was covered. It towered, aloof, impressive and mysterious against the night. A guardian walked noiselessly on his naked feet, an old man was lighting a row of candles before an image of the Buddha; they gave an emphasis to the solitude. Here and there a yellow-robed monk muttered a husky invocation; his droning punctuated the silence.

IV

So that the reader of these pages may be under no misapprehension I hasten to tell him that he will find in them little information. This book is the record of a journey through Burmah, the Shan States, Siam and Indo-China. I am writing it for my own diversion and I hope that it will divert also such as care to spend a few hours in reading it. I am a professional writer and I hope to get from it a certain amount of money and perhaps a little praise.

Though I have travelled much I am a bad traveller. The

good traveller has the gift of surprise. He is perpetually interested by the differences he finds between what he knows at home and what he sees abroad. If he has a keen sense of the absurd he finds constant matter for laughter in the fact that the people among whom he is do not wear the same clothes as he does, and he can never get over his astonishment that men may eat with chop-sticks instead of forks or write with a brush instead of with a pen. Since everything is strange to him he notices everything, and according to his humour can be amusing or instructive. But I take things for granted so quickly that I cease to see anything unusual in my new surroundings. It seems to me so obvious for the Burman to wear a coloured *paso* that only by a deliberate effort can I make the observation that he is not dressed as I am. It seems to me just as natural to ride in a rickshaw as in a car, and to sit on the floor as on a chair, so that I forget that I am doing something odd and out-of-the-way. I travel because I like to move from place to place, I enjoy the sense of freedom it gives me, it pleases me to be rid of ties, responsibilities, duties, I like the unknown; I meet odd people who amuse me for a moment and sometimes suggest a theme for a composition; I am often tired of myself and I have a notion that by travel I can add to my personality and so change myself a little. I do not bring back from a journey quite the same self that I took.

It is true that should the historian of the Decline and Fall of the British Empire come across this book on the shelves of some public library he will have hard things to say of me. 'How can one explain,' he will ask, 'that this writer who in other places showed that he was not devoid of observation, could have gone through so many parts of this Empire and not noticed (for by never a word is it apparent that suspicion of anything of the sort crossed his mind) with what a nerveless hand the British held the power that their fathers had conquered? A satirist in his day, was there no matter for his derision

9

in the spectacle of a horde of officials who held their positions only by force of the guns behind them trying to persuade the races they ruled that they were there only on sufferance? They offered efficiency to people to whom a hundred other things were of more consequence and sought to justify themselves by the benefits they conferred on people who did not want them. As if a man in whose house you have forcibly quartered yourself will welcome you any the more because you tell him you can run it better than he can! Did he go through Burmah and not see how the British power was tottering because the masters were afraid to rule? Did he not meet judges, soldiers, commissioners who had no confidence in themselves and therefore inspired no respect in those they were placed over? What had happened to the race that had produced Clive, Warren Hastings and Stamford Raffles that it must send out to govern its colonies, men who were afraid of the authority entrusted to them, men who thought to rule the Oriental by cajolery and submissiveness, by being unobtrusive, by pocketing affronts and giving the natives powers they were unfit to use and must inevitably turn against their masters? But what is a master whose conscience is troubled because he is a master? They prated of efficiency and they did not rule efficiently, for they were filled with an uneasy feeling that they were unfit to rule. They were sentimentalists. They wanted the profits of Empire, but would not assume the greatest of its responsibilities, which is power. But all this, which was staring him in the face, seems to have escaped this writer, and he contented himself with jotting down little incidents of travel, describing his emotions and inventing little stories about the persons he met; he produced a book that can be of no value to the historian, the political economist or the philosopher: it is deservedly forgotten.'

I cock a snook at the historian of the Decline and Fall of the British Empire. On my side I venture to express the wish that when the time comes for him to write this great work he will write it with sympathy, justice and magnanimity. I would have him eschew rhetoric, but I do not think a restrained emotion would ill become him. I would have him write lucidly and yet with dignity; I would have his periods march with a firm step. I should like his sentences to ring out as the anvil rings when the hammer strikes it; his style should be stately but not pompous, picturesque without affectation or effort, lapidary, eloquent and yet sober; for when all is said and done he will have a subject upon which he may well expend all his pains: the British Empire will have been in the world's history a moment not without grandeur.

V

A light rain was falling and the sky was dark with heavy clouds when I reached Pagan. In the distance I saw the pagodas for which it is renowned. They loomed, huge, remote and mysterious, out of the mist of the early morning like the vague recollections of a fantastic dream. The river steamer set me down at a bedraggled village some miles from my destination, and I waited in the drizzle while my servant found an ox-wagon to take me on my way. It was a springless cart on solid wooden wheels, covered with a coconut matting. Inside, it was hot and breathless, but the rain had increased to a steady downpour and I was thankful for its shelter. I lay full length and when I was tired of this sat cross-legged. The oxen went at a snail's pace, with cautious steps, and I was shaken and jolted as they ploughed their way through the tracks made by the carts that had gone before, and every now and then I was given a terrific jerk as the cart passed over a great stone. When I reached the circuit-house I felt as though I had been beaten and pummelled.

The circuit-house stood on the river bank, quite close

to the water, and all round it were great trees, tamarinds, banyans and wild gooseberries. A flight of wooden steps led to a broad verandah, which served as a living-room, and behind this were a couple of bedrooms, each with a bath-room. I found that one of these was occupied by another traveller, and I had but just examined the accommodation and talked to the Madrassi in charge about meals and taken stock of what pickles and canned goods and liquor he had on the premises when a little man appeared in a mackintosh and a topee dripping with rain. He took off his soaking things and presently we sat down to the meal known in this country as brunch. It appeared that he was a Czecho-Slovak, employed by a firm of exporters in Calcutta, and was spending his holiday seeing the sights of Burmah. He was a short man with wild black hair, a large face, a bold hooked nose and gold-rimmed spectacles. His stingah-shifter fitted tightly over a corpulent figure. He was evidently an active and an energetic sightseer; for the rain had not prevented him from going out in the morning and he told me that he had visited no less than seven pagodas. But the rain stopped while we were eating and soon the sun shone brightly. We had no sooner finished than he set out again. I do not know how many pagodas there are at Pagan; when you stand on an eminence they surround you as far as the eye can reach. They are almost as thickly strewn as the tombstones in a cemetery. They are of all sizes and in all states of preservation. Their solidity and size and magnificence are the more striking by reason of their surroundings, for they alone remain to show that here a vast and populous city once flourished. To-day there is only a straggling village with broad untidy roads lined with great trees, a pleasant enough little place with matting houses, neat and trim, in which live the workers in lacquer; for this is the industry on which Pagan, forgetful of its ancient greatness, now modestly thrives.

But of all these pagodas only one, the Ananda, is still a place of pilgrimage. Here are four huge gilded Buddhas standing against a gilded wall in a lofty gilded chamber. You look at them one by one through a gilded archway. In that glowing dimness they are inscrutable. In front of one a mendicant in his yellow robe chants in a high-pitched voice some litany that you do not understand. But the other pagodas are deserted. Grass grows in the chinks of the pavement and young trees have taken root in the crannies. They are the refuge of birds. Hawks wheel about their summits and little green parrots chatter in the eaves. They are like bizarre and monstrous flowers turned to stone. There is one in which the architect has taken as his model the lotus, as the architect of St John's, Smith Square, took Queen Anne's footstool, and it has a baroque extravagance that makes the Jesuit churches in Spain seem severe and classical. It is preposterous, so that it makes you smile to look at it, but its exuberance is captivating. It is quite unreal, shoddy but strange, and you are staggered at the fantasy that could ever have devised it. It looks like the fabric of a single night made by the swarming hands of one of those wayward gods of the Indian mythology. Within the pagodas images of the Buddha sit in meditation. The gold leaf has long since worn away from the colossal figures and the figures are crumbling to dust. The fantastic lions that guard the entrance ways are rotting on their pedestals.

A strange and melancholy spot. But my curiosity was satisfied with a visit to half-a-dozen of the pagodas, and I would not let the vigour of my Czecho-Slovak be a reproach to my indolence. He divided them into various types and marked them down in his notebook according to their peculiarities. He had theories about them, and in his mind they were neatly ticketed to support a theory or clinch an argument. None was so ruined that he did not think it worth while to give it his close and enthusiastic attention; and to examine the make and shape of tiles he climbed up broken places like a mountain goat. I preferred to sit idly on the verandah of the circuit-house and watch the scene before me. In the full tide of noon the sun burned all the colour from the landscape so that the trees and the dwarf scrub that grew wildly, where in time past were the busy haunts of men, were pale and grey; but with the declining day the colour crept back, like an emotion that tempers the character and has been submerged for a while by the affairs of the world, and trees and scrub were again a sumptuous and living green. The sun set on the other side of the river and a red cloud in the west was reflected on the tranquil bosom of the Irrawaddy. There was not a ripple on the water. The river seemed no longer to flow. In the distance a solitary fisherman in a dug-out plied his craft. A little to one side but in full view was one of the loveliest of the pagodas. In the setting sun its colours, cream and fawn-grey, were soft like the silk of old dresses in a museum. It had a symmetry that was grateful to the eye; the turrets at one corner were repeated by the turrets at every other; and the flamboyant windows repeated the flamboyant doors below. The decoration had a sort of bold violence, as though it sought to scale fantastic pinnacles of the spirit and in the desperate struggle, with life and soul engaged, could not concern itself with reticence or good taste. But withal it had at that moment a kind of majesty and there was majesty in the solitude in which it stood. It seemed to weigh upon the earth with too great a burden. It was impressive to reflect that it had stood for so many centuries and looked down impassively upon the smiling bend of the Irrawaddy. The birds were singing noisily in the trees; the crickets chirped and the frogs croaked, croaked, croaked. Somewhere a boy was whistling a melancholy tune on a rude pipe and in the compound the natives were chattering loudly. There is no silence in the East.

It was at this hour that the Czecho-Slovak returned

to the circuit-house. He was very hot and dusty, tired but happy, for he had missed nothing. He was a mine of information. The night began gradually to enfold the pagoda and it looked now unsubstantial, as though it were built of lath and plaster, so that you would not have been surprised to see it at the Paris exhibition housing a display of colonial produce. It was a strangely sophisticated building in that exquisitely rural scene. But the Czecho-Slovak told me when it was built and under what king, and then, gathering way, began to tell me something of the history of Pagan. He had a retentive memory. He marshalled his facts with precision and delivered them with the fluency of a lecturer delivering a lecture he has repeated too often. But I did not want to know the facts he gave me. What did it matter to me what kings reigned there, what battles they fought and what lands they conquered? I was content to see them as a low relief on a temple wall in a long procession, with their hieratic attitudes, seated on a throne and receiving gifts from the envoys of subjugated nations, or else, with a confusion of spears, in the hurry and skelter of chariots, in the turmoil of battle. I asked the Czecho-Slovak what he was going to do with all the information he had acquired.

'Do? Nothing,' he replied. 'I like facts. I want to know things. Whenever I go anywhere I read everything about it that has been written. I study its history, the fauna and flora, the manners and customs of the people, I make myself thoroughly acquainted with its art and literature. I could write a standard book on every country I have visited. I am a mine of information.'

'That is just what I was saying to myself. But what is the good of information that means nothing to you? Information for its own sake is like a flight of steps that leads to a blank wall.'

'I do not agree with you. Information for its own sake is like a pin you pick up and put in the lapel of your coat or the piece of string that you untie instead of cutting and put away in a drawer. You never know when it will be useful.'

And to show me that he did not choose his metaphors at random the Czecho-Slovak turned up the bottom of his stingah-shifter (which has no lapel) and showed me four pins in a neat row.

VI

From Pagan, wishing to go to Mandalay, I took the steamer once more, and a couple of days before I arrived there, the boat tying up at a riverside village, I made up my mind to go ashore. The skipper told me that there was there a pleasant little club in which I had only to make myself at home; they were quite used to having strangers drop off like that from the steamer, and the secretary was a very decent chap; I might even get a game of bridge. I had nothing in the world to do, so I got into one of the bullock-carts that were waiting at the landscape-stage and was driven to the club. There was a man sitting on the verandah and as I walked up he nodded to me and asked whether I would have a whisky and soda or a gin and bitters. The possibility that I would have nothing at all did not even occur to him. I chose the longer drink and sat down. He was a tall, thin, bronzed man, with a big moustache, and he wore khaki shorts and a khaki shirt. I never knew his name, but when we had been chatting a little while another man came in who told me he was the secretary, and he addressed my friend as George.

'Have you heard from your wife yet?' he asked him.

The other's eyes brightened.

'Yes, I had letters by this mail. She's having no end of a time.'

'Did she tell you not to fret?'

George gave a little chuckle, but was I mistaken in thinking that there was in it the shadow of a sob?

'In point of fact she did. But that's easier said than done. Of course I know she wants a holiday, and I'm glad she should have it, but it's devilish hard on a chap.' He turned to me. 'You see, this is the first time I've ever been separated from my missus, and I'm like a lost dog without her.'

'How long have you been married?'

'Five minutes.'

The secretary of the club laughed.

'Don't be a fool, George. You've been married eight years.'

After we had talked for a little George, looking at his watch, said he must go and change his clothes for dinner and left us. The secretary watched him disappear into the night with a smile of not unkindly irony.

'We all ask him as much as we can now that he's alone,' he told me. 'He mopes so terribly since his wife went home.'

'It must be very pleasant for her to know that her husband is as devoted to her as all that.'

'Mabel is a remarkable woman.'

He called the boy and ordered more drinks. In this hospitable place they did not ask you if you would have anything; they took it for granted. Then he settled himself in his long chair and lit a cheroot. He told me the story of George and Mabel.

They became engaged when he was home on leave, and when he returned to Burmah it was arranged that she should join him in six months. But one difficulty cropped up after another; Mabel's father died, the war came, George was sent to a district unsuitable for a white woman; so that in the end it was seven years before she was able to start. He made all arrangements for the marriage, which was to take place on the day of her arrival, and went down to Rangoon to meet her. On the morning on which the ship was due he borrowed a motor-car and drove along to the dock. He paced the quay.

Then, suddenly, without warning, his nerve failed him. He had not seen Mabel for seven years. He had forgotten what she was like. She was a total stranger. He felt a terrible sinking in the pit of his stomach and his knees began to wobble. He couldn't go through with it. He must tell Mabel that he was very sorry, but he couldn't, he really couldn't marry her. But how could a man tell a girl a thing like that when she had been engaged to him for seven years and had come six thousand miles to marry him? He hadn't the nerve for that either. George was seized with the courage of despair. There was a boat at the quay on the very point of starting for Singapore; he wrote a hurried letter to Mabel, and without a stick of luggage, just in the clothes he stood up in, leaped on board.

The letter Mabel received ran somewhat as follows:

Dearest Mabel,

I have been suddenly called away on business and do not know when I shall be back. I think it would be much wiser if you returned to England. My plans are very uncertain.

Your loving George.

But when he arrived at Singapore he found a cable waiting for him.

Quite understand. Don't worry. Love. Mabel.

Terror made him quick-witted.

'By Jove, I believe she's following me,' he said.

He telegraphed to the shipping-office at Rangoon and sure enough her name was on the passenger list of the ship that was now on its way to Singapore. There was not a moment to lose. He jumped on the train to Bangkok. But he was uneasy; she would have no difficulty in finding out that he had gone to Bangkok and it was just as simple for her to take the train as it had been for him. Fortunately there was a French tramp sailing next day for Saïgon. He took it. At Saïgon he would be safe; it would never occur to her that he had gone there; and if it did, surely by now she would have taken the hint. It is five days journey from Bangkok to Saïgon and the boat is dirty, cramped and uncomfortable. He was glad to arrive and took a rickshaw to the hotel. He signed his name in the visitors' book and a telegram was immediately handed to him. It contained but two words: *Love. Mabel.* They were enough to make him break into a cold sweat.

'When is the next boat for Hong-Kong?' he asked.

Now his flight grew serious. He sailed to Hong-Kong, but dared not stay there; he went to Manila; Manila was ominous; he went on to Shanghai: Shanghai was nerve-racking; every time he went out of the hotel he expected to run straight into Mabel's arms; no, Shanghai would never do. The only thing was to go to Yokohama. At the Grand Hotel at Yokohama a cable awaited him.

'So sorry to have missed you at Manila. Love. Mabel.'

He scanned the shipping intelligence with a fevered brow. Where was she now? He doubled back to Shanghai. This time he went straight to the club and asked for a telegram. It was handed to him.

'Arriving shortly. Love. Mabel.'

No, no, he was not so easy to catch as all that. He had already made his plans. The Yangtze is a long river and the Yangtze was falling. He could just about catch the last steamer that could get up to Chungking and then no one could travel till the following spring except by junk. Such a journey was out of the question for a woman alone. He went to Hankow and from Hankow to Ichang, he changed boats here and from Ichang through the rapids went to Chungking. But he was desperate now, he was not going to take any risks: there was a place called Cheng-tu, the capital of Szechuan, and it was four hundred miles away. It could only be reached by road, and the road was infested with brigands. A man would be safe there.

George collected chair-beaters and coolies and set out. It was with a sigh of relief that he saw at last the crenellated walls of the lonely Chinese city. From those walls at sunset you could see the snowy mountains of Tibet.

He could rest at last: Mabel would never find him there. The Consul happened to be a friend of his and he stayed with him. He enjoyed the comfort of a luxurious house, he enjoyed his idleness after that strenuous escape across Asia, and above all he enjoyed his divine security. The weeks passed lazily one after the other.

One morning George and the Consul were in the courtyard looking at some curios that a Chinese had brought for their inspection when there was a loud knocking at the great door of the Consulate. The doorman flung it open. A chair borne by four coolies entered, advanced, and was set down. Mabel stepped out. She was neat and cool and fresh. There was nothing in her appearance to suggest that she had just come in after a fortnight on the road. George was petrified. He was as pale as death. She went up to him.

'Hulloa, George, I was so afraid I'd missed you again.'

'Hulloa, Mabel,' he faltered.

He did not know what to say. He looked this way and that: she stood between him and the doorway. She looked at him with a smile in her blue eyes.

'You haven't altered at all,' she said. 'Men can go off so dreadfully in seven years and I was afraid you'd got fat and bald. I've been so nervous. It would have been terrible if after all these years I simply hadn't been able to bring myself to marry you after all.'

She turned to George's host.

'Are you the Consul?' she asked.

'I am.'

'That's all right. I'm ready to marry him as soon as I've had a bath.'

And she did.

VII

First of all Mandalay is a name. For there are places whose names from some accident of history or happy association have an independent magic and perhaps the wise man would never visit them, for the expectations they arouse can hardly be realised. Names have a life of their own, and though Trebizond may be nothing but a poverty-stricken village the glamour of its name must invest it for all right-thinking minds with the trappings of Empire; and Samarkand: can anyone write the word without a quickening of the pulse and at his heart the pain of unsatisfied desire. The very name of the Irrawaddy informs the sensitive fancy with its vast and turbid flow. The streets of Mandalay, dusty, crowded and drenched with a garish sun, are broad and straight. Tram-cars lumber down them with a rout of passengers; they fill the seats and gangways and cling thickly to the footboard like flies clustered upon an over-ripe mango. The houses, with their balconies and verandahs, have the slatternly look of the houses in the Main Street of a Western town that has fallen upon evil days. Here are no narrow alleys nor devious ways down which the imagination may wander in search of the unimaginable. It does not matter: Mandalay has its name; the falling cadence of the lovely word has gathered about itself the chiaroscuro of romance.

But Mandalay has also its fort. The fort is surrounded by a high wall, and the high wall by a moat. In the fort stands the palace, and stood, before they were torn down, the offices of King Thebaw's government and the dwelling-places of his ministers. At intervals in the wall are gateways washed white with lime and each is surmounted by a sort of belvedere, like a summer-house in a Chinese garden; and on the bastions are teak pavilions too fanciful to allow you to think they could ever have served a warlike purpose. The wall is made of huge sun-baked bricks and the colour of it is old rose. At its foot is a broad stretch of sward planted quite thickly with tamarind, cassia and acacia; a flock of brown sheep, advancing with tenacity, slowly but intently grazes the luscious grass; and here in the evening you see the Burmese in their coloured skirts and bright handkerchiefs wander in twos and threes. They are little brown men of a solid and sturdy build, with something a trifle Mongolian in their faces. They walk deliberately as though they were owners and tillers of the soil. They have none of the sidelong grace, the deprecating elegance, of the Indian who passes them; they have not his refinement of features, nor his languorous, effeminate distinction. They smile easily. They are happy, cheerful and amiable.

In the broad water of the moat, the rosy wall and the thick foliage of the trees and the Burmese in their bright clothes, are sharply reflected. The water is still, but not stagnant, and peace rests upon it like a swan with a golden crown. Its colours, in the early morning and towards sunset, have the soft fatigued tenderness of pastel; they have the translucency without the stubborn definiteness, of oils. It is as though light were a prestidigitator and in play laid on colours that he had just created and were about with a careless hand to wash them out again. You hold your breath for you cannot believe that such an effect can be anything but evanescent. You watch it with the same expectancy with which you read a poem in some complicated metre when your ear awaits the long delayed rhyme that will fulfil the harmony. But at sunset, when the clouds in the west are red and splendid so that the wall, the trees and the moat are drenched in radiance; and at night under the full moon when the white gateways drip with silver and the belvederes above them are shot with silhouetted glimpses of the sky, the assault on your senses is shattering. You try to guard yourself by saying it is not real. This is not a beauty that steals upon you unawares, that flatters and soothes your bruised spirit, this is not a beauty that you can hold in your hand and call your own and put in its place among familiar beauties that you know; it is a beauty that batters you and stuns you and leaves you breathless, there is no calmness in it nor control, it is like a fire that on a sudden consumes you and you are left shaken and bare and yet by a strange miracle alive.

VIII

The palace of Mandalay is built within a great square, surrounded by a low whitewashed wall, and you go up to the terrace on which it stands by an inconsiderable stairway. In old days this expanse was thickly covered with buildings, but now many of them, the lodgings of inferior queens and of maids of honour, have been pulled down and where they stood are pleasant green spaces.

First then you come upon a long audience chamber, then a throne room, robing chambers, other throne rooms and private apartments. On each side of these are the dwelling-places of the king, the queens and the princesses. The throne room is a barn, a roof supported by tall posts, but the posts are great teak trees on which you can still see the marks of the tools with which they were rudely shaped, and they are lacquered and gilt; the walls are mere planks roughly planed and they are lacquered and gilt too. The gold is worn and discoloured. The contrast of this crudeness of workmanship with all this gilt and lacquer gives, I know not how, an effect of peculiar magnificence. Each building, too much like a Swiss chalet, by itself is unimpressive, but in the mass they have a dark splendour that takes the fancy. The carving that adorns the roofs, the balustrades and the partitions between chamber and chamber, is coarse, but the designs have often grace and a luxurious elegance. The builders of the palace in the most unexpected way, by the use of the most incongruous elements, have achieved a palatial effect so that you feel that here Oriental monarchs might fitly dwell. Much of the decoration is obtained by the use in various patterns of a mosaic of innumerable little pieces of mirror and of white and brightly coloured glass: you would have said that nothing could be more hideous (it reminds you of the kind of thing you saw on Margate pier in your childhood and took back with pride after a day's outing as a present to a dismayed relation), yet oddly enough the impression is not only sumptuous but pleasing. So rudely carved are the screens and partitions on which these artful fragments of glass are thus inlaid that they have none of the effect of tinsel, but on their solid ground glitter dimly with the secret radiance of tarnished gems. This is not a barbarous art, which has a greater strength and vitality, a more rugged force, but a savage or if you like a childlike art; it is in a way trifling and effeminate and it is its roughness (as though with uncertain touch the artists were creating each familiar pattern afresh from their own heads) that gives it character. You have a notion of a people fumbling confusedly with the very beginning of the beautiful and they are charmed with shining objects as a bushman might be or a child.

The palace now is despoiled of the rich hangings and the gilded furniture with which it was adorned. You walk through chamber after chamber and it is like a house that has been long to let. No one seems to visit it. Towards evening these gilded, jewelled, deserted chambers are sombre and ghostly. You wander softly so that you may not disturb the faintly scented silence. You stand and look at all that emptiness in amaze and it is incredible that so short a while ago this was the scene of unimaginable intrigue and of turbulent passion. For here romance is within the memory of men still alive. It is not fifty years since this palace saw incidents as dramatic and to us as remote as those of the Renaissance in Italy or of Byzantium. I was taken to see an old lady who in her day had made history. She was a rather stout, short person, dressed soberly in black and white, and she looked at me through gold-rimmed spectacles with quiet, slightly ironic eyes. Her father, a Greek, had been in the service of King Mindon and she was appointed maid of honour to Queen Supalayat. Presently she married the English captain of one of the king's river boats, but he died, and after a decent interval she became engaged to a Frenchman. (She spoke in a low voice, with the very faintest trace of a foreign accent; the flies buzzing about her did not seem to incommode her, she held her hands clasped demurely on her lap.) The Frenchman went home and at Marseilles married one of his own countrywomen. After so long a time she did not remember very much about him; she remembered his name, of course, and she remembered that he had a very handsome moustache, and that was all. But then she loved him madly. (When she laughed it was a little ghostly chuckle as though her mirth were a shadow and what she laughed at an illusion of the comic.) She made up her mind to be revenged on him. She still had her entrée to the palace. She got hold of the draft of a treaty that King Thebaw had made with the French by the terms of which every sphere of influence in Upper Burma passed into their hands. She gave it to the Italian Consul to take to the Chief Commissioner of Lower Burma, and so caused the English advance on Mandalay and the dethronement and exile of King Thebaw. Was it not Alexandre Dumas who said that in the theatre there is nothing so dramatic as something that is happening behind a closed door? The quiet, ironic eyes of that old lady, behind their gold-rimmed spectacles, were a closed door, and who could tell what bizarre thoughts, what a welter of fantastic passions, still dwelt behind them? She spoke of Queen Supalayat: she was a very nice woman, and people had been so unkind about her; all those stories of the massacres she had instigated, stuff and nonsense!

'I know for a fact that she did not murder more than two or three people at the outside.' The old lady faintly shrugged her fat little shoulders. 'Two or three people! What is that to make a fuss about? Life is cheap.'

I sipped a cup of tea and someone turned on the gramophone.

IX

Though not an indomitable sight-seer I went to Amarapura, once the capital of Burma, but now a straggling village, where the tamarind trees grow lofty on each side of the road and in their shade the silk-weavers ply their trade. The tamarind is a noble tree. Its trunk is rough and gnarled, pale like the teak logs that have been floating down the river, and its roots are like great serpents that writhe upon the earth with a convulsive violence; but its foliage is lacy and fern-like, so thick that notwithstanding the delicacy of the leaves it yields a dense shade. It is like an old farmer's wife, full of years, but rugged and hale, who is clothed incongruously in fleecy muslins. Green pigeons roost in its branches. Men and women sit outside their little houses, spinning or winding the silk on bobbins, and they have soft friendly eyes. Children play about them and pariah dogs lie sleeping in the middle of the road. It is a gently industrious, happy and peaceful life that they seem to lead, and the thought crosses your mind that here are people who have found at least one solution to the mystery of existence.

Then I went to see the great bell at Mengon. Here

is a Buddhist convent and as I stood looking a group of nuns surrounded me. They wore robes of the same shape and size as the monks', but instead of the monks' fine yellow of a grimy dun. Little old toothless women, their heads shaven but covered with an inch of thin grey stubble, and their little old faces deeply lined and wrinkled. They held out skinny hands for money and gabbled with bare pale gums. Their dark eyes were alert with covetousness and their smiles were mischievous. They were very old and they had no human ties or affections. They seemed to look upon the world with a humorous cynicism. They had lived through every kind of illusion and held existence in a malicious and laughing contempt. They had no tolerance for the follies of men and no indulgence for their weakness. There was something vaguely frightening in their entire lack of attachment to human things. They had done with love, they had finished with the anguish of separation, death had no terrors for them, they had nothing left now but laughter. They struck the great bell so that I might hear its tone; boom, boom, it went, a long low note that travelled in slow reverberations down the river, a solemn sound that seemed to call the soul from its tenement of clay and reminded it that though all created things were illusion, in the illusion was also beauty; and the nuns, following the sound, burst into ribald cackles of laughter, hi, hi, hi, that mocked the call of the great bell. Dupes, their laughter said, dupes and fools. Laughter is the only reality.

X

When I left Colombo I had no notion of going to Keng Tung, but on the ship I met a man who told me he had spent five years there. He said it had an important market, held every five days, whither came natives of half a dozen countries and members of half a hundred tribes. It had pagodas darkly splendid and a remoteness that liberated the questing spirit from its anxiety. He said he would sooner live there than anywhere in the world. I asked him what it had offered him and he said, contentment. He was a tall, dark fellow with the aloofness of manner you often find in those who have lived much alone in unfrequented places. Men like this are a little restless in the company of others and though in the smoking room of a ship or at the club bar they may be talkative and convivial, telling their story with the rest, joking and glad sometimes to narrate their unusual experiences, they seem always to hold something back. They have a life in themselves that they keep apart, and there is a look in their eyes, as it were turned inwards, that informs you that this hidden life is the only one that signifies to them. And now and then their eyes betray their weariness with the social round into which hazard or the fear of seeming odd has for a moment forced them. They seem then to long for the monotonous solitude of some place of their predilection where they can be once more alone with the reality they have found.

It was as much the manner of this chance acquaintance as what he told me that persuaded me to make the journey across the Shan States on which I now set out. From the rail-head in Upper Burma to the rail-head in Siam, whence I could get down to Bangkok, it was between six and seven hundred miles. Kind people had done everything possible to render the excursion easy for me and the Resident at Taunggyi had wired to me that he had made arrangements for mules and ponies to be ready for me on my arrival. I had bought in Rangoon such stores as seemed necessary, folding chairs and a table, a filter, lamps and I know not what. I took the train from Mandalay to Thazi, intending there to hire a car for Taunggyi, and a man I had met at the club at Mandalay and who lived at Thazi asked me to have brunch (the pleasant meal of Burma that combines breakfast and lunch) with him before I started. His name was Masterson. He was a man in the early thirties, with a pleasant friendly face, curling dark hair speckled with grey, and handsome dark eyes. He spoke with a singularly musical voice, very slowly, and this, I hardly know why, inspired you with confidence. You felt that a man who took such a long time to say what he had to say and had found the world with sufficient leisure to listen to him must have qualities that made him sympathetic to his fellows. He took the amiability of mankind for granted and I suppose he could only have done this because he was himself amiable. He had a nice sense of humour, without of course a quick thrust and parry, but agreeably sarcastic; it was of that agreeable type that applies commonsense to the accidents of life and so sees them in a faintly ridiculous aspect. He was engaged in a business that kept him travelling up and down Burma most of the year and in his journeyings he had acquired the collector's habit. He told me that he spent all his spare money on buying Burmese curiosities and it was especially to see them that he asked me to have a meal with him.

The train got in early in the morning. He had warned me that, having to be at his office, he could not meet me; but brunch was at ten and he told me to go to his house as soon as I was finished with the one or two things I had to do in the town.

'Make yourself at home,' he said, 'and if you want a drink ask the boy for it. I'll get back as soon as I've got through with my business.'

I found out where there was a garage and made a bargain with the owner of a very dilapidated Ford to take me and my baggage to Taunggyi. I left my Madrassi servant to see that everything was stowed in it that was possible and the rest tied on to the footboards, and strolled along to Masterson's house. It was a neat little bungalow in a

29

road shaded by tall trees, and in the early light of a sunny day looked pretty and homelike. I walked up the steps and was hailed by Masterson.

'I got done more quickly than I expected. I shall have time to show you my things before brunch is ready. What will you have? I'm afraid I can only offer you a whisky and soda.'

'Isn't it rather early for that?'

'Rather. But it's one of the rules of the house that nobody crosses the threshold without having a drink.'

'What can I do but submit to the rule?'

He called the boy and in a moment a trim Burmese brought in a decanter, a syphon and glasses. I sat down and looked about the room. Though it was still so early the sun was hot outside and the jalousies were drawn. The light was pleasant and cool after the glare of the road. The room was comfortably furnished with rattan chairs and on the walls were water-colour paintings of English scenes. They were a little prim and old-fashioned and I guessed that they had been painted in her youth by the maiden and elderly aunt of my host. There were two of a cathedral I did not know, two or three of a rose garden and one of a Georgian house. When he saw my eyes for an instant rest upon this, he said:

'That was our house at Cheltenham.'

'Oh, is that where you come from?'

Then there was his collection. The room was crowded with Buddhas and with figures, in bronze or wood, of the Buddha's disciples; there were boxes of all shapes, utensils of one kind and another, curiosities of every sort, and although there were far too many they were arranged with a certain taste so that the effect was pleasing. He had some lovely things. He showed them to me with pride, telling me how he had got this object and that, and how he had heard of another and hunted it down and the incredible astuteness he had employed to induce an unwilling owner to part with it. His kindly eyes shone when he described a great bargain and they flashed darkly when he inveighed against the unreasonableness of a vendor who rather than accept a fair price for a bronze dish had taken it away. There were flowers in the room, and it had not the forlorn look that so many bachelors' houses have in the East.

'You've made the place very comfortable,' I said.

He gave the room a sweeping glance.

'It *was* all right. It's not much now.'

I did not quite know what he meant. Then he showed me a long wooden gilt box, decorated with the glass mosaic that I had admired in the palace at Mandalay, but the workmanship was more delicate than anything I had seen there, and this with its gem-like richness had really something of the ornate exquisiteness of the Italian Renaissance.

'They tell me it's about a couple of hundred years old,' he said. 'They've not been able to turn out anything like this for a long time.'

It was a piece made obviously for a king's palace and you wondered to what uses it had been put and what hands it had passed through. It was a jewel.

'What is the inside like?' I asked.

'Oh, nothing much, it's just lacquered.'

He opened it and I saw that it contained three or four framed photographs.

'Oh, I'd forgotten those were there,' he said.

His soft, musical voice had a queer sound in it, and I gave him a sidelong look. He was bronzed by the sun, but his face notwithstanding flushed a deeper red. He was about to close the box, and then he changed his mind. He took out one of the photographs and showed it to me.

'Some of these Burmese girls are rather sweet when they're young, aren't they?' he said.

The photograph showed a young girl standing some-what self-consciously against the conventional background of a photographer's studio, a pagoda and a group of palm-trees. She was wearing her best clothes and she had a flower in her hair. But the embarrassment you saw she felt at having her picture taken did not prevent a shy smile from trembling on her lips and her large solemn eyes had nevertheless a roguish twinkle. She was very small and very slender.

'What a ravishing little thing,' I said.

Then Masterson took out another photograph in which she sat with a child standing by her side, his hand timidly on her knee, and a baby in her arms. The child stared straight in front of him with a look of terror on his face; he could not understand what that machine and the man behind it, his head under a black cloth, were up to.

'Are those her children?' I asked.

'And mine,' said Masterson.

At that moment the boy came in to say that brunch was ready. We went into the dining-room and sat down.

'I don't know what you'll get to eat. Since my girl went away everything in the house has gone to blazes.'

A sulky look came into his red honest face and I did not know what to reply.

'I'm so hungry that whatever I get will seem good,' I hazarded.

He did not say anything and a plate of thin porridge was put before me. I helped myself to milk and sugar. Masterson ate a spoonful or two and pushed his plate aside.

'I wish I hadn't looked at those damned photographs,' he said. 'I put them away on purpose.'

I did not want to be inquisitive or to force a confidence my host had no wish to give, but neither did I desire to seem so unconcerned as to prevent him from telling me something he had in his heart. Often in some lonely post in the jungle or in a stiff grand house, solitary in the midst of a teeming Chinese city, a man has told me stories about himself that I was sure he had never told to a living soul. I was a stray acquaintance whom

32

he had never seen before and would never see again, a wanderer for a moment through his monotonous life, and some starved impulse led him to lay bare his soul. I have in this way learned more about men in a night (sitting over a syphon or two and a bottle of whisky, the hostile, inexplicable world outside the radius of an acetylene lamp) than I could have if I had known them for ten years. If you are interested in human nature it is one of the great pleasures of travel. And when you separate (for you have to be up betimes) sometimes they will say to you:

'I'm afraid I've bored you to death with all this nonsense. I haven't talked so much for six months. But it's done me good to get it off my chest.'

The boy removed the porridge plates and gave each of us a piece of pale fried fish. It was rather cold.

'The fish is beastly, isn't it?' said Masterson. 'I hate river fish, except trout; the only thing is to smother it with Worcester sauce.'

He helped himself freely and passed me the bottle.

'She was a damned good housekeeper, my girl; I used to feed like a fighting-cock when she was here. She'd have had the cook out of the house in a quarter of an hour if he'd sent in muck like this.'

He gave me a smile, and I noticed that his smile was very sweet. It gave him a peculiarly gentle look.

'It was rather a wrench parting with her, you know.'

It was quite evident now that he wished to talk and I had no hesitation in giving him a lead.

'Did you have a row?'

'No. You could hardly call it a row. She lived with me five years and we never had a tiff even. She was the best-tempered little thing that ever was. Nothing seemed to put her out. She was always as merry as a cricket. You couldn't look at her without her lips breaking into a smile. She was always happy. And there was no reason why she shouldn't be. I was very good to her.'

'I'm sure you were,' I answered.

'She was mistress here. I gave her everything she wanted. Perhaps if I'd been more of a brute she wouldn't have gone away.'

'Don't make me say anything so obvious as that women are incalculable.'

He gave me a deprecating glance and there was a trace of shyness in the smile that just flickered in his eyes.

'Would it bore you awfully if I told you about it?'

'Of course not.'

'Well, I saw her one day in the street and she rather took my fancy. I showed you her photograph, but the photograph doesn't begin to do her justice. It sounds silly to say about a Burmese girl, but she was like a rose-bud, not an English rose, you know, she was as little like that as the glass flowers on that box I showed you are like real flowers, but a rose grown in an Eastern garden that had something strange and exotic about it. I don't know how to make myself plain?'

'I think I understand what you mean all the same,' I smiled.

'I saw her two or three times and found out where she lived. I sent my boy to make enquiries about her, and he told me that her parents were quite willing that I should have her if we could come to an arrangement. I wasn't inclined to haggle and everything was settled in no time. Her family gave a party to celebrate the occasion and she came to live here. Of course I treated her in every way as my wife and put her in charge of the house. I told the boys that they'd got to take their orders from her and if she complained of any of them out they went. You know, some fellows keep their girls in the servants' quarters and when they go away on tour the girls have a rotten time. Well, I think that's a filthy thing to do. If you are going to have a girl to live with you the least you can do is to see that she has a good time.

'She was a great success and I was as pleased as Punch.

34

She kept the house spotless. She saved me money. She wouldn't let the boys rob me. I taught her to play bridge and believe me, she learned to play a damned good game.'

'Did she like it?'

'Loved it. When people came here she couldn't have received them better if she'd been a duchess. You know, these Burmese have beautiful manners. Sometimes it would make me laugh to see the assurance with which she would receive my guests, government officials, you know, and soldiers who were passing through. If some young subaltern was rather shy she'd put him at his ease at once. She was never pushing or obtrusive, but just there when she was wanted and doing her best to see that everything went well and everyone had a good time. And I'll tell you what, she could mix the best cocktail you'd get anywhere between Rangoon and Bhamo. People used to say I was lucky.'

'I'm bound to say I think you were,' I said.

The curry was served and I piled my plate with rice and helped myself to chicken and then chose from a dozen little dishes the condiments I fancied. It was a good curry.

'Then she had her babies, three in three years, but one died when it was six weeks old. I showed you a photograph of the two that are living. Funny looking little things, aren't they? Are you fond of children?'

'Yes. I have a strange and almost unnatural passion for new-born babies.'

'I don't think I am, you know. I couldn't even feel very much about my own. I've often wondered if it showed that I was rather a rotter.'

'I don't think so. I think the passion many people affect for children is merely a fashionable pose. I have a notion that children are all the better for not being burdened with too much parental love.'

'Then my girl asked me to marry her, legally I mean,

35

in the English way. I treated it as a joke. I didn't know how she'd got such an idea in her head. I thought it was only a whim and I gave her a gold bracelet to keep her quiet. But it wasn't a whim. She was quite serious about it. I told her there was nothing doing. But you know what women are, when they once set their mind on getting something they never give you a moment's peace. She wheedled and sulked, she cried, she appealed to my compassion, she tried to extract a promise out of me when I was rather tight, she was on the watch for me when I was feeling amorous, she nearly tripped me when she was ill. She watched me more carefully, I should think, than a stockbroker ever watched the market, and I knew that, however natural she seemed, however occupied with something else, she was always warily alert for the unguarded moment when she could pounce on me and gain her point.'

Masterson gave me once more his slow, ingenuous smile.

'I suppose women are pretty much the same all the world over,' he said.

'I expect so,' I answered.

'A thing I've never been able to understand is why a woman thinks it worth while to make you do something you don't want to. She'd rather you did a thing against the grain than not do it at all. I don't see what satisfaction it can be to them.'

'The satisfaction of triumph. A man convinced against his will may be of the same opinion still, but a woman doesn't mind that. She has conquered. She has proved her power.'

Masterson shrugged his shoulders. He drank a cup of tea.

'You see, she said that sooner or later I was bound to marry an English girl and turn her out. I said I wasn't thinking of marrying. She said she knew all about that. And even if I didn't I should retire some day and go back to England. And where would she be then? It went on for a year. I held out. Then she said that if I wouldn't marry her she'd go and take the kids with her. I told her not to be a silly little fool. She said that if she left me now she could marry a Burman, but in a few years nobody would want her. She began to pack her things. I thought it was only a bluff and I called it; I said, "Well, go if you want to, but if you do you won't come back." I didn't think she'd give up a house like this, and the presents I made her, and all the pickings, to go back to her own family. They were as poor as church mice. Well, she went on packing her things. She was just as nice as ever to me, she was gay and smiling; when some fellows came to spend the night here she was just as cordial as usual, and she played bridge with us till two in the morning. I couldn't believe she meant to go and yet I was rather scared. I was very fond of her. She was a damned good sort.'

'But if you were fond of her why on earth didn't you marry her? It would have been a great success.'

'I'll tell you. If I married her I'd have to stay in Burma for the rest of my life. Sooner or later I shall retire and then I want to go back to my old home and live there. I don't want to be buried out here, I want to be buried in an English churchyard. I'm happy enough here, but I don't want to live here always. I couldn't. I want England. Sometimes I get sick of this hot sunshine and these garish colours. I want grey skies and a soft rain falling and the smell of the country. I shall be a funny fat elderly man when I go back, too old to hunt even if I could afford it, but I can fish. I don't want to shoot tigers, I want to shoot rabbits. And I can play golf on a proper course. I know I shall be out of it, we fellows who've spent our lives out here always are, but I can potter about the local club and talk to retired Anglo-Indians. I want to feel under my feet the grey pavement of an English country town, I want to be able to go and have a row with the butcher because the steak he sent me in yesterday was tough, and I want to browse about second-hand bookshops. I want to be said how d'you do to in the street by people who knew me when I was a boy. And I want to have a walled garden at the back of my house and grow roses. I daresay it all sounds very humdrum and provincial and dull to you, but that's the sort of life my people have always lived and that's the sort of life I want to live myself. It's a dream if you like, but it's all I have, it means everything in the world to me, and I can't give it up.'

He paused for a moment and looked into my eyes.

'Do you think me an awful fool?'

'No.'

'Then one morning she came to me and said that she was off. She had her things put on a cart and even then I didn't think she meant it. Then she put the two children in a rickshaw and came to say good-bye to me. She began to cry. By George, that pretty well broke me up. I asked her if she really meant to go and she said yes, unless I married her. I shook my head. I very nearly yielded. I'm afraid I was crying too. Then she gave a great sob and ran out of the house. I had to drink about half a tumbler of whisky to steady my nerves.'

'How long ago did this happen?'

'Four months. At first I thought she'd come back and then because I thought she was ashamed to make the first step I sent my boy to tell her that if she wanted to come I'd take her. But she refused. The house seemed awfully empty without her. At first I thought I'd get used to it, but somehow it doesn't seem to get any less empty. I didn't know how much she meant to me. She'd twined herself round my heart.'

'I suppose she'll come back if you agree to marry her.'

'Oh, yes, she told the boy that. Sometimes I ask myself if it's worth while to sacrifice my happiness for a dream. It is only a dream, isn't it? It's funny, one of the things that holds me back is the thought of a muddy lane I know, with great clay banks on both sides of it, and above, beech

38

trees bending over. It's got a sort of cold, earthy smell that I can never quite get out of my nostrils. I don't blame her, you know. I rather admire her. I had no idea she had so much character. Sometimes I'm awfully inclined to give way.' He hesitated for a little while. 'I think, perhaps, if I thought she loved me I would. But of course, she doesn't; they never do, these girls who go and live with white men, I think she liked me, but that's all. What would you do in my place?'

'Oh, my dear fellow, how can I tell? Would you ever forget the dream?'

'Never.'

At that moment the boy came in to say that my Madrassi servant with the Ford car had just come up. Masterson looked at his watch.

'You'll want to be getting off, won't you? And I must get back to my office. I'm afraid I've rather bored you with my domestic affairs.'

'Not at all,' I said.

We shook hands, I put on my topee, and he waved to me as the car drove off.

XI

I spent a few days at Taunggyi completing my preparations and then early one morning started. It was the end of the rainy season and the sky was overcast, but the clouds were high in the heavens and bright. The country was wide and open, sparsely covered with little trees; but now and then, a giant among them, you came upon a huge banyan with wide-spreading roots. It stood upon the earth, a fit object for worship, with a kind of solemnity, as though it were conscious of victory over the blind force of nature and now like a great power aware of its enemy's strength, rested in armed peace. At its foot were the offerings that the Shans had placed to the spirit that dwelt in it. The road wound tortuously up and down gentle declivities and on each side of it, stretching over the upland plains, swayed the elephant grass. Its white fronds waved softly in the balmy air. It was higher than a man and I rode between it like the leader of an army reviewing countless regiments of tall green soldiers.

I rode at the head of the caravan, and the mules and ponies that carried the loads followed at my heels. But one of the ponies, unused perhaps to a pack, was very wild. It had savage eyes. Every now and then it bolted wildly among the mules, hitting them with its packs; then the leading mule headed it off, rounding it into the long grass at the side of the road, and stopped it. They both stood still for a moment and then the mule led the pony quietly back to its place in the file. It walked along quite contentedly. It had had its scamper and for a little while at all events was prepared to behave reasonably. The idea in the mulish brain of the pack-leader was as clear and distinct as any idea of Descartes. In the train was peace, order and happiness. To walk with your nose at the tail of the mule in front of you and to know that the nose of the mule behind you was at your tail, was virtue. Like some philosophers the mule knew that the only liberty was the power to do right; any other power was only licence. Theirs not to reason why, theirs but to do and die.

But presently I came face to face with a buffalo standing stock still in the middle of the road. Now I knew that the Shan buffalo had none of that dislike of my colour that makes white men give the Chinese buffalo a wide berth, but I was not certain whether this particular animal had a very exact notion of nationality, and since his horns were enormous and his eyes far from friendly I thought it prudent to make a slight detour: whereupon the whole file, though neither mules nor muleteers could have had my reason for anxiety, followed me into the elephant grass. I could not but reflect that an undue observance of the law may put you to a good deal of unnecessary trouble.

With abundant leisure before me and nothing to distract, I had promised myself to think out on this journey various things that had been on my mind for a long time. There were a number of subjects, error and evil, space, time, chance and mutability, which I felt I should really come to some conclusion about. I had a great deal to say to myself about art and life, but my ideas were higgledy-piggledy like the objects in an old junk shop and I did not know where to put my hands on them when I wanted them. They were in corners of my mind, like oddments stowed away at the back of a chest of drawers, and I only just knew they were there. Some of them hadn't been taken out and brushed for so long that it was a disgrace, the new and the old were all jumbled together, and some were of no use any more and might just as well be thrown on the dust heap, and some (like a pair of Queen Anne spoons long forgotten that with the four a dealer has just found you in an auction room make up the half dozen) would fit very well with new ones. It would be pleasant to have everything cleaned and dusted, neatly put away on shelves, ordered and catalogued so that I knew what my stock consisted of. I resolved that while I rode through the country I would have a regular spring-cleaning of all my ideas. But the pack-leader had round his neck a raucous bell and it clanged so loudly that my reflections were very much disturbed. It was like a muffin bell and it made me think of Sunday afternoon in the London of my youth, with its empty streets and its grey, cold and melancholy sky. I put the spurs to my pony so that I might trot on and escape the dreary sound, but as soon as I began to do so the leader trotted too and the whole cavalcade trotted after him; I galloped and in a moment mules and ponies, their packs jangling and bumping, were galloping helter-skelter after me, and the muffin bell rattled madly at my heels as though it were knelling the death agonies of all the muffin-makers in

London. I gave it up as a bad job and settled down again to walk; the train slowed down and just behind me the pack-leader shuffled up and down the empty, respectable street offering muffins for tea, muffins and crumpets. I could not put two thoughts together. I resigned myself at least for that day to make no attempt at serious meditation and instead, to pass the time, invented Blenkinsop.

There can be nothing so gratifying to an author as to arouse the respect and esteem of the reader. Make him laugh and he will think you a trivial fellow, but bore him in the right way and your reputation is assured. There was once a man called Blenkinsop. He had no talent, but he wrote a book in which his earnestness and his sincerity, his thoughtfulness and his integrity were so evident that, although it was quite unreadable, no one could fail to be impressed by it. Reviewers were unable to get through it, but could not but recognise the author's high aim and purity of purpose. They praised it with such an enthusiastic unanimity that all the people who flatter themselves they are in the movement felt bound to have it on their tables. The critic of *The London Mercury* said that he would have liked to have written it himself. This was the highest praise he knew. Mr Blenkinsop deplored the grammar but accepted the compliment. Mrs Woolf paid it a generous tribute at Bloomsbury, Mr Osbert Sitwell admired it in Chelsea and Mr Arnold Bennett was judicious about it in Cadogan Square. Smart women of easy morals bought it so that people should not think they had no mind above the Embassy Club and banting. The poets who go to luncheon parties talked of it exactly as though they had read it from cover to cover. It was bought in the great provincial towns where the virtuous young are gathered together at high tea to improve their minds. Mr Hugh Walpole wrote a preface to the American edition. The booksellers placed it in piles in their shop windows with a photograph of the author on one side and a card with long extracts from the more important reviews on the other. In short the vogue of the book was so great that its pubisher said that if it did not stop selling soon he would have to read it himself. Mr Blenkinsop became a celebrity. He was asked to its annual dinner by the Lyceum Club.

Now it happened that just about the time when Mr Blenkinsop's book reached this dizzy height of success, the Prime Minister's secretary presented the Prime Minister with the list of birthday honours. This high dignitary of the Crown looked at it with misgiving.

'A pretty mangy lot,' he said. 'The public will raise a stink about this.'

The secretary was a democrat.

'Who cares?' he said. 'Let the public go and boil itself.'

'Couldn't we do something for arts and letters?' suggested the Prime Minister.

The secretary remarked that almost all the RA's were knights already and those that were kicked up the devil of a row if any others were knighted.

'The more the merrier, I should have thought,' said the Prime Minister flippantly.

'Not at all,' answered the secretary. 'The more titled RA's there are the less is their financial value.'

'I see,' said the Prime Minister. 'But are there no authors in England?'

'I will inquire,' replied the secretary, who had been at Balliol.

He asked at the National Liberal Club and was told that there were Sir Hall Caine and Sir James Barrie. But honours had already been heaped upon them so freely that there seemed nothing more to offer them than the Garter and it was evident that the Lord Mayor of London would be very much put out if they were offered that. The Prime Minister, was, however, insistent and his secretary was in a quandary. But one day when he was being shaved his barber asked him if he had read Blenkinsop's book.

'I'm not much of a reader meself,' he said, 'but our Miss Burroughs, she done your nails last time you was here, she says it's simply divine.'

The Prime Minister's secretary was a man who made it his business to be abreast of the current movements in art and literature, and he was well aware that Blenkinsop's book was a sound piece of work. In honouring him the State would honour itself and the public might swallow without a wry face the baronetcies and peerages that rewarded services of a less obvious character. But he could afford to take no risks and so sent for the manicurist.

'Have you read it?' he asked her point blank.

'No, sir, I haven't exactly what you might call read it, but all the gentlemen who talk about it when I'm doing their nails say it's absolutely priceless.'

The result of this conversation was that the secretary placed Blenkinsop's name before the Prime Minister and told him of his book.

'What do you think about it yourself?' asked the great man.

'I haven't read it, I don't read books,' replied the secretary frigidly, 'but there's nothing about it that I don't know.'

Blenkinsop was offered a KCVO.

'We may just as well do the thing well if we're going to do it at all,' said the Prime Minister.

But Blenkinsop, true to his character, begged to be allowed to refuse the distinction. Here was a pretty kettle of fish! The Prime Minister's secretary was at his wits' end. But the Prime Minister was a man of determination. When he had once made up his mind to do a thing he would allow no obstacle to stand in his way. He discovered the solution in a flash of his fertile brain and literature after all found a place in the birthday honours. A viscounty was conferred on the Editor of Bradshaw's Railway Time Tables.

44

XII

But even when I had learned by experience that if I wanted a quiet ride I must give the mules an hour's start of me I found it impossible to concentrate my thoughts on any of the subjects that I had selected for meditation. Though nothing of the least consequence happened my attention was distracted by a hundred trifling incidents of the wayside. The two big butterflies in black and white fluttered along in front of me, and they were like young war widows bearing the loss they had sustained for their country's sake with cheerful resignation: so long as there were dances at Claridge's and dressmakers in the Place Vendôme they were ready to swear that all was well with the world. A little cheeky bird hopped down the road turning round every now and then jauntily as though to call my attention to her smart suit of silver grey. She looked like a neat typist tripping along from the station to her office in Cheapside. A swarm of saffron butterflies upon the droppings of an ass reminded me of pretty girls in evening frocks hovering round an obese financier. At the roadside grew a flower that was like the Sweet William that I remember in the cottage gardens of my childhood and another had the look of a more leggy white heather. I wish, as many writers do, I could give distinction to these pages by the enumeration of the birds and flowers that I saw as I ambled along on my little Shan pony. It has a scientific air and though the reader skips the passage it gives him a slight thrill of self-esteem to know that he is reading a book with solid fact in it. It puts you on strangely familiar terms with your reader when you tell him you came across P. Johnsonii. It has a significance that is almost cabalistic; you and he (writer and reader) share a knowledge that is not common to all and sundry and there is the sympathy between you that there is between men who wear masonic aprons or Old Etonian ties. You communicate with one another in a secret language. I should be proud to read in a footnote of a learned work on the botany or ornithology of Upper Burma, *Maugham, however, states that he observed F. Jonesia in the Southern Shan States.* But I know nothing of botany and ornithology. I could, indeed, fill a page with the names of all the sciences of which I am completely ignorant. A yellow primrose to me, alas! is not *primula Vulgaris*, but just a small yellow flower, ever so faintly scented with the rain, and grey balmy mornings in February when you have a funny little flutter in your heart, and the smell of the rich wet Kentish earth, and kind dead faces, and the statue of Lord Beaconsfield in his bronze robes in Parliament Square, and the yellow hair of a girl with a sweet smile, hair now grey and shingled.

I passed a party of Shans cooking their dinner under a tree. Their wagons were placed in a circle round them, making a kind of laager, and the bullocks were grazing a little way off. I went on a mile or two and came upon a respectable Burman sitting at the side of the road and smoking a cheroot. Round him were his servants, with their loads on the ground beside them, for he had no mules and they were carrying his luggage themselves. They had made a little fire of sticks and were cooking the rice of his midday meal. I stopped while my interpreter had a chat with the respectable Burman. He was a clerk from Keng Tung on his way to Taunggyi to look for a situation in a government office. He had been on the road for eighteen days and with only four more to go looked upon his journey as nearly at an end. Then a Shan on horseback threw confusion among the thoughts I tried to marshal. He rode a shaggy pony and his feet were bare in his stirrups. He wore a white jacket and his coloured skirt was tucked up so that it looked like gay riding breeches. He had a yellow handkerchief bound round his head. He was a romantic figure cantering through that wide upland, but not so romantic as Rembrandt's *Polish Rider* who rides through space and time with so gallant a bearing. No living horseman has ever achieved that effect of mystery so that when you look at him you feel that you stand on the threshold of an unknown that lures you on and yet closes the way for you. Nor is it strange, for nature and the beauty of nature are dead and senseless things and it is only art that can give them significance.

But with so much to distract me I could not but suspect that I should reach my journey's end without after all having made up my mind upon a single one of the important subjects that I had promised myself to consider.

XIII

The day's march was no more than from twelve to fifteen miles, that being the distance that a mule can comfortably do, and the distance from one another at which the PWD bungalows are placed. But because it is the daily routine it gives you just as much the sensation of covering space as if you had been all day in an express train. When you arrive at your destination you are in reality just as far from your starting place, though you have gone but a few miles, as if you had travelled from Paris to Madrid. When you have ridden along a stream for a couple of days it seems to you of quite imposing length; you ask its name and are surprised to find that it has none, until you stop to reflect that you have followed it for no more than five and twenty miles. And the differences between the upland that you rode through yesterday and the jungle that you are riding through to-day impress themselves upon you as much

47

as the differences between one country and another.

But because the bungalows are built on the same pattern, though you have been riding for several hours (your caravan does little more than two miles an hour) you seem always to arrive at the same house. It stands on piles in a compound a few yards away from the road. There is a large living-room, and behind, two bedrooms with their bath-rooms. In the middle of the living-room is a handsome teak table. There are two easy-chairs with extensions for the legs and four stout, severe armchairs to set round the table. There is a chiffonier on which are copies of the Strand Magazine for 1918 and two tattered much read novels by Phillips Oppenheim. On the walls there is a longitudinal section of the road, a summary of the Burma Game rules and a list of the furniture and the household utensils of the bungalow. In the compound are the servants' quarters, stalls for the ponies and a cook-house. It is certainly not very pretty, it is not very comfortable, but it is solid, substantial and serviceable; and though I had never seen any one bungalow before and after that day should never see it again, I seldom caught sight of it at the end of the morning's journey without a little thrill of content. It was like coming home and when I got my first glimpse of its trim roof I put the spurs to my pony and galloped helter-skelter to the door.

The bungalow stands generally on the outskirts of a village, and when I arrived at the confines of the commune I found waiting to greet me the headman with his clerk and an attendant, a son or nephew, and the elders. When I approached they went down on their haunches, shikoed and offered me a cup of water, a few marigolds and a little rice. I drank the water with misgiving. But once I was handed on a tray eight thin tapers and was told that this was the highest mark of respect that could be shown me, for they were the tapers that were set before the image of Buddha. I could not but be conscious that I little deserved such a compliment. I settled down in the bungalow and then my interpreter informed me that the headman and the elders stood without, desiring to tender the customary presents. They brought them in on lacquer trays, eggs, rice and bananas. I sat down in a chair and they knelt on the floor in a half-circle in front of me. The headman, with abundant gestures but with composure, made me a long harangue. Through the translation that my interpreter gave me I thought I perceived certain phrases that were not unfamiliar to me, and I seemed to discern something about one flag, hands across the sea and the desire that I should take back to my own country not only a greeting from this distant land, but the urgent request of the inhabitants that the government would build a metal road. I felt it became me to make a reply if not as eloquent at least as long. I was only a wandering stranger, and if by the instructions they had received to make easy my way they had been misled into thinking me a person of any consequence I could at least do myself the justice of not behaving like one. I am no politician and I was too shamefaced to utter the imperial platitudes that fall so trippingly from the mouth of those who make it their business to govern empires. Perhaps I might have told my listeners that they were fortunate in being under the control of a power that was content to leave them alone. Once a year the Resident of the district came round and composed the differences that they could not compose themselves, listened to their complaints, appointed a new headman when one was needed, and then left them to their own devices. They governed themselves according to their own customs and they were free to grow their rice, to marry, bring forth children, and die, to worship the gods they chose, without let or hindrance. They saw no soldiers and had no jail. But I felt that these matters were not of my competence and so contented myself with the smaller office of amusing them. Though no speaker (I can count on one hand the speeches that on public occasions

49

I have been induced to make), it was not hard to devise a few graceful and humorous remarks in return for the eggs, bananas and rice which were presented to me.

It is not easy, however, to make forty different speeches about eggs, bananas and rice, and the eggs I soon learnt by experience were far from fresh. But thinking my interpreter would despise me if I said the same thing every day, in the morning as I rode along I racked my brain for new ways of expressing my gratification at my welcome and my present. I invented as one day followed another more than thirty different speeches and when I sat there while my interpreter translated what I had said, it was a satisfaction for me to see the little nods the headman and the elders gave me when a point had gone home and the way they shook themselves when they saw a joke. Now one morning I suddenly thought of an entirely new jest. It was a very good one and I saw in the twinkling of an eye how I could bring it into my speech. The lot of the English and the American humorist is hard, for pornography rather than brevity is the soul of wit, but the prudishness of his audience (and perhaps their sentimentality) has forced him to look for a laugh everywhere but where it is most easily to be found. But just as the poet may beat out more exquisite verse when he is constrained by the complicated measures of a Pindaric ode than when he has the elbow room of blank verse, so the difficulties placed in the way of our humorists have often resulted in their making unexpected discoveries in the ludicrous. They have found a rich load of laughter where but for the taboos they would never have sought it. The two pitfalls that threaten the humorist are the inane on one side and the disgusting on the other; and it is a regrettable fact, which the English or American humorist has to put up with, that the inane enrages more than the disgusting revolts.

But by this time I knew my public and this joke, though

I hope not coarse, just touched the obscene as a mosquito touches your face and then flies away buzzing when you slap. It amused me very much, and as I rode along I thought of the headman and the elders of the village I was approaching, on their knees on the floor in front of me, shaking with laughter and rolling from side to side.

We arrived. The village chief was a man of fifty-seven and he had been headman for thirty years. He brought his nephew, a shy youth with the beginnings of a beard, four or five elders and the clerk, who sat a little by himself, a man of immeasurable age, wrinkled, with a sparse grey beard, a man so old that he seemed hardly human. He looked like a pagoda which is tumbling into ruin and soon the encroaching jungle will fall upon it and it will be no more.

In due time I made my speech and when I came to my good joke the interpreter giggled and his eyes glistened. I was pleased. I finished and sat back in my chair while he translated my winged words. The little half-circle of listeners turned from me to him and watched him with dark, attentive eyes. He was a good speaker, my interpreter, fluent, with a gift of easy and descriptive gesture. I always felt that he did me justice. I had never made a wittier speech. I was surprised that it did not seem to go down. Not a smile rewarded any of my sallies; they listened politely, but no change in their expression suggested that they were either interested or amused. I had kept my best joke for the last and as I reckoned that it was approaching, a smile on my lips, I leaned forward. The interpreter finished. Not a laugh, not a chuckle. I will admit that I was put out. I signified to the headman that the ceremony was at an end, they shikoed, struggled to their feet, and one after the other left the bungalow.

For a moment I hesitated.

'They didn't seem to me very intelligent,' I hazarded.

'They were the stupidest lot of people we've come across,' said my interpreter, and there was indignation in his tone. 'I've made the same jokes every day and this is the first time they've never laughed.'

I was a trifled startled. I was not sure that I understood.

'I beg your pardon?' I said.

'What for you say all sorts of different things, sir? You take too much trouble for ignorant men like that. I make the same speech every day and they like it very much.'

I was silent for a moment.

'For all you care I might just as well say the multiplication table,' I said then, with what I thought a certain irony.

My interpreter smiled brightly, flashing a great many white teeth at me.

'Yes, sir, that will save you a lot of trouble,' he said. 'You say the multiplication table and then I make my speech.'

The worst of it was that I could not be quite certain that I remembered it.

XIV

When I set out in the early morning the dew was so heavy that I could see it falling, and the sky was grey; but in a little while the sun pierced through and in the sky, blue now, the cumulus clouds were like white sea-monsters gambolling sedately round the North Pole. The country was thinly peopled and on each side of the road was the jungle. For some days we went through pleasant uplands by a broad track, unmetalled but hard, its surface deeply furrowed by the passage of bullock-carts. Now and then I saw a pigeon and now and then a crow, but there were few birds. Then leaving the open spaces we passed through secluded hills and forests of bamboo. A bamboo forest is a graceful thing. It has the air of an enchanted wood and you can imagine that in its green shade the princess, heroine of an Eastern story, and the prince her lover might very properly undergo their incredible and fantastic adventures. When the sun shines through and a tenuous breeze flutters its elegant leaves, the effect is charmingly unreal: it has a beauty not of nature, but of the theatre.

At last we arrived at the Salween. This is one of the great rivers that rise far up in the Tibetan steppes, the Bramahputra, the Irrawaddy, the Salween and the Mehkong, and roll southwards in parallel courses to pour their mighty waters into the Indian Ocean. Being very ignorant I had never heard of it till I went to Burma and even then it was nothing to me but a name. It had none of the associations that are for ever attached to such rivers as the Ganges, the Tiber and the Guadalquiver. It was only as I went along that it gained a meaning to me and with a meaning mystery. It was a measure of distance, we were seven days from the Salween, then six; it seemed very remote; and at Mandalay I had heard people say:

'Don't the Rogers live on the Salween? You must go and stay with them when you cross.'

'Oh, my dear fellow,' someone expostulated, 'they live right down on the Siamese frontier, he won't be going within three weeks' journey of them.'

And when we passed some rare traveller on the road perhaps my interpreter after talking to him would come and tell me that he had crossed the Salween three days before. The water was high, but was going down; in bad weather it was no joke crossing. 'Beyond the Salween' had a stirring sound and the country seemed dim and aloof. I added one little impression to another, a detached fact, a word, an epithet, the recollection of an engraving in an old book, enriching the name with associations as the lover in Stendhal's book decks his beloved with the jewels of his fancy, and soon the thought of the Salween intoxicated my imagination. It became the Oriental river of my dreams, a broad stream, deep and secret, flowing through wooded hills, and it had romance, and a dark mystery so that you could scarcely believe that it rose here and there poured itself into the ocean, but like a symbol of eternity flowed from an unknown source to lose itself at last in an unknown sea.

We were two days from the Salween; then one. We left the high road and took a rocky path that wound through the jungle in and out of the hills. There was a heavy fog and the bamboos on each side were ghostly. They were like the pale wraiths of giant armies that had fought desperate wars in the beginning of the world's long history and now, lowering, waited in ominous silence, waited and watched for one knew not what. But every now and then, straight and imposing, rose dimly the shadow of a tall, an immensely tall tree. An unseen brook babbled noisily, but for the rest silence surrounded one. No birds sang and the crickets were still. One seemed to go stealthily, as though one had no business there, and dangers encompassed one all about. Spectral eyes seemed to watch one. Once when a branch broke and fell to the ground it was with so sharp and unexpected a sound that it startled one like a pistol shot.

But at last we came out into the sunshine and soon passed through a bedraggled village. Suddenly I saw the Salween shining silvery in front of me. I was prepared to feel like stout Cortez on his peak and was more than ready to look upon that sheet of water with a wild surmise, but I had already exhausted the emotion it had to offer me. It was a more ordinary and less imposing stream than I had expected; indeed then, and there, it was no wider than the Thames at Chelsea Bridge. It flowed without turbulence, swiftly and silently.

The raft (two dug-outs on which was built a platform of bamboos) was at the water's edge and we set about unloading the mules. One of them, seized with a sudden panic, bolted for the river and before anyone could stop him plunged in. He was carried away on the current,

54

I would never have thought that that turbid, sluggish stream had such a power; he was swept along the reach, swiftly, swiftly, and the muleteers shouted and waved their arms. We could see the poor brute struggling desperately, but it was inevitable that he would be drowned and I was thankful when a bend of the river robbed me of the sight of him. When with my pony and my personal effects I was ferried across the stream I looked at it with more respect, and since the raft seemed to me none too secure I was not sorry when I reached the other side.

The bungalow was on the top of the bank. It was surrounded by lawns and flowers. Poinsettias enriched it with their brilliant hues. It had a little less than the austerity common to the bungalows of the PWD and I was glad that I had chosen this place to linger for a day or two in order to rest the mules and my own weary limbs. From the windows the river shut in by the hills looked like an ornamental water. I watched the raft going backwards and forwards bringing over the mules and their loads. The muleteers were cheerful because they were to get their rest and I had given the headman a trifling sum so that they could have a treat.

Then, their duties accomplished and the servants having unpacked my things, peace descended upon the scene, and the river, empty as though man had never adventured up its winding defiles, regained its dim remoteness. There was not a sound. The day waned and the peace of the water, the peace of the tree-clad hills and the peace of the evening were three exquisite things. There is a moment just before sundown when the trees seem to detach themselves from the dark mass of the jungle and become individuals. Then you cannot see the wood for the trees. In the magic of the hour they seem to acquire a life of a new kind so that it is not hard to imagine that spirits inhabit them and with dusk they will have the power to change their places.

You feel that at some uncertain moment some strange thing will happen to them and they will be wondrously transfigured. You hold your breath waiting for a marvel the thought of which stirs your heart with a kind of terrified eagerness. But the night falls; the moment has passed and once more the jungle takes them back. It takes them back as the world takes young people who, feeling in themselves the genius which is youth, hesitate for an instant on the brink of a great adventure of the spirit, and then engulfed by their surroundings sink back into the vast anonymity of human kind. The trees again become part of the wood; they are still and if not lifeless, alive only with the sullen and stubborn life of the jungle.

The spot was so lovely and the bungalow with its lawns and trees so homelike and peaceful that for a moment I toyed with the notion of staying there not a day, but a year, not a year but all my life. Ten days from a railhead and my only communication with the outside world the trains of mules that passed occasionally between Taunggyi and Keng Tung, my only intercourse the villagers from the bedraggled village on the other side of the river, and so to spend the years away from the turmoil, the envy and bitterness and malice of the world, with my thoughts, my books, my dog and my gun and all about me the vast, mysterious and luxuriant jungle. But alas, life does not consist only of years, but of hours, the day has twenty-four and it is no paradox that they are harder to get through than a year; and I knew that in a week my restless spirit would drive me on, to no envisaged goal it is true, but on as dead leaves are blown hither and thither to no purpose by a gusty wind. But being a writer (no poet, alas! but merely a writer of stories) I was able to lead for others a life I could not lead for myself. This was a fit scene for an idyll of young lovers and I let my fancy wander as I devised a story to fit the tranquil and lovely scene. But, I do not know why unless it is that in beauty is always something tragic, my

56

invention threw itself into a perverse mould and disaster fell upon the thin wraiths of my imagination.

But on a sudden I heard a commotion in the compound and my Ghurka servant coming in at that moment with a gin and bitters, with which I was accustomed to bid the departing day farewell, I asked him what was the matter. He spoke tolerable English.

'The mule that was drowned, he come back,' he said.

'Dead or alive?' I asked.

'Oh, he alive all right. The mule fellow he give mule a damn good beating.'

'Why?'

'Teach him not to show off.'

Poor mule! Freedom from the heavy load and the saddle that galled his sores, and that wild excitement when he saw the broad river before him and the green hills on the other side. Oh, for an escapade! Just a fling after all those days of humdrum labour and the joy of feeling the strength of one's limbs. The dash down to the river and then the irresistible force of the stream that carried one off, the desperate effort and the panting, the sudden fear of death, and at last a couple of miles down, the struggle to the safe shore. The scamper along a jungle path and then the approach of night. Well, one had had one's fling and one felt all the better for it, now one could go back quite quietly to the compound where all the other mules were and one was ready next day or the day after to take up one's load again and go quietly on one's way in the file, one's nose at the tail of the mule ahead of one; and when one got back, happy and rested after the adventure, they beat one because they said one had been showing off. As if one cared enough for them to bother to show off. Oh, well, it was worth a hiding. Whoops, dearie!

XV

I took to the road once more. One day followed another with a monotony in which was nothing tedious. At dawn a cock, crowing loudly, woke me; and the various sounds in the compound, first one and then after a pause another, stealing upon the silence of the night a little uncertainly, as in a symphony one instrument takes up after another the first notes of a theme, the theme of the day and the labour of man, the various sounds in the compound prevented me from going to sleep again: there was the bell around the neck of a mule that tinkled as he stirred or the shake another gave himself and the hee-haw of an ass; there were the lazy movements of the muleteers, their muffled talk, and their cries as they called their beasts. The gathering light crept into my room. Then I heard my servants moving and in a little while my Ghurka boy, Rang Lal by name, brought me my tea and took down my mosquito curtains. I drank the tea and smoked the first delicious cigarette of the day. Pleasant thoughts crowded upon me, scraps of dialogue, a metaphor or a sonorous phrase, a trait or two to add to a character, an episode, and it was charming to lie there idly and let my fancy wander. But Rang Lal brought in my shaving water, silently, and the thought that it would soon grow cold urged me to get up. I shaved and had my bath and breakfast was ready. If I was in luck the headman of the village or the *durwan* of the bungalow had made me a present of a papaia. This is a fruit that many people dislike and it is true that it needs getting used to; but when you have, you cannot but acquire a passion for it. It combines a clean and delicate savour with medicinal virtues (for does it not contain some almost incredible

58

percentage of pepsine?) so that in eating it you not only satisfy the grossness of your appetite, but attend likewise to your soul's welfare. It is like a beautiful woman whose conversation is instructive and elevating.

Then I smoked my pipe and to clear my mind read, idly enough, I fear, some philosophical treatise that was not too heavy to hold in one hand. The first lot of mules had already got away, and now my bedding was rolled up, the things I had used for breakfast were put into the proper boxes, and everything was loaded on such of the mules as had remained behind. I let them get ahead. I was left alone in the bungalow, my pony tethered to a fence, and I watched with the eyes of my mind, so to say, while the village about me, the trees outside the bungalow, the chairs and tables, returned to the humdrum repose from which for a few hours the arrival of myself and my caravan had rudely snatched them. When I went down the steps and untethered my pony, silence, like an old mad woman with a finger on her lips, crept past me into the room that I had left. The map of the road hung on its nail more solidly because I was gone and the long chair in which I had been sitting gave a creaky sigh.

I started riding.

I caught up with the mules as they were nearing the bungalow and knowing it was close they increased their pace. They went along now with a sort of bustle, the bells ringing, the loads jangling, and the muleteers shouted to them and called out to one another. The muleteers were Yunnanese, strapping fellows, with bronzed faces, ragged and unwashed, but they bore themselves with a bold insouciance. Up and down Asia they marched with a lazy stride, hundreds upon hundreds of miles, and in their dark eyes were open spaces and the dim blue of far-off mountains. The mules crowded round them in the compound, each wanting his own load taken off first, and there was a shouting and a kicking and a jostling. The load is lashed to the yokes with leather thongs and it needs two men to take it off. When this was done the mule retreated a step or two and bowed his head as though he were bowing his thanks for the release. Then the pack-saddle was taken off him and he lay down on the ground and rolled over and over to ease his back of the irritation. One after the other as they were freed the mules wandered out of the compound to the herbage and their liberty.

Gin and bitters waited for me on the table, then my curry was served, and I flung myself in a long chair and went to sleep. When I woke I went out with my gun. The headman had designated two or three young men to show me where I could shoot pigeon or jungle-fowl, but game was shy and I am a bad shot and I came back generally with nothing for my pains but a scramble in the bush. The light was failing. The muleteers called the mules to shut them up for the night in the compound. They called in a shrill falsetto, a sound wild and barbaric that seemed scarcely human; it was a peculiar, even a terrifying cry, and it suggested vaguely the vast distances of Asia and the nomad tribes of heaven knows how many ages back from which they were descended.

I read till my dinner was ready. If I had crossed a river that day I ate a bony, tasteless fish; if not, sardines or tunny; a dish of tough meat, and one of the three sweets that my Indian cook knew how to make. Then I played patience.

I reproached myself as I set out the cards. Considering the shortness of life and the infinite number of important things there are to do during its course, it can only be the proof of a flippant disposition that one should waste one's time in such a pursuit. I had with me a number of books that would have improved my mind and others, masterpieces of style, by the study of which I might have made progress in the learning of this difficult language in which we write. I had a volume, small enough to carry in my pocket, that contained all the tragedies of

Shakespeare and I had resolved to read one act of one play on every day of my journey. I promised myself thus both entertainment and profit. But I knew seventeen varieties of patience. I tried the Spider and never by any chance got it out; I tried the patience they play at the Florence Club (and you should hear the shout of triumph which goes up when some Florentine of noble family, Pazzi or Strozzi, accomplishes it) and I tried a patience, the most incredibly difficult of all, that was taught me by a Dutch gentleman from Philadelphia. Of course the perfect patience has never been invented. This should take a long time to do; it should be complicated, calling forth all the ingenuity you have; it should require profound thought and demand from you solid reasoning, the exercise of logic and the weighing of chances; it should be full of hairbreadth escapes so that your heart palpitates as you see what disaster might have befallen you had you put down the wrong card; it should poise you dizzy on the topmost peak of suspense when you consider that your fate hangs on the next card you turn up; it should wring your withers with apprehension; it should have desperate perils that you must avoid and incredible difficulties that only a reckless courage can surmount; and at the end, if you have made no mistake, if you have seized opportunity by the forelock and wrung unstable fortune by the neck, victory should always crown your efforts.

But since such a patience does not exist, in the long run I generally returned to that which has immortalised the name of Canfield. Though it is of course very difficult to get out, you are at least sure of some result, and when all seems lost the turning of a sudden happy card may grant you a respite. I have heard that this estimable gentleman was a gambler in New York and he sold you the pack for fifty dollars and gave you five dollars for every card you got out. The establishment was palatial, supper was free and champagne flowed freely; negroes shuffled the packs for you. There were Turkey carpets on the floors and pictures by Meissonier and Lord Leighton on the walls, and there were life-sized statues in marble. I think it must have been very like Lansdowne House.

Looking back on it from this distance it had for me something of the charm of a genre picture and as I set out the seven cards, and then the six, I saw from my quiet room in the jungle bungalow (as it were through the wrong end of a telescope) the rooms brightly lit with glass chandeliers, the crowd of people, the haze of smoke and the tense, strained, tragic feeling of the gambling-hell. I was held for a moment in the great world with its complications, vice and dissipation. It is one of the mistakes that people make to think that the East is depraved; on the contrary the Oriental has a modesty that the ordinary European would find fantastic. His virtue is not the same as the European's, but I think he is more virtuous. Vice you must look for in Paris, London or New York, rather than in Benares or Peking. But whether this is due to the fact that the Oriental, not being oppressed as we are by the sense of sin, feels no need to transgress the rules that during the long course of his history he has found it convenient to make, or whether, as is shown by his art and literature (which after all are only complicated, but monotonous variations on a single theme) he is unimaginative, who am I to say?

It was time for me to go to bed. I got under my mosquito curtain, lit my pipe and read the novel which I kept for that particular moment. I had looked forward to it all day. It was *Du Côte de Guermantes* and in my fear of coming to the end of it too quickly (I had read it before and could not really start on it again the moment I had finished it) I limited myself rigidly to thirty pages at a time. A great deal of course was exquisitely boring, but what did I care? I would sooner be bored by Proust than amused by anybody else, and I finished the thirty pages all too soon; I seemed to have to hold back my eyes not

62

to run along the lines too quickly. I put out my lamp and fell into a dreamless sleep.

But I could have sworn I had not been asleep ten minutes when a cock, crowing loudly, woke me; and the various sounds in the compound, first one and then after a pause another, broke in upon the silence of the night. The gathering light crept into my room. Another day began.

XVI

I lost count of time. The track now could no longer be called a road and a bullock-cart could not have gone along it; it was no more than a narrow path and we went in single file. We began to climb, and a river, a tributary of the Salween, ran over rocks boisterously below us. The track wound up and down hills through the defiles of the range we were crossing, now at the level of the river, and then high above it. The sky was blue, not with the brilliant, provocative blue of Italy, but with the Eastern blue, which is milky, pale and languorous. The jungle now had all the air of the virgin forest of one's fancy: tall trees, rising straight, without a branch, for eighty or a hundred feet flaunted their power majestically in the sun. Creepers with gigantic leaves entwined them and the smaller trees were covered with parasitic plants as a bride is covered by her veil. The bamboos were sixty feet high. The wild plantains grew everywhere. They seemed set in their places by some skilful gardener, for they had the air of consciously completing the decoration. They were magnificent. The lower leaves were torn and yellow and bedraggled; they were like wicked old women who looked with envy and malice on the beauty of youth; but the upper ones, lissom, green and lovely, lifted their splendour proudly. They had the haughtiness and the callous indifference of youthful beauty; their ample surface took the sun like water.

One day, looking for a short cut, I ventured along a path that led straight into the jungle. There was more life than I had seen while I kept to the highway; the jungle-fowl scurried over the tops of the trees as I passed, pigeons cooed all about me, and a hornbill sat quite still on a branch to let me look at it. I can never quite get over my surprise at seeing at liberty birds and beasts whose natural habitation seems a Zoological Garden, and I remember once in a far island away down in the South East of the Malay Archipelago, when I saw a great cockatoo staring at me I looked about for the cage from which it had escaped and could not realise for a moment that it was at home there and had never known confinement.

The jungle was not very thick and the sun finding its bold way through the trees diapered the ground with a coloured and fantastic pattern. But after a while it began to dawn on me that I was lost, not seriously and tragically lost as may happen to one in the jungle, but astray as one might be in the squares and terraces of Bayswater; I did not want to retrace my steps and the pathway, with the sun shining on it, was tempting: I thought I would go on a little further and see what happened. And suddenly I came upon a tiny village; it consisted of no more than four or five houses surrounded by a stockade of bamboos. I was as surprised to find it there, right in the jungle and six or seven miles from the main road, as its inhabitants must have been to see me, but neither they nor I would betray by our demeanour that there was anything odd about it. Small children playing on the dry, dusty ground scattered at my approach (I remembered how in one place I was asked if two little boys who had never seen a white man might be brought to have a look at me and were promptly carried away screaming with terror at the revolting sight); but the women, carrying buckets of water or pounding rice, went on unconcernedly with their tasks; and the men, sitting on their verandahs, gave me but an indifferent glance. I wondered how those people had found their way there and what they did; they were self-subsistent, living a life entirely of their own, and as much cut off from the outside world as though they dwelt on an atoll in the South Seas. I knew and could know nothing of them. They were as different from me as though they belonged to another species. But they had passions like mine, the same hopes, the same desires, the same griefs. To them, too, I suppose, love came like sunshine after rain, and to them too, I suppose, came satiety. But for them the days unchanging added their long line to one another without haste and without surprise; they followed their appointed round and led the lives their fathers had led before them. The pattern was traced and all they had to do was to follow it. Was that not wisdom and in their constancy was there not beauty?

I urged my pony on and in a few yards I was once more in the thick of the jungle. I continued to climb, the path crossing and recrossing little rushing streams, and then wound down, wound round the hills, the trees growing upon them so densely that you felt you could walk upon the tree-tops as though upon a green floor, until all sunny I saw the plain and the village for which I was bound that day.

It was called Mong Pying and I had made up my mind to rest there for a little. It was very warm and in the afternoon I sat in shirt sleeves on the verandah of the bungalow. I was surprised to see approaching me a white man. I had not seen one since I left Taunggyi. Then I remembered that before leaving they had told me that somewhere along the road I should meet an Italian priest. I rose to meet him. He was a thin man, tall for an Italian, with regular features and large handsome eyes. His face, sallow from malaria, was covered almost to the eyes with a luxuriant black beard that curled as boldly as the beard of an Assyrian king. And his hair was abundant, black and curling. I guessed him to be somewhere between thirty-five and forty. He was dressed in a shabby black cassock, stained and threadbare, a battered khaki helmet, white trousers and white shoes.

'I heard you were coming,' he said to me. 'Just think, I haven't seen a white man for eighteen months.'

He spoke fluent English.

'What will you have?' I asked him. 'I can offer you whisky, or gin and bitters, or tea or coffee.'

He smiled.

'I haven't had a cup of coffee for two years. I ran out of it, and I found I could do without it very well. It was an extravagance and we have so little money for this mission. But it is a deprivation.'

I told the Ghurka boy to make him a cup and when he tasted it his eyes glistened.

'Nectar,' he cried. 'It is real nectar. People should do without things more. It is only then that you really enjoy them.'

'You must let me give you two or three tins.'

'Can you spare them? I will send you some lettuces from my garden.'

'But how long have you been here then?' I asked.

'Twelve years.'

He was silent for a moment.

'My brother, who is a priest in Milan, offered to send me the money to go back to Italy so that I might see my mother before she died. She is an old woman and she cannot live much longer. They used to say I was her favourite son and indeed when I was a child she used to spoil me. I should have liked to see her once more, but to tell you the truth I was afraid to go; I thought that if I did I should not have the courage to come back here to my people. Human nature is very weak, do you not think so? I could not trust myself.' He smiled and gave

66

a gesture that was oddly pathetic. 'Never mind, we shall meet again in Paradise.'

Then he asked me if I had a camera. He was very anxious to send a photograph of his new church to the lady in Lombardy through whose pious generosity he had been able to build it. He took me to it, a great wooden barn, severe and bare; the reredos was decorated with an execrable picture of Jesus Christ painted by one of the nuns at Keng Tung, and he begged me to take a photograph of this also so that when I went there and visited the convent I could show the nun how her work looked in place. There were two little pews for the scanty congregation. He was proud, as well he might be, because the church, the altar and the pews had been built by himself and his converts. He took me to his compound and showed me the modest building which served as school-room and as sleeping-quarters for the children in his charge. I think he told me that there were six and thirty of them. He led me into his own little bungalow. The living-room was fairly spacious and this till the church was built he had used also as a chapel. At the back was a tiny bedroom no larger than a monk's cell, in which was nothing but a small wooden bed, a washing-stand and a book-shelf. Alongside of this was a tiny, rather dirty and untidy kitchen. There were two women in it.

'You see I am very grand now, I have a cook and a kitchen-maid,' he said.

The younger woman had a hare-lip and, giggling, took pains to hide it with her hand. The father said something to her. The other was squatting on the ground pounding some herb in a mortar and he patted her kindly on the shoulder.

'They have been here nearly a year now,' he said. 'They are mother and daughter. The woman, poor thing, had a malformed hand and the girl, as you see, that terrible lip.'

67

The woman had had a husband and two children besides the girl with the hare-lip; but they had died suddenly, within a few weeks of one another, and the people of her village, thinking that she was possessed of an evil spirit, drove her out, her and her daughter, penniless, into a world of which she knew nothing. She went to another village in the jungle where lived a catechist, for she had heard that the Christians did not fear the spirits, and the catechist was willing to give her lodging; but he was very poor and could not provide her with food. He told her to go to the father. This was a five-day journey and it was the beginning of the rainy season. She and her daughter shouldered their small possessions, they were no more than they could carry in a little bundle on their backs, and set out, walking along the jungle paths, up and down the hills, and at night they slept in a village if they came upon one and if not in such resting-place, in the shadow of a rock or under the branches of a tree, as they found by the wayside. But the people of the villages through which they passed sought to dissuade them from their purpose, for it was well known that the father took children into his house and after a while bore them away to Rangoon where he offered them to the spirit of the sea and received money for them. They were terrified, but no village would keep them and the father was their only refuge. They went on and at last, desperate but panic-stricken, presented themselves to him. He told them that they could live in an out-house and cook the rice of the children in the school.

We went into the living-room and sat down. It was bare of every sort of comfort. There was a large table and two or three wooden chairs, straight-backed and severe; there were shelves on which were a number of religious books, paper-bound and musty, and a great many Catholic periodicals. The only secular book I saw was that dreary masterpiece *I Promessi Sposi*. (When

68

Manzoni met Sir Walter Scott who complimented him on his work he, acknowledging his debt to the Waverley Novels, said that it was not his book, but Sir Walter's, upon which Sir Walter replied, then it is my best book. But he spoke from his generous heart; it is of an almost intolerable tediousness.) But the father received a daily paper from Italy, the *Corriere della Sera*, arriving in bundles once a month, and he told me that he read every word of every one.

'It amuses me,' he said, 'of course, but I do it also as well, as a spiritual exercise, for I cannot afford to let my faculties rust. I know everything that is happening in Italy, what operas they are doing at the Scala, what plays are given, and what books are published. I read the political speeches. Everything. In that way I keep abreast of the world. My mind remains active. I do not suppose I shall ever return to Italy, but if I do I shall step back in my environment as though I had never been away. In this kind of life one must never let go of oneself for a minute.'

He talked fluently, in a resonant voice, and he was quick to smile; he had a loud and hearty laugh. When first he came to this place he put up at the PWD bungalow and set about learning the language. The rest of his time he spent building the little house in which I now sat. Then he went out into the jungle.

'I can do nothing with the Shans,' he told me. 'They are Buddhists and they are satisfied with Buddhism. It suits them.' He gave me a deprecating look of his fine black eyes and with a smile made a statement that I could see was so bold to his mind that he was a trifle startled at it himself. 'You know, one must admit that Buddhism is a beautiful religion. I have long talks sometimes with the monk at the Pongyi Chaun, he is not an uneducated man, and I cannot but respect him and his faith.'

He soon discovered that he could hope to influence only the people in the little lonely villages in the jungle, for they were spirit-worshippers and their lives were perplexed by the unceasing dread of the malignant powers that lay in wait to ensnare them. But the villages were far away, in the mountains, and often he had to go twenty, thirty or even forty miles to reach them.

'Do you ride?' I asked.

'No, I walk. I don't say I wouldn't ride if I could afford a pony, but I am glad to walk. In this country you need plenty of exercise. I suppose that when I get old I shall have to have a pony, and by then I may have the money to buy one, but as long as I am in the prime of life there is no reason I should not travel on the legs God gave me.'

It was his custom on arriving at a village to go to the headman's house and ask for lodging. When the people came back in the evening from their work he gathered them together on the verandah and talked to them. Now, after all these years, they knew him for forty miles around and they made him welcome. Sometimes a message came to ask him to go to some distant village that he had not yet visited so that they could hear what he had to say.

I remembered the lonely little village, shut off by the pressing growth of that dense verdure, that I had come upon in the jungle. I wanted to form in my mind's eye some picture of the lives those people led in it. The father shrugged his shoulders when I questioned him.

'They work. Men and women work together. It is a constant round of unceasing toil. Believe me, life is not easy in the jungle villages up in the mountains. They sow their rice, and you know what time and trouble it takes, and then they reap it; they cultivate opium, and when they have an interval they go into the jungle to gather the jungle produce. They do not starve, but they only save themselves from starvation because they never rest.'

As I wandered through the country, fording rivers or crossing them by rustic bridges, going up and down the tree-clad hills, passing between the rice fields, stopping for a night at one village of bamboo houses after another,

70

talking with that long succession of headmen, their faces wizened or hardy, I seemed to myself like a figure in a tapestry that lined the halls of some old, infinitely deserted palace, an interminable tapestry of a sombre green in which you see dimly dark stiff trees and faded streams, hamlets of strange houses and shadowy people occupied without pause with actions that have a mystical, hieratic and obscure significance. But sometimes when I arrived at a village and the headman and the elders, kneeling on the ground, gave me their presents, I had seemed to read in their large dark eyes a strange hunger. They looked at me humbly, as though they were expecting from me a message for which they had been long eagerly waiting. I wished that I could make them a discourse that would stir them; I wished that I could deliver to them the glad tidings for which they seemed to hanker. I could tell them nothing of a Beyond of which I knew nothing. The priest at least could give them something. I saw him arriving, footsore and weary, at some village, and when the approach of night prevented the people from working any longer, sitting on the floor on the verandah, lit by the moon perhaps, but perhaps only by the stars, and telling them, silent shadows in the darkness, things strange and new.

I do not think he was a very intellectual man; he had character, of course, and shrewdness. He knew quite well that the hill Shans let their children come to him only because he clothed, lodged and fed them, but he shrugged his shoulders tolerantly; they would return to their hills when they were of a proper age, and though some would revert to the savage beliefs of their fathers, others would retain the faith he had taught them and by their influence perhaps lighten the darkness that surrounded them. He led too busy a life to have much time for reflection, and certainly there was in his mind no mystical strain; his faith was strong, as an athlete's arms are muscular, and he accepted the dogmas of his religion as unquestioningly

71

as you and I accept the fact of single vision or the flushing cheek. He told me that he had had a desire to come to the East as a missionary when he was still a seminarist and had studied in Milan to that end. He showed me a photograph of the group, sitting round the bishop, who had come out with him, twelve of them, and pointed out to me those that were dead. This one had been drowned crossing a river in China, that one had died of cholera in India, and the other had been killed by the wild Was up in the north of the Shan States. I asked him when he had sailed and without a moment's hesitation he gave me the day of the week, the day of the month and the year; whatever anniversaries they may forget, these nuns, monks and secular priests, the date on which they left Europe remains on the tip of their tongues. Then he showed me a photograph of his family, a typical group of lower middle-class people, such as you may see in the window of any cheap photographer in Italy. They were stiff, formal and self-conscious, the father and mother sitting in the middle in their best clothes, two younger children arranged on the floor at their feet, a daughter on each side of them and behind, standing according to their heights, a row of sons. The priest pointed out to me those that had entered religion.

'More than half,' I commented.

'It has been a great happiness to our mother,' he said. 'It is her doing.'

She was a stout woman, in a black dress, with her hair parted in the middle and large, soft eyes. She looked like a good housekeeper and I had little doubt that when it came to buying and selling she could drive a hard bargain. The priest smiled affectionately.

'She is a wonderful creature, my mother, she has had fifteen children and eleven of them are still alive. She is a saint, and goodness is as natural to her as a fine voice is to a *cantatrice*; it is no more difficult for her to do a beautiful action than it was for Adelina Patti to take C in alt. *Cara.'*

He put the photograph back on the table.

When the next day but one I set out again the father said he would walk with me till we came to the hills and so, slinging my pony's bridle over my arm, we trudged along while he gave me messages for the nuns at Keng Tung and impressed upon me not to forget to send him prints of the photographs I had taken. He walked with his gun on his shoulder, an old weapon that looked to me much more dangerous to himself than to the beasts of the field; he was an odd figure in his battered helmet and his black cassock trussed up round his waist in order not to impede his gait, his white trousers tucked into his heavy boots. He walked with a long slow stride and I could well imagine that the miles sagged away under it. But presently his sharp eyes caught sight of a kingfisher that sat on the low branch of a tree, green and blue, a little quivering, beautiful thing, poised there for a moment like a living gem; the father put his hand on my arm to stop me and crept forward very softly, noiselessly, till he got to within ten feet; then he fired and when the bird dropped he sprang forward with a cry of triumph and picking it up he threw it in the bag he carried slung to his side.

'That will help to make my rice tasty,' he said.

But we reached the jungle and he stopped again.

'I shall leave you here,' he said. 'I must get back to my work.'

I mounted my pony, we shook hands, and I trotted off. I turned back when I came to a bend of the path and waved as I saw him still standing where I had left him. He had his hand on the trunk of a tall tree and the green of the forest surrounded him. I went on and soon, I suppose, with that heavy tread of his that seemed not to spurn the earth but to stamp upon it with a jovial energy, as though it were friendly and would take his affectionate violence in good part (like a great strong dog who wags his tail when you give him a hearty slap on the buttock)

73

soon, I suppose, he trudged back to the life from which for a day or two I had lured him. I knew that I should never see him again. I was going on to I knew not what new experiences and presently I should return to the great world with its excitement and vivid changes, but he would remain there always.

Much time has passed since then and sometimes, at a party when women, their cheeks painted, with pearls round their necks, sit listening to a broad-bosomed *prima donna* singing the songs of Schumann or at a first night when the curtain falls after an act and the applause is loud, and the audience bursts into amused conversation, my thoughts go back to the Italian priest, a little older now and greyer, a little thinner, for since then he has had two or three bouts of fever, who is jogging up the Shan hills along the forest paths, the same to-day and to-morrow as when I left him; and so it will be till one day, old and broken, he is taken ill in one of those little mountain villages, and too weak to be moved down to the valley is presently overtaken by death. They will bury him in the jungle, with a wooden cross over him, and perhaps (the beliefs of generations stronger than the new faith he had taught) they will put little piles of stone about his grave and flowers so that his spirit may be friendly to the people of the village in which he died. And I have sometimes wondered whether at the end, so far from his kin, the headman of the village and the elders sitting round him silently, frightened to see a white man die, whether in a last moment of lucidity (those strange brown faces bending over him) fear will seize him and doubt, so that he will look beyond death and see that there is nothing but annihilation and whether then he will have a feeling of wild revolt because he has given up for nothing all that the world has to offer of beauty, love and ease, friendship and art and the pleasant gifts of nature, or whether even then he will think his brave life of toil and abnegation and endurance worth while.

74

It must be a terrifying moment for those whom faith has sustained and supported all their lives, the moment when they must finally know whether their belief was true. Of course he had a vocation. His faith was robust and it was as natural to him to believe as to us to breathe. He was no saint to work miracles and no mystic to endure the pain and the ineffable pleasure of union with the Godhead, but as it were the common labourer of God. The souls of men were like the fields of his native Lombardy and without sentimentality, without emotion even, taking the rough with the smooth, he ploughed them and sowed, he protected the growing corn from the birds, he took advantage of the sunshine and grumbled because the rain was too much or too little, he shrugged his shoulders when the yield was scanty and took it as his due when it was abundant. He looked upon himself as a wage-earner like any other (but his wages were the glory of God and a world without end), and it gave him a sort of satisfaction to feel that he earned his keep. He gave the people his heart, and made no more fuss about it than did his father when he sold macaroni over the counter of his little shop in the Milanese.

XVII

I entered upon the last lap of the journey to Keng Tung. For two or three days I went along the valleys by a level path, with a pretty stream flowing by the side of it; on its banks grew huge trees and now and again I saw a nimble monkey leaping from branch to branch; then I began to climb. I had to cross the divide between the basins of the Salween and the Mehkong and soon it grew very cold. Up and up we went. In the morning the mist swathed the surrounding hills, but here and there their tops emerged from it so that they looked like little green islets in a grey sea. The sun shining on the mist made a rainbow, and it was like the bridge that led to the gate of some fairy region of the underworld. A bitter wind blew around those bleak heights, and soon I was chilled to the bone. The mule track was muddy and very slippery, so that my pony kept his feet with difficulty and dismounting I walked. The mist was heavy now, and I could see but a few yards in front of me. The bell on the leader of my caravan was muffled and plaintive and the muleteers shivering trudged along by their beasts' sides in silence. The path wound through one defile after another, and at each bend I thought I had reached the pass, but the way still went uphill and it seemed interminable. Then suddenly I found myself sloping down. I had crossed the pass, which had needed so prolonged an effort to reach, without noticing it; it gave me a slight shock of disillusion. So when you have spent all your labour to achieve some ambition and have achieved it, it seems nothing to you and you go on somewhither without any sense of a great thing accomplished. And it may be that death is like that also. I should add that this pass being no more than seven thousand feet high, to reach it was perhaps not so extraordinary a feat as to merit these pregnant reflections.

A similar incident occurred to Mr Wordsworth when with his friend, Mr Jones (*Jones, as from Calais South ward you and I*) he crossed the Alps; but being a poet he wrote:

> *. . . whether we be young or old,*
> *Our destiny, our being's heart and home,*
> *Is with infinitude, and only there;*
> *With hope it is, hope that can never die,*
> *Effort, and expectation, and desire,*
> *And something ever more about to be.*

So simple is it when you know just how to put the best words in the best order to achieve beauty. The elephant can with his trunk pick up a sixpence and uproot a tree.

Then I came to a point from which they told me I could see Keng Tung, but the whole country was bathed in a silvery vapour and though I strained my eyes I could see nothing. I wound down and down and gradually emerged from the mountain mist and the sun was warm on my back. In the afternoon I came into the plain. The hills I had left were dark and the grey clouds were entangled in the trees that clad them. I trotted along a straight road, wide enough for a bullock wagon, with rice fields, now only a brown and dusty stubble, on each side; I passed peasants with loads on their backs, or suspended on bamboos, going to town for the market next day; and at last I reached a broken brick gateway. It was the gate of Keng Tung. I had been twenty-six days on the journey.

Here I was met by a magistrate, a stoutish man of dignified aspect but of friendly reception, riding a mettlesome white pony, and some other official, who had come to greet me on behalf of the Sawbwa, the chieftain of that state. After we had exchanged the proper civilities we rode on through the main street of the town (but as the houses stood each in its compound with trees growing in it, it had no air of a street but rather of a road in a garden suburb), till we came to the circuit-house, at which I was to lodge. This was a long brick bungalow, placed on a hill without the town, whitewashed, with a verandah in front of it, and from the verandah I saw among trees the brown roofs of Keng Tung. All round were the green hills that surround it.

XVIII

I rode down to the market on my little Shan pony. It was held on a great flat space in which were four rows of open booths and here the people jostled one another in a serried throng. I had wandered so long through country almost uninhabited that I was dazzled by the variety and the colour of the crowd. The sun shone brightly. In the wayside villages the peasants were dressed in sombre hues, in blue or maroon, and often in black, but here the colours were brilliant. The women were neat and small and pretty, with flattened faces, and sallow rather than swarthy, but their hands were beautiful, as delicate as the flowers they wore in their hair, and finely attached to their slender wrists. They were dressed in a sort of skirt, called a *lungyi*, a long strip of silk wound round and tucked in at the waist, the upper part of which was in stripes of gay colours and the lower part pale green, maroon or black, and they wore a little white bodice, very neat and modest, and over this a padded jacket, pale green or pink or black like a Spanish bolero, with tight sleeves and little wings on the shoulders which suggested that at any moment they might fly smilingly away. The men wore coloured *lungyis* too or baggy Shan trousers. And a great many wore huge hats of finely plaited straw, like candle extinguishers, with enormous curved brims, and they perched uneasily on the abundant hair and handkerchiefs of men and women. These extravagant hats, hundreds of them, swaying, bobbing up and down, with the restless movements of their wearers, were so fantastic that you could not persuade yourself that these people were busy with the serious affairs of life, but rather, engaged in a frolic, were having an enormous joke with one another.

As is usual in the East the sellers of the same things

78

congregated together. The stalls were merely tiled roofs on posts, speaking well for the clemency of the climate, and the floor was either the trodden earth or a very low wooden platform. The selling was done for the most part by women; there were generally three or four of them in each stall, and they sat smoking long green cheroots. But in the medicine stalls the vendors were very old men, with wrinkled faces and blood-shot eyes, who looked like wizards. I observed their wares with consternation. There were piles of dried herbs and large boxes of powders of various colours, blue, yellow, red and green, and I could not but think he must be a brave man who ventured upon them. In my childhood I have been beguiled into taking a dose of salts under the impression that as a reward for virtue I was being treated to a spoonful of plum jam (and have never been able to stomach plum jam since), but I cannot imagine how a fond Shan mother would conceal from her little Shan boy that she was administering to him a large spoonful of a gritty emerald powder. There were pills so large that I asked myself what throat was ever so capacious as to be able to wash them down with a drink of water. There were small dried animals that looked like the roots of plants that had been dug out of the ground and left to rot, and there were roots of plants that looked like dried animals. But the aged apothecaries suffered from no lack of custom. Trade was brisk that morning, and they were kept busy weighing out drugs not with the flaky weights we use at home but with large pieces of lead cast in the form of the Buddha. At last my patience was rewarded, and having seen a man buy a dozen pills as large as bantams' eggs, I watched him take one in finger and thumb, open his mouth, drop it in and swallow. There was a struggle, for a moment his face bore a strained look, then he gave himself a jerk, and the pill was gone. The apothecary watched him with rheumy eyes.

XIX

In the market was to be found everything, to eat to wear, and to furnish his house that was necessary to the needs of the simple Shan. There were silks from China, and the Chinese hucksters, sedately smoking their water pipes, were dressed in blue trousers, tight-fitting black coats and black silk caps. They were not lacking in elegance. The Chinese are the aristocracy of the East. There were Indians in white trousers, a white tunic that fitted closely to their thin bodies and round caps of black velvet. They sold soap and buttons, and flimsy Indian silks, rolls of Manchester cotton, alarm clocks, looking-glasses and knives from Sheffield. The Shans retailed the goods brought down by the tribesmen from the surrounding hills and the simple products of their own industry. Here and there a little band of musicians occupied a booth and a crowd stood round idly listening. In one three men beat on gongs, one played the cymbals and another thumped a drum as long as himself. My uneducated ear could discern no pattern in that welter of sound, but only a direct and not unexhilarating appeal to crude emotion; but a little further on I came across another band, not of Shans this time but of hillmen who played on long wind instruments of bamboo and their music was melancholy and tremulous. Every now and then I seemed in its vague monotony to catch a few notes of a wistful melody. It gave you an impression of something immensely old. Every violence of statement had been worn away from it and every challenge to an energetic reaction, and there remained but subdued suggestions on which the imagination might work and references, as it were, to desires and hopes and despairs deep buried in the heart.

You had the feeling of a music recollected at night by the camp-fires of nomad tribes on their wanderings from the grass-lands of their ancient homes and begotten of the scattered sounds of the jungle and the silence of flowing rivers; and to my fancy (worked up now, as is the writer's way, by the power of the words, so difficultly controlled, that throng upon his imagination) it suggested the perplexity in the midst of strange and hostile surroundings of men who came they knew not whence and went they knew not whither, a plaintive, questioning cry and a song sung together (as men at sea in a storm tell one another lewd stories to drive away the uneasiness of the battering waves and the howling wind) to reassure themselves by the blessed solace of human companionship against the loneliness of the world.

But there was nothing doleful or forlorn in the throng that crowded the streets of the market. They were gay, voluble and blithe. They had come not only to buy and sell, but to gossip and pass the time of day with their friends. It was the meeting-place not only of Keng Tung, but of the whole countryside for fifty miles around. Here they got the news and heard the latest stories. It was as good as a play and doubtless much better than most. Among the Shans, who were in the majority, wandered in their distinctive costumes members of many tribes. They held together in little groups as though, feeling shy in this foreign environment, they were afraid of being parted from one another. To them it must have seemed a vast and populous city, and they kept themselves to themselves with the countryman's odd mingling of awe and contempt for the inhabitants of a city. There were Tais, Laos, Kaws, Palaungs, Was and heaven knows what else. The Was are divided by people wise in these matters into wild and tame, but the wild ones do not leave their mountain fastnesses. They are head-hunters, not from vainglory like the Dyaks, nor for aesthetic reasons like the people of the Mambwe country, but for the purely

utilitarian purpose of protecting their crops. A fresh skull
will guard and strengthen the growing grain, and so at the
approach of spring from each village a small party of men
goes out to look for a likely stranger. A stranger is sought
since he does not know his way about the country and
his spirit will not wander away from his earthly remains.
It is said that travel in those parts is far from popular
during the hunting season. But the tame Was have the
air of amiable and kindly people and certainly their
appearance, though wild enough, is picturesque. The
Kaws stand out from among the others by reason of
their fine physique and swarthy colour. The authorities,
however, state that the darkness of their complexion is
due for the most part to their dislike of the use of water.
The women wear a headdress covered with silver beads
so that it looks like a helmet; their hair is parted in the
middle and comes down over the ears as one sees it in
the portraits of the Empress Eugénie, and in middle age
they have funny little wrinkled faces full of humour.
They wear a short coat, a kilt and leggings; and there
is quite an interval between the coat and the kilt; I
could not fail to notice how much character it gives a
woman's face to display her navel. The men are dressed
in dingy blue, with turbans, and in these the young lads
put marigolds as a sign that they are bachelors and want
to marry. I wondered indeed if they kept them there or
only put them in when the urge was strong upon them.
For presumably no one feels inclined to marry on a cold
and frosty morning. I saw one with half a dozen flowers
in his turban. He was not going to leave his intentions
in doubt. He cut a gay and jaunty figure, but the girls
seemed to take no more notice of him than he, I am
bound to confess, took of them. Perhaps they thought
his eagerness was exaggerated and he, I suppose, having
put his advertisement in the paper, as it were, was willing
to leave it at that. He was a pleasant creature, of a dusky
complexion, with large dark eyes, bold and shining, and

82

he stood, with his back a trifle arched, as though all his muscles quivered with strength. There were peasants threading their way among the throng with pigeons on a perch tied by the leg with a string, which you might either buy to release and so acquire merit or add to the next day's curry. One of these men passing him the young Kaw, evidently a careless fellow with his money, on a sudden impulse (and you saw on his mobile face how unexpectedly it came into his head) bought a pigeon, and when it was given to him he held it for a moment in both his hands, a grey wood pigeon with a pink breast, and then throwing up his arms with the gesture of the bronze boy from Herculaneum flung it high into the air. He watched it fly rapidly away, fly back to its native woods, and there was a boyish smile on his handsome face.

XX

I spent the best part of a week in Keng Tung. The days were warm and sunny and the circuit-house neat, clean and roomy. After so many strenuous days on the road it was pleasant to have nothing much to do. It was pleasant not to get up till one felt inclined and to breakfast in pyjamas. It was pleasant to lounge through the morning with a book. For it is an error to think that because you have no train to catch and no appointments to keep your movements on the road are free. Your times for doing this and that are as definite as if you lived in a city and had to go to business every morning. Your movements are settled not by your own whim, but by the length of the stages and the endurance of the mules. Though you would not think it mattered if you arrived half an hour sooner or later at your day's destination, there is always a rush to get up in the morning, a bustle of preparation and an urgent compulsion to get off without delay.

I kept the emotion with which Keng Tung filled me

well under control. It was a village, larger than those I had passed on the way, but a village notwithstanding, of wooden houses, spacious, with wide dirt streets, and I was put to it to find objects of interest to visit. On other than market days it was empty. In the main street you saw nothing but a few gaunt pariah dogs. In one or two shops a woman, smoking a cheroot, sat idly on the floor; she had no thought that on such a day there would ever be a customer; in another four Chinamen crouched on their heels were gambling. Silence. The dusty road had great ruts in it, and the sun beat down on it from a clear blue sky. Three little women suddenly appeared in monstrous, diverting hats and passed along in single file; they had a couple of baskets suspended by a bamboo over the shoulder and they walked with bent knees, speedily, as though if they went more slowly they would sink under their burdens. And against the emptiness of the street they made a quick and evanescent pattern.

And there was silence too in the monasteries. There are perhaps a dozen of them in Keng Tung and their high roofs stand out when you look at the town from the little hill on which is the circuit-house. Each one stands in its compound and in the compound are a number of crumbling pagodas. The great hall in which the Buddha, enormous, sits in his hieratic attitude, surrounded by others, eight or ten, hardly smaller, is like a barn, but its roof is supported by huge columns of teak, gilt or lacquered, and the wooden walls and the rafters are gilt or lacquered too. Rude paintings of scenes in the Master's life hang from the eaves. It is dark and solemn, but the Buddhas sit on their great lotus leaves in the gloaming like gods who have had their day, and now neglected, but indifferent to neglect, in their decaying grandeur of gilt and mosaic continue to reflect on suffering and the end of suffering, transitoriness and the eightfold path. Their aloofness is almost terrifying. You tread on tiptoe in order not to disturb their meditations and when you close behind you the carved and gilded doors and come out once more into the friendly day it is with a sigh of relief. You feel like a man who has gone by accident to a party at the wrong house and on realising his mistake makes his escape quickly and hopes that no one has noticed him.

XXI

Musing upon the odd chance that had brought me to that distant spot, my idle thoughts gathered about the tall, aloof figure of the casual acquaintance whose words spoken at random had tempted me to make the journey. I tried from the impressions he had left upon me to construct the living man. For when we meet people we see them only in the flat, they offer us but one side of themselves, and they remain shadowy; we have to give them our flesh and our bones before they exist in the round. That is why the characters of fiction are more real than the characters of life. He was a soldier and for five years had been in command of the Military Police Post at Loimwe, which is a few miles south-east of Keng Tung. Loimwe signifies the Hill of Dreams.

I do not think he was a great hunter, for I have noticed that most men who live in places were game is plentiful acquire a distaste for killing the wild creatures of the jungle. When on their arrival they have shot this animal or that, the tiger, the buffalo, or the deer, for the satisfaction of their self-esteem, they lose interest. It suggests itself to them that the graceful creatures, whose habits they have studied, have as much right to life as they; they get a sort of affection for them, and it is only unwillingly that they take their guns to kill a tiger that is frightening the villagers, or woodcock or snipe for the pot.

Five years is a big slice out of a man's life. He spoke

of Keng Tung as a lover might speak of his bride. It had been an experience so poignant that it had set him apart for ever from his fellows. He was reticent, and as is the English way could tell but in clumsy words what he had found there. I do not know whether even to himself he was able to put into plain language the vague emotions that touched his heart when in a secluded village at night he sat and talked with the elders and whether he asked himself the questions, so new and strange to one of his circumstances and profession, that stood in silence (like homeless men in winter outside a refuge for the destitute) waiting to be answered. He loved the wild wooded hills and the starry nights. The days were interminable and monotonous, and on them he embroidered a vague and misty pattern. I do not know what it was. I can only guess that it made the world he went back to, the world of clubs and mess-tables, of steam-engines and motor cars, dances and tennis-parties, politics, intrigue, bustle, excitement, the world of the newspapers, strangely without meaning. Though he lived in it, though he even enjoyed it, it remained utterly remote. I think it had lost its sense for him. In his heart was the reflection of a lovely dream that he could never quite recall.

We are gregarious, most of us, and we resent the man who does not seek the society of his fellows. We do not content ourselves with saying that he is odd, but we ascribe to him unworthy motives. Our pride is wounded that he should have no use for us and we nod to one another and wink and say that if he lives in this strange way it must be to practise some secret vice and if he does not inhabit his own country it can only be because his own country is too hot to hold him. But there are people who do not feel at home in the world, the companionship of others is not necessary to them and they are ill-at-ease amid the exuberance of their fellows. They have an invincible shyness. Shared emotions abash them. The thought of community singing, even though it be but *God Save the King*, fills them with embarrassment, and if they sing it is plaintively in their baths. They are self-sufficient and they shrug a resigned and sometimes, it must be admitted, a scornful shoulder because the world uses that adjective in a depreciatory sense. Wherever they are they feel themselves 'out of it'. They are to be found all over the surface of this earth, members of a great monastic order bound by no vows and cloistered though not by walls of stone. If you wander up and down the world you will meet them in all sorts of unexpected places. You are not surprised when you hear that an elderly English lady is living in a villa on a hill outside a small Italian town that you have happened on by an accident to the car in which you were driving, for Italy has always been the preferred refuge of these staid nuns. They have generally adequate means and an extensive knowledge of the *cinque cento*. You take it as a matter of course when a lonely *hacienda* is pointed out to you in Andalusia and you are told that there has dwelt for many years an English lady of a certain age. She is usually a devout Catholic and sometimes lives in sin with her coachman. But it is more surprising when you hear that the only white person in a Chinese city is an Englishwoman, not a missionary, who has lived there, none knows why, for a quarter of a century; and there is another who inhabits an islet in the South Seas and a third who has a bungalow on the outskirts of a large village in the centre of Java. They live solitary lives, without friends, and they do not welcome the stranger. Though they may not have seen one of their own race for months they will pass you on the road as though they did not see you, and if, presuming on your nationality, you call, the chances are that they will decline to receive you; but if they do they will give you a cup of tea from a silver tea-pot and on a plate of old Worcester you will be offered hot scones. They will talk to you politely, as though they were entertaining you in a drawing-room overlooking a London square, but when

87

you take your leave they express no desire ever to see you again.

The men are at once shyer and more friendly. At first they are tongue-tied and you see the anxious look on their faces as they rack their brains for topics of conversation, but a glass of whisky loosens their minds (for sometimes they are inclined to tipple) and then they will talk freely. They are glad to see you, but you must be careful not to abuse your welcome; they get tired of company very soon and grow restless at the necessity of making an effort. They are more apt to run to seed than women, they live in a higgledy-piggledy manner, indifferent to their surroundings and their food. They have often an ostensible occupation. They keep a little shop, but do not care whether they sell anything, and their goods are dusty and fly-blown; or they run, with lackadaisical incompetence, a coconut plantation. They are on the verge of bankruptcy. Sometimes they are engaged in metaphysical speculation, and I met one who had spent years in the study and annotation of the works of Immanuel Swedenborg. Sometimes they are students and take endless pains to translate classical works which have been already translated, like the dialogues of Plato, or of which translation is impossible, like Goethe's *Faust*. They may not be very useful members of society, but their lives are harmless and innocent. If the world despises them they on their side despise the world. The thought of returning to its turmoil is a nightmare to them. They ask nothing but to be left in peace. Their satisfaction with their lot is sometimes a trifle irritating. It needs a good deal of philosophy not to be mortified by the thought of persons who have voluntarily abandoned everything that for the most of us makes life worth living and are devoid of envy of what they have missed. I have never made up my mind whether they are fools or wise men. They have given up everything for a dream, a dream of peace or happiness or

88

freedom, and their dream is so intense that they make it true.

XXII

But I had idled long enough and so, bright and early one morning, I set out with my caravan from Keng Tung. I was accompanied by an official of the Sawbwa's court who was to escort me to the frontier of the Sawbwa's dominions. He was a corpulent gentleman and he rode a very small and scraggy pony. For the first day I rode through the plain with rice fields on either side of the road and then plunged once more into the hills. I had finished now with the PWD bungalows, but the Sawbwa had been good enough to order houses to be built for me on the way and messengers had been sent on to the various villages with the necessary instructions. I felt very grand to have a house built for me to spend a single night in and the first one I lodged at filled me with delight. It was like a toy. It would hardly have kept out the wet if it rained or the wind if it blew, but in fine weather it was a place for young lovers to live in rather than a middle-aged writer. It was very neat and clean, for the bamboos of which it was made had been cut that morning, and it had the pleasant, fresh smell of growing things. It was all green, walls, floor and roof. It consisted of two rooms and a broad verandah. The walls and the floor, raised about three feet from the ground, were of split bamboos. The supporting pillars and the beams were of whole bamboos, and the roof was neatly thatched with rice straw. The floor was resilient so that, accustomed to an unyielding surface underfoot, I had at first a feeling of some insecurity and walked gingerly; but there was a network of solid bamboos under it and it was really as strong as could be desired. Within a few feet was a rushing mountain stream (I had crossed it half-a-dozen times during the day either by a ford or a rickety bridge) and its banks were thickly grown with trees. In front was a little open space where cattle grazed and the view was shut in by a green hill. It was an enchanting spot.

One day, the letter sent on ahead to arrange accommodation having been received but that morning, on arriving at the end of the stage I found the villagers, gathered from a village some miles off, for this was in the middle of the jungle, still busy with the construction of my house. It was of course very curious to watch the speed and deftness with which with their rude knives they cut and split the bamboos in order to make the floor, the ingenuity with which they fitted the rafters and the neatness with which they thatched the roof; but it did not interest me. I was tired and hungry, I wanted a cook-house so that my dinner could be prepared, and I wanted a place for my bed so that I could lie down and rest. I lost my temper and my commonsense. I sent for the Sawbwa's official and abused him roundly for his slackness. I vowed I would send him back to his master and threatened him with every sort of punishment my angry imagination could devise. I would not listen to his excuses. I stamped and raved. Now no one had ever troubled in my life before to treat me with such consideration and though I have travelled much in out-of-the-way parts of the world I have had to shift for myself and lodge at haphazard wherever I could find a lodging. I have slept quite happily for seven days in an open rowing boat and in South Sea islands shared a native hut open to the wind and rain with a family of Kanakas. No one had even thought of building a house for me, and in the middle of the jungle besides, and it was an attention to which I had no right. The moral is that even the most sensible person can very easily get above himself: grant him certain privileges and before you know where you are he will claim them as his inalienable right; lend him a little authority and he will play the tyrant. Give a fool a

90

uniform and sew a tab or two on his tunic and he thinks that his word is law.

But when my house was finished, a green house in a green glade with the torrent splashing noisily between its green banks, and I had eaten, I laughed at myself. At Keng Tung I had bought some rum off a Ghurka when I discovered that my supply of gin was running low and feared that I should have to finish my journey on tea and coffee; it was good rum, home-made, but I did not like it; so to mark the sincere contrition I felt for having behaved with so little sense I sent the Sawbwa's official two bottles.

XXIII

In reading the books of explorers I have been very much struck by the fact that they never tell you what they eat and drink unless they are driven to extremities and shoot a deer or a buffalo that replenishes their larder when they have drawn in their belts to the last hole; or are so much in want of water that their pack animals are dying and it is only by the merest chance that at the very last moment they come across a well, or by the exercise of the most ingenious ratiocination hit upon a spot where in the evening and the distance they see a shining that tells them that after a few more weary miles they will find ice to quench their thirst. Then a look of relief crosses their set grim faces and perchance a grateful tear courses down their unwashed cheeks. But I am no explorer and my food and drink are sufficiently important matters to me to persuade me in these pages to dwell on them at some length. I keep a pleasant place in my memory for the *durwan* of a bungalow on the way to Keng Tung who brought me with obsequious gestures a lordly dish covered with a napkin, removing which he craved my acceptance of two large cabbages. I had eaten no green vegetables for a fortnight and they tasted to me more delicious than peas fresh from a Surrey garden or young asparagus from Argenteuil. It is a charming sight and wonderfully exalting to the soul, when you ride wearily into a village, to come upon a duck-pond on which are swimming fat ducks, unconscious of the fact that next day one of them, the fattest, the youngest, the most tender, with baked potatoes and abundant gravy is destined (who can escape his fate?) to make you a succulent dinner. Late in the afternoon, just before the sun is setting, you take an easy stroll and a little way from the compound you catch sight of two green pigeons flying about the trees. They run along the pathway, seeming playfully to chase each other, they are tame and friendly, and unless you have a heart of stone you cannot but be touched by the sight of them. You reflect on the innocence and bliss of their lives. You remember vaguely the fable of La Fontaine which in your childhood you learned by heart and shyly repeated when visitors came to see your mother.

> Deux pigeons s'aimaient d'amour tendre.
> L'un d'eux, s'ennuyant au logis
> Fut assez fou pour entreprendre
> Un voyage en lointain pays.

The charming and obscene Lawrence Sterne would have been moved to tears by the sight of the dainty creatures and he would have written a passage that would have wrung your heart. But you are made of sterner stuff. You have a gun in your hands and though you are a bad shot they are an easy mark. In a little while the native who has accompanied you holds them in his hand, but he is unconcerned and sees nothing pathetic in those pretty little birds, but a moment ago full of life, dead before him. How good they are, fat, succulent and juicy, when Rang Lal, the Gurkha, brings them roasted to a turn for your breakfast next morning!

My cooks was a Telegu, a man of mature age; his face, of a dark mahogany, was thin, ravaged and lined, and his thick hair was dully streaked with silver. He was very lean, a tall, saturnine creature of a striking appearance in his white turban and white tunic. He walked with long strides and a swinging step, covering the twelve to fourteen miles of the day's march without fatigue or effort. It startled me at first to see this bearded and dignified person nimbly shin up a tree in the compound and shake down the fruit he needed for some sauce. Like many another artist his personality was more interesting than his work; his cooking was neither good nor varied, one day he gave me trifle for my dinner and the next cabinet pudding; they are the staple sweets of the East, and as one sees them appear on table after table, made by a Japanese at Kyoto, a Chinese at Amoy, a Malay at Alor Star or a Madrassi at Mulmein, one's sympathetic heart feels a pang at the thought of the drab lives of those English ladies in country vicarages or seaside villas (with the retired Colonel their father) who introduced them to the immemorial East. My own knowledge of these matters is small, but I made so bold as to teach my Telegu how to make a corned beef hash. I trusted that after he left me he would pass on the precious recipe to other cooks and that eventually one more dish would be added to the scanty repertory of Anglo-Eastern cuisine. I should be a benefactor of my species.

It had occurred to me that the cook-house was very disorderly and none too clean, but in these matters it is unwise to be squeamish; when you think of all the disagreeable things that go on in your inside it seems absurd to be too particular about the way in which is prepared what you put into it. It must be accepted that from a kitchen that is neat and shining like a new pin you do not often get food that is very good to eat. But I was taken aback when Rang Lal came to me with complaints that the Telegu was so dirty that no one could eat what he prepared. I went into the cook-house again and saw for myself; it was impossible not to notice also that my cook was very much the worse for liquor. I was told then that he was often so drunk that Rang Lal had to do the cooking himself. We were a fortnight's journey from any place where I might have replaced him, so I contented myself with such vituperation (not very effective since it had to be translated into Burmese which he understood but little) as I was master of. I think the most biting thing I said was that a drunken cook should at least be a good one, but he merely looked at me with large mournful eyes. He did not wince. At Keng Tung he went on a terrific spree and did not appear for three days: I looked about for someone to take his place, for I had four weeks' journey ahead of me before I could reach the rail-head in Siam, but there was no one to be found, so when he reappeared very sorry for himself and woe-begone, I assumed the part of one who is cut to the quick, but magnanimous. I forgave him and he promised that for the rest of the journey he would abstain. One should be tolerant of the vices of others.

Now, passing through the villages, I had often seen little pigs scurrying about the posts on which the houses were built and about a week after I left Keng Tung it occurred to me that a sucking-pig would make a pleasant change to my daily fare; so I gave instructions to buy one at the next opportunity, and one day on arriving at the bungalow I was shown a little black pig lying at the bottom of a basket. It did not look more than a week old. For a few days it was carried in its basket from stage to stage by a young Chinese boy I had engaged at Keng Tung to help my drunken cook, and the boy and Rang Lal played with it. It was a pet. I meant to keep it for a special occasion and often, as I rode along, I indulged in a pleasing reverie on the excellent dinner it would make; I could not hope for apple sauce, but my mouth watered at the thought of the crackling, and I told myself that the flesh would be sweet and tender. Anxiously I asked the Telegu if he was quite certain he knew how to cook it. He swore by the heads of all his ancestors that there was nothing about roasting a pig that he did not know. Then I halted for a day to give the mules and the men a rest, and I ordered the sucking-pig to be killed. But when it came to the table (how vain are human hopes!) there was no crackling, there was no white tender meat, it was just a brown sloppy stinking mess, it was uneatable. For a moment I was dismayed. I wondered what on earth the great explorers would do in such a pass. Would a frown darken the stern face of Stanley and would Dr Livingstone preserve unruffled his Christian temper? I sighed. Not for this was the little black sucking-pig reft untimely from his mother's breast. It had been better to leave him to lead a happy life in his Shan village. I sent for the cook. Presently he came supported on one side by Rang Lal and on the other by Kyuzaw, my interpreter. When they let go of him he swayed slowly from side to side like a schooner at anchor in a swell.

'He's drunk,' I said.

'He's as drunk as a lord,' answered Kyuzaw, who had been to the rajah's school at Taunggyi and knew many a racy English idiom.

(Once upon a time somebody called upon one of the most eminent of the Victorians early one morning and was told by the butler:

'His lordship isn't up yet, sir.'

'Oh, at what time does he have breakfast?'

Then the butler imperturbable: 'He doesn't have breakfast sir. His lordship is generally sick about eleven.')

The Telegu looked at me and I looked at the Telegu. There was no understanding in his lustrous eyes.

'Take him away,' I said. 'Give him his wages in the morning and tell him to get out.'

'Very good, sir,' said Kyuzaw. 'I think that's best.'

They removed him and there was a great clatter and a

thud outside on the steps, but whether the Telegu had fallen down or whether Kyuzaw and Rang Lal had thrown him I did not think it necessary to ask.

Next morning while I was having breakfast on my verandah Kyuzaw came in to ask for the day's instructions and to gossip. The bungalow was on the edge of a considerable village. And there was more life and movement than you see generally in the Shan villages. The day before when I arrived, perhaps a little before I was expected, the women wore nothing but their *lungyis*, drawn up just to cover their breasts, and the upper part of their bodies were naked, but to-day, I fear in deference to the importance they were good enough to ascribe to me, they wore little bodices and were less pleasing of aspect. Suddenly the cook appeared in front of the bungalow. He had a bundle on his shoulder and this he put down on the ground beside him. He gave me a deep and solemn bow, then quickly took up his bundle, turned round and walked off.

'I gave him his wages and money for his keep,' said Kyuzaw.

'Is he going?' I asked.

'Yes, sir. You said he was to go the first thing this morning. He cooked your breakfast and now he is going.'

I did not say anything. My word was law, and I suppose it bound me more sternly than anyone else. It was twelve days to Keng Tung, and the Telegu would foot it day after day seldom seeing a human face, and then it was twenty-three days more to Taunggyi. He took the path that led into the jungle and my eyes followed him. I had often noticed his long swinging stride. But now, emaciated, in his dingy Eastern clothes, his turban slovenly tied, he looked incredibly forlorn and under the weight of his bundle seemed to walk with lassitude. I did not really care if he was dirty and drunken, and I had dined just as happily off tinned tongue as off a sucking-pig. He seemed now very small and frail as he trudged on and soon he would be lost to sight in the immensity of Asia. There was something immeasurably pathetic, nay, tragic even, in the sight of that old man stepping out thus into the unknown. In his lagging gait I seemed to read the despair of one who had been beaten by life. I suppose that Kyuzaw saw my uneasiness, for with his frank and tolerant smile he said:

'You were very patient with him, sir. I would have sent him away long ago.'

'Was he upset when you told him?'

'Oh, no, sir. He knew he deserved it. He is not a bad man, a thief, drunken and very dirty, but that is all. He will find another place when he gets back to Taunggyi.'

XXIV

The uneventful days followed one another like the rhymed couplets of a didactic poem. The country was sparsely inhabited. On the road we met no one but a few Kaws, and now and then we saw their villages perched on the side of a hill. The stages were long and when we arrived at the end of the day's journey we were exhausted. There was no road, but only a narrow pathway, and where it ran under the trees it was thick with mud, and the ponies stumbled through it splashing; sometimes it came up to their knees and it was impossible to go at more than a snail's pace. It was hard work and dreary. We went up and down low hills, winding in and out by the side of the river, and this, which at first was but a narrow stream that one could ford easily, grew day by day into a broad and rushing torrent. The last time we forded it, it was deep enough to come up to the bellies of the ponies. Then it became a great flow of water, tumultuous in places where it dashed over rocks, and then flowing calm and swift. We crossed it on a bamboo raft attached to each bank by a bamboo rope and pulled ourselves over. Most of the tropical rivers that the traveller sees are very wide, but this one, overhung with an immense luxuriance of vegetation, was as narrow as the Wey. But you could never have mistaken it for an English river, it had none of the sunny calm of our English streams, nor their smiling nonchalance; it was dark and tragic and its flow had the sinister intensity of the unbridled lusts of man.

We camped beside it, among lofty trees, and at night the noise of the crickets and the frogs and the cries of the birds were loud and insistent. There is a notion abroad that the jungle at night is silent and writers have often been eloquent on the subject; but the silence they have described is spiritual; it is a translation of the emotion of solitude and of distance from the world of men and of the sense of awe that comes from the darkness and the solemn trees and the pressing growth of the greenwood; in sober fact the din is tremendous, so that till you become accustomed to it you may find it hard to sleep. But when you lie awake listening to it there is a strange uneasiness in your heart that does feel oddly like a terrible, an unearthly stillness.

But at last we reached the end of the jungle and the track, though uneven and bad, was wide enough for a bullock-cart. From my rest-house there was a broad view of the paddy fields and the hills in the distance were blue. Though they were the same hills that I had been crossing for I do not know how many days they had now a strangely romantic air. In their depths was magic. It was surprising to find what a difference it made to one's spirits to be once more in the open country. It was not till then that one realised how much the long days of travelling through the jungle had depressed them. One felt on a sudden content and well-disposed towards one's fellows.

Then we came to a large and prosperous village, called Hawng Luk, with a spacious and well-built rest-house, and this was the last place we stayed at before reaching Siam. The hills in front of us were Siamese hills. I think we all had a feeling of elation as we approached the frontier. We passed through a trim little village (as we neared Siam the villages, touched by the greater civilisation of the country we were entering, seemed more prosperous) over a quaint covered bridge and then came to a small, sluggish stream. This was the boundary. We forded it and were in Siam.

XXV

We came to a wood of young teak-trees and rode through this till we reached the village at which I had arranged to pass the night. Here there was a police post, neat and trim, with flowers in the garden; the sergeant in charge, notwithstanding his khaki uniform and the tidy little soldiers under him somewhat flustered at the sight of a white man and such an imposing retinue, telling us that there was no rest-house, directed us to the monastery. It was about a quarter of a mile from the main road and I rode up to it through the rice fields. It was a very poor little monastery, consisting only of a sort of barn of sun-baked bricks, in which were the images, and a wooden bungalow, in which lived the monks and their pupils. Here my bed was set up and my camp equipment, in the temple itself, with the images looking down on me. It caused no scandal to the monks or the novices. They scanned my possessions with eager interest, they watched me eat as the crowd watches the wild beasts eat at the Zoo, and in the evening they stood round me with wondering eyes when I played patience. After a little while they caught the sense of my complicated motions and a little gasp was wrung from them (like that flattering, anguished sob that breaks from a silent audience as a trapezist a hundred feet from the ground does the *salto mortale*) when with a bold gesture I transferred a dozen fitting cards to a line when there was a place for them. But such is the infirmity of human nature that no sooner had one of them got an inkling of what I was doing and in an agitated whisper explained to the others, than all with excited cries and gestures of delight pressed round about me; they snatched at my arm to point out to me a card that I should move (and how was I who knew no Siamese to explain that you could never, never put a six of hearts on a seven of diamonds?); I had to restrain them by force from moving a card, which I meant to move myself when I had sufficiently considered the matter, and when I did so my action was greeted with applause. No man, be he a monk in a Buddhist monastery or Prime Minister of England, can forbear to give advice when he watches somebody else doing a patience.

At eight the novices said their prayers, in a sing-song monotonous tone, some of them smoking cheroots the while, and then I was left alone for the night. There was no door to the temple and the blue night entered and the images on their tables shone dimly. The floor was clean, swept by women to acquire merit, but there were thousands of ants, attracted I suppose by the rice brought in offering by the devout, and they made sleep difficult. After a while I gave it up as a bad job and got up. I went to the doorway and looked out at the night. The air was balmy. I saw someone moving about and presently discovered that it was Kyuzaw. He also could not sleep. I offered him a cheroot and we sat down on the steps of the temple. He was a trifle contemptuous of this Siamese Buddhism. The monks did not go out with their begging bowls, it appeared, as the Blessed One had directed, but let the faithful bring them their rice and food to the monastery. Kyuzaw, like most Shans, had at one time been a novice and he told me, not without complacency, that he had never failed to go out with the begging bowl. He gave a little chuckle.

'I always went to my own house first and got a well-cooked meal put in the bottom of my bowl. I covered it with a leaf and went on my round till the bowl was filled. Then I went back to the monastery, threw away to the dogs all that was above the leaf and ate my own good dinner.'

I asked him if he liked the life. He shrugged his shoulders.

'There was nothing to do,' he said. 'Two hours' work in the morning and there were prayers at night, but all the rest of the day nothing. I was glad when the time came for me to go home again.'

I inveigled him to speak of transmigration.

'There was a man in a village near my house who remembered his old life. He had been dead eighteen years and he came to the village and he recognised his wife and he told her where they used to keep their money and he reminded her of things that she had long forgotten. He went into the house and said that one of the pots had been mended in such a way and they looked at it and it had been mended in the way he said. The woman cried and all the neighbours were amazed and people came to see him from all over the country. They wrote about it in the paper. They asked him questions and to every question he had an answer. He knew everything that had happened in the village during his previous existence and the people remembered that what he said was true. But it did not end well.'

'Why, what happened?' I asked.

'Well, his sons were grown up and they had divided the land and the buffaloes. They did not want to give everything back again. They said he had had his time and now it was their turn. He said he would go to the law and the mother said she would testify that what he said was true. You see, sir, she liked to have a fine young husband again, but the sons did not want to have a fine young father, so they took him aside and said that if he did not go away they would beat him till he died, so he took the money that was in the house and everything he could lay his hands on and went away.'

'Did he take his wife, too?'

'No, he did not take her. He did not tell her he was going. He just went away. She was very sorry. And of course she had nothing any more.'

We talked till we had finished our cheroots and then Kyuzaw got me some paraffin and we put it on the legs of my bed to keep the ants away and I went back to bed and slept. But the door of the temple looked due East and the dawn woke me and I saw a huge expanse of rose and purple. Then a little novice came in with a platter on which were four or five cakes of rice. He went down on his heels, a tiny little figure in yellow, with large black eyes, and uttered a brief invocation and then left the platter before the images. He had hardly gone before a pariah dog, evidently on the watch, slipped in quickly, seized one of the cakes in his mouth and ran out again. The early sun caught the gold on the Buddha and gave it a richness not its own.

XXVI

I travelled leisurely down Siam. The country was pleasant, open and smiling, scattered with neat little villages, each surrounded with a fence, and fruit trees and areca palms growing in the compounds gave them an attractive air of modest prosperity. There was a good deal of traffic on the road, but it was carried on not, as in the little inhabited Shan States by mules, but by bullock-carts. Where the country was flat rice was cultivated, but where it undulated teak forests grew. The teak is a handsome tree, with a large smooth leaf; it does not make a very dense jungle and the sun shines through. To ride in a teak forest, so light, graceful and airy, is to feel yourself a cavalier in an old romance. The rest-houses were clean and trim. During this part of my journey I came across but one white man and this was a Frenchman on his way north who came into the bungalow in which I had settled myself for the night. It belonged to a French teak company, of which he was a servant, and he seemed to look upon it as very natural that I, a stranger, should have made myself at home in it. He was cordial; there are few French in this business and the men, out in the jungle constantly to superintend the native labourer, live lives even more lonely than the English forest men, so that he was glad to have someone to talk to. We shared our dinner. He was a man of robust build, with a large fleshy red face and a warm voice that seemed to wrap his fluent words in a soft rich fabric of sound. He had just come from short leave in Bangkok and with the Frenchman's ingenuous belief that you are any more impressed by the number of his amours than by the number of his hats, talked much of the sexual experiences he had had there. He was a coarse fellow, ill-bred and stupid. But he caught sight of a torn, paper-bound book that was lying on the table.

'*Tiens*, where did you get hold of this?'

I told him that I had found it in the bungalow and had been glancing through it. It was that selection of Verlaine's poems which has for a frontispiece Carrière's misty, but not uninteresting portrait of him.

'I wonder who the devil can have left it here,' he said.

He took up the volume and idly fingering the pages told me various gross stories about the unhappy poet. They were not new to me. Then his eyes caught a line that he knew and he began to read

'*Voici des fruits, des fleurs, des feuilles et des branches.*
Et puis voici mon coeur qui ne bat que pour vous.'

And as he read his voice broke and tears came into his eyes and ran down his face.

'*Ah, merde,*' he cried, '*ça me fait pleurer comme un veau.*'

He flung the book down and laughed and gave a little sob. I poured him out a drink of whisky, for there is nothing better than alcohol to still or at least to enable one to endure that particular heartache from which at the moment he was suffering. Then we played piquet. He went to bed early, since he had a long day before him and was starting at dawn, and by the time I got up he was gone. I did not see him again.

But as I rode along in the sunshine, bustling and quick like women gossiping at their spinning-wheels, I thought of him. I reflected that men are more interesting than books, but have this defect that you cannot skip them; you have at least to skim the whole volume in order to find the good page. And you cannot put them on a shelf and take them down when you feel inclined; you must read them when the chance offers, like a book in a circulating library that is in such demand that you must take your turn and keep it no more than four and twenty hours. You may not be in the mood for them then or it may be that in your hurry you miss the only thing they had to give you.

And now the plain spread out with a noble spaciousness. The rice fields were no longer little patches laboriously wrested from the jungle, but broad acres. The days followed one another with a monotony in which there was withal something impressive. In the life of cities we are conscious but of fragments of days; they have no meaning of their own, but are merely parts of time in which we conduct such and such affairs; we begin them when they are already well on their way and continue them without regard to their natural end. But here they had completeness and one watched them unroll themselves with stately majesty from dawn to dusk; each day was like a flower, a rose that buds and blooms and, without regret but accepting the course of nature, dies. And this vast sun-drenched plain was a fit scene for the pageant of that ever-recurring drama. The stars were like the curious who wander upon the scene of some great event, a battle or an earthquake, that has just occurred, first one by one timidly and then in bands, and stand about gaping or look for traces of what has passed.

The road became straight and level. Though here and there deep with ruts and when a stream crossed it muddy, great stretches could have been traversed by car. Now it is all very well to ride a pony at the rate of twelve or fifteen miles a day when you go along mountain paths, but when the road is broad and flat this mode of travel sorely tries your patience. It was six weeks now that I had been on the way. It seemed endless. Then on a sudden I found myself in the tropics. I suppose that little by little, as one uneventful day followed another, the character of the scene had been changing, but it had been so gradual that I had scarcely noticed it, and I drew a deep breath of delight when, riding into a village one noon, I was met, as by an unexpected friend, with the savour of the harsh, the impetuous, the flamboyant South. The depth of colour, the hot touch of the air on one's cheek, the dazzling, yet strangely veiled light, the different walk of the people, the lazy breadth of their gestures, the silence, the solemnity, the dust – this was the real thing and my jaded spirits rose. The village street was bordered by tamarinds and they were like the sentences of Sir Thomas Browne, opulent, stately and self-possessed. In the compounds grew plantains, regal and bedraggled, and the crotons flaunted the riches of their sepulchral hues. The coconut trees with their dishevelled heads were like long lean old men suddenly risen from sleep. In the monastery was a grove of areca palms and they stood, immensely tall and slender, with the gaunt precision and the bare, precise, and intellectual nakedness of a collection of apothegms. It was the South.

We had now to get the day's journey over as early as possible and we started just as the first grey light stole into the Eastern sky. The sun rose and it was pleasantly warm on one's back, but in a little while it grew fierce and by ten it was overwhelming. It seemed to me that I had been riding along that broad white road since the beginning of time and still it stretched interminably before me. Then we arrived at a handsome village where the township officer, a neat Siamese, smiling and polite, offered to put me up in his own spacious house; and when he took me into his compound I saw waiting for me, shaded by palm trees and diapered by the sun, red, substantial, reliable but unassuming – a Ford car. My journey was over. It ended without any flourish of trumpets, quietly, like the anti-climax of a play; and next morning, in the chilly dawn, leaving my mules and ponies with Kyuzaw, I started. The metal road was building and where it was impassable the Ford car took the bullock track; here and there we splashed through shallow streams. I was bumped and shaken and tossed from side to side; still it was a road, a motor road, and I sped along vertiginously at the rate of eight miles an hour. It was the first car in the history of man that had ever passed that way and the peasants in their fields looked at us in amaze. I wondered whether it occurred to any of them that in it they saw the symbol of a new life. It marked the end of an existence they had led since time immemorial. It heralded a revolution in their habits and their customs. It was change that came down upon them panting and puffing, with a slightly flattened tyre but blowing a defiant horn, Change.

And a little before sunset we arrived at the railhead. There was a new, gaily-painted rest-house at the station, and it might almost have been called a hotel. There was a bath-room, with a bath you could lie down in, and on the verandah long chairs in which you could loll. It was civilisation.

XXVII

I was within forty-eight hours by rail of Bangkok, but before going there I wanted to see Lopburi and Ayudha, which at one time were capitals of Siam. In these Eastern countries cities are founded, increase to greatness and are destroyed in a manner that cannot but fill the Western traveller, accustomed for many centuries now to a relative stability, with a certain misgiving. A king, forced by the hazards of war or maybe only to gratify a whim, will change his capital and founding a new city, build a palace and temples and richly ornament them; and in a few generations the seat of government, owing to another hazard or another whim, moving elsewhere, the city is abandoned and desolation usurps the place of so much transitory splendour. Here and there in the jungle, far from any habitation, you will find ruined temples, overgrown with trees, and among the dank verdure broken gods and elaborate bas-reliefs as the only sign that here was once a thriving city, and you will come across poverty-stricken villages that are all that remain of the capital of a rich and powerful kingdom. It is a sombre reminder of the mutability of human things.

Lopburi is now but a narrow winding street of Chinese houses, built along one bank of the river; but all about are the ruins of a great city, mouldering temples and crumbling pagodas with here and there a fragment of florid carving, and in the temples are broken images of the Blessed One, and in their courtyards bits of heads and arms and legs. The plaster is grey as though it had been discoloured by London fogs and it peels off the bricks so that you think of old men with loathsome diseases. There is no elegance of line in these ruins and the decoration of doors and windows, robbed by time of their gold and tinsel, is mean and tawdry.

But I had come to Lopburi chiefly to see what remained of the grand house of Constantine Faulkon, who was, I suppose, one of the most amazing of the adventurers who have made the East the scene of their exploits. The son of a Cephalonian innkeeper, he ran away to sea in an English ship, and after many hazards arriving in Siam rose to be the chief minister of the King. The world of his day rang with the tale of his unlimited power, splendour and enormous wealth. There is an account of him in a little book by the Père d'Orléans of the Company of Jesus, but it is a work of edification and dilates unduly upon the tribulations of Constantine's widow when after his death she sought to preserve her virtue from the rude onslaughts of a Siamese prince. In her laudable efforts she was supported by her saintly grandmother, who at the age of eighty-eight, having lost nothing of the ardour and vivacity of her faith, talked to her continually of the famous Martyrs of Japan, from whom she had the honour to be descended. *My daughter, she said to her, what glory there is in being a martyr! You have here the advantage that martyrdom seems to be an heirloom in your family: if you have so much reason to expect it, what pains should you not take to deserve it!*

It is satisfactory to learn that, sustained by these counsels and fortified by the incessant admonitions of the Jesuit fathers, the widow resisted all temptations to become the bejewelled inmate of an almost royal seraglio and ended her virtuous days as dish-washer in the house of a gentleman of no social consequence.

One could have wished that the Père d'Orléans had been a little more circumstantial in his account of his hero's career. The vicissitudes in the course of which he ascended from his lowly station to such a pinnacle surely deserved to be saved from oblivion. He represents him as a pious catholic and an upright minister devoted to the interests of his king; but his account of the revolution that overthrew both king and dynasty and delivered the Greek into the hands of the outraged patriots of Siam, reads as though a certain arrangement of the facts had seemed necessary so that neither *le grand roi* nor various persons in high places should incur reproach. A decent veil is thrown over the sufferings of the fallen favourite, but his death at the hands of the executioners is vastly edifying. Reading between the jejune lines you receive notwithstanding the impression of a powerful and brilliant character. Constantine Faulkon was unscrupulous, cruel, greedy, faithless, ambitious; but he was great. His story reads like one of Plutarch's lives.

But of the grand house which he built nothing remains but the high brick wall that surrounded it and three or four roofless buildings, crumbling walls and the shapes of doors and windows. They have still the vague dignity of the architecture of Louis XIV. It is an unhandsome ruin that reminds you of nothing but a group of jerry-built villas destroyed by fire.

I went back to the river. It was narrow and turbid, deep between high banks, and on the other side were thick clumps of bamboo behind which the red sun was setting. The people were having their evening bath; fathers and mothers were bathing their children, and monks, having washed themselves, were rinsing out their yellow robes. It was a pleasant sight and grateful to the sensibility jarred by those sordid ruins and perplexed.

I have not the imagination to clothe dead bones with life nor the capacity to feel emotion over and over again about the same thing. I have known people who read *The Egoist* once a year and others who never go to Paris without having a look at Manet's *Olympe*. When once I have received from a work of art its peculiar thrill I have done with it till after the lapse of years, having become a different person, I can in *The Egoist* read a book I have never read before and in Manet's *Olympe* see a picture that has only just been hung in the Louvre. I had a notion that Ayudha would offer me nothing more than Lopburi and so made up my mind to give it a miss. Besides, I like my ease. I had gone from rest-house to rest-house long enough to hanker for the modest comfort of an Eastern hotel. I was getting a trifle tired of tinned sausages and canned pears. I had neither had a letter nor seen a paper since I left Taunggyi and I thought with pleasure of the huge packet that must be awaiting me in Bangkok.

I determined to go there without lingering on the way. The train passed leisurely through wide and open country with jagged blue hills in the distance. There were rice fields on both sides of the line, as far as the eye could reach, but a good many trees, too, so that the landscape had a certain friendliness. The rice was in all stages of growth, from the young green shoots in little patches to the grain nearly ripe and yellowing in the sun. Here and there they were cutting it and sometimes you saw three or four peasants in line laden with great sheaves. I suppose that there is none of the staple foods of man that needs so much labour first to grow and then to prepare for consumption. In the stream by the side of the track buffaloes in herds, under the charge of a small boy or a bronzed, dwarfish man in a large hat, wallowed luxuriously. Little flocks of rice-birds flew white and shining and sometimes grey cranes with outstretched necks. At the wayside stations there was always a crowd of idlers, and their *panaungs*, bright yellow, plum or emerald green, made lovely splashes of colour against the dust and the sunshine.

The train arrived at Ayudha. I was content to satisfy my curiosity about this historic place by a view of the railway-station (after all if a man of science can reconstruct a prehistoric animal from its thigh-bone why cannot a writer get as many emotions as he wants from a railway-station? In the Pennsylvania Depot is all the mystery of New York and in Victoria Station the grim, weary vastness of London), and with nonchalant eyes I put my head out of the carriage window. But a young man sprang to the door and opened it so promptly that I was nearly precipitated on to the platform. He wore a small round topee, a white drill coat, a black silk *panaung* so arranged as to make breeches, black silk stockings and patent-leather pumps. He spoke voluble English. He had been sent to meet me, he said, and would show me everything there was to be seen at Ayudha; there was a launch waiting at the landing-stage to take me up and down the river; and he had ordered a carriage; and the rest-house had been swept and cleaned that morning; and he ended up:

'Everything in the garden is lovely.'

He smiled at me with large flashing white teeth. A young man with a yellow face as smooth as a new plate, high cheek-bones, and very black gleaming eyes. I had not the heart then to tell him that I would not stay at Ayudha and indeed he gave me no time, for calling porters he told them to take my traps out of the carriage.

He took his duties seriously. He spared me nothing. From the station we walked along a broad street shaded with tamarind trees, on each side of which were Chinese shops, and the light was lovely and the people made attractive little pictures so that I would willingly have lingered; but my guide told me that there was nothing to see there, you had to go to Bangkok for shops, there they had everything you could buy in Europe; and with gentle determination led me to the landing-stage. We got into the launch. The river was broad and yellow. All along it were houseboats in which were shops, and above the muddy banks were houses on piles among fruit-trees. My guide took me to a walled enclosure on the river bank where had been a royal palace, and in what might have been once a throne-room, for it was but a ruin, there was a royal bed and a royal chair and some fragments of carved wood. He showed me innumerable heads of Buddha in bronze and stone, which had been brought from Lopburi or excavated from the numerous wats of Ayudha. We walked along a road for a little and there waiting for us was a tiny carriage and an obstinate pony. What organisation! We drove for two or three miles, along a pleasantly shady road with peasants' houses on piles on each side of it and outside each gateway was a little paper pagoda stuck over with little white flags in order to preserve the inmates of the house from cholera. We came to a vast park, with its green glades and grassy clearings, a pleasant place to picnic in, and here were the remains of a palace and great temples, many ruined pagodas and in one of the temples, deserted of all and lonely but indifferent, an enormous bronze figure of a sitting Buddha. Here and there under the trees children were playing. The little Siamese boys, with their wide eyes, curling hair and roguish looks, were very pretty. In passing my guide pointed out to me a shrub with a pale violet flower. He told me that when you found it you might be sure that there were no tigers.

'You have no tigers in England,' he laughed, not, I thought, without condescension.

I answered with deprecating modesty.

'No, we lead safe and peaceful lives in that tight little island. We are exposed to no dangers more alarming than the recklessness of a drunken motorist or the fury of a woman scorned.'

When we got back to the river I thanked the young Siamese warmly for showing me such interesting things and said that I would now go to the rest-house, upon which he opened his large gleaming eyes still larger and with his voice rising shrilly told me that I had not yet seen half of what he had to show me. I looked at him archly and murmured that enough was as good as a feast. He laughed brightly at this, evidently with the flattering belief that I had just invented the epigrammatic phrase, but floored me with the observation that enough was a purely relative term. I let him take me to another ruined temple, a scene untidy with desolation, and I gave an impatient glance at another Buddha of enormous size. And another and another. At last we came to a temple that was still a place of pilgrimage. I drew a breath of relief. It was like coming out of an unfurnished house to let, with its dead emptiness, into the busy street. At the landing-stage were women in sampans selling gold leaf, papers and incense sticks. On each side of the walk that led to the temple were little tables on which were displayed the same wares and sweets and cakes besides, and the vendors were plying a busy trade. The chapel was not very large and it was almost filled with a gigantic image of the Blessed One, and as you walked up the steps and looked through the door (your eyes still dazzled by the sunlight) it was awe-inspiring to discern vaguely that enormous gilded figure looming out of the darkness. In front of him were large figures of two disciples and the altar table was covered with burning incense. In a corner was a large teak bed on which were sitting two monks, smoking the fat Siamese cigarettes, drinking tea and chewing betel; they seemed not to notice the people who were there; some, men, women and children, in order to acquire merit were applying gold leaf to the pediment, a gigantic lotus, on which the Buddha sat. One woman, a spare, middle-aged person with a thin, intelligent face, with genuflections and prayers was consulting fortune by means of large wooden beans, which she threw on the ground and which, by falling on their flat or their concave side, answered her questions. There was an old man who came in with half-a-dozen members of his family and as soon as the middle-aged woman had finished with the beans he took them and when after the prescribed rites he threw them on the ground the whole party watched anxiously. Having finished he lit a cigarette and the rest rose from their knees, but whether the fates had promised good fortune or ill you could tell from not one of those impassive faces.

Now at last my guide took me to the rest-house that had been swept and cleaned for my visit. It was a houseboat with a narrow verandah looking on the river, a long sitting-room of dark wood and a bedroom and bath-room on each side. I very much liked the look of it. The young Siamese asked me to go to his house after dinner, saying he would ask his friends, but I told him I was tired, and with many expressions of goodwill he left me. The day was waning and, alone at last, sitting on the verandah I watched the traffic of the river. There were pedlars going along in their sampans with an easy stroke, pots and pans in their boats, vegetables for sale or food cooking in little stoves. Peasants passed me with a load of rice or an old woman with a shrivelled grey head paddling herself as unconcernedly in a tiny dug-out as though she were walking along the street. The rest-house was at a bend of the river and the bank to which it was moored turned sharply; it was thick with mangoes and palms and arecas. The sun set and they were silhouetted against the redness of the sky: the areca with its bedraggled crown looks like a feather duster very much the worse for wear, but at night against the sapphire of the sky it has the distinction of a Persian miniature. With the last light of day a white flock of egrets, like haphazard thoughts that flit through the mind without reason or sequence, fluttered disorderly down the tranquil stream. Darkness fell and at first the houseboats on the other side of the broad river were bright with lights, but they went out one by one and only here and there was a red gleam reflected on the water. One by one the stars came out and the sky blazed with them. The traffic of the river ceased and only now and then did you hear the soft splash of a paddle as someone silently passed on his way home. When I awoke in the night I felt a faint motion as the houseboat rocked a little and heard a little gurgle of water, like the ghost

114

of an Eastern music travelling not through space but through time. It was worth while for that sensation of exquisite peace, for the richness of that stillness, to have endured all that sight-seeing.

XXVIII

A few hours later I was in Bangkok.

It is impossible to consider these populous modern cities of the East without a certain malaise. They are all alike, with their straight streets, their arcades, their tramways, their dust, their blinding sun, their teeming Chinese, their dense traffic, their ceaseless din. They have no history and no traditions. Painters have not painted them. No poets, transfiguring dead bricks and mortar with their divine nostalgia, have given them a tremendous melancholy not their own. They live their own lives, without associations, like a man without imagination. They are hard and glittering and as unreal as a backcloth in a musical comedy. They give you nothing. But when you leave them it is with a feeling that you have missed something and you cannot help thinking that they have some secret that they have kept from you. And though you have been a trifle bored you look back upon them wistfully; you are certain that they have after all something to give you which, had you stayed longer or under other conditions, you would have been capable of receiving. For it is useless to offer a gift to him who cannot stretch out a hand to take it. But if you go back the secret still evades you and you ask yourself whether after all their only secret is not that the glamour of the East enwraps them. Because they are called Rangoon, Bangkok or Saïgon, because they are situated on the Irrawaddy, the Menam or the Mehkong, those great turbid rivers, they are invested with the magic spell that the ancient and storied East has cast upon the imaginative West. A hundred travellers may seek in them the answer to a question they cannot put and that yet torments them, only to be disappointed, a hundred travellers more will continue to press. And who can so describe a city as to give a significant picture of it? It is a different place to everyone who lives in it. No one can tell what it really is. Nor does it matter. The only thing of importance – to me – is what it means to me; and when the money-lender said, you can 'ave Rome, he said all there was to be said, by him, about the Eternal City. Bangkok. I put my impressions on the table, as a gardener puts the varied flowers he has cut in a great heap, leaving them for you to arrange, and I ask myself what sort of pattern I can make out of them. For my impressions are like a long frieze, a vague tapestry, and my business is to find in it an elegant and at the same time moving decoration. But the materials that are given me are dust and heat and noise and whiteness and more dust. The New Road is the main artery of the city, five miles long, and it is lined with houses, low and sordid, and shops, and the goods they sell, European and Japanese for the most part, look shop-soiled and dingy. A leisurely tram crowded with passengers passes down the whole length of the street, and the conductor never ceases to blow his horn. Gharries and rickshaws go up and down ringing their bells and motors sounding their claxons. The pavements are crowded and there is a ceaseless clatter of the clogs the people wear. Clopperty-clop they go and it makes a sound as insistent and monotonous as the sawing of the cicadas in the jungle. There are Siamese. The Siamese, with short bristly hair, wearing the *panaung*, a wide piece of stuff which they tuck in to make baggy and comfortable breeches, are not a comely race, but old age gives them distinction; they grow thin, emaciated even, rather than fat, and grey rather than bald, and then their dark eyes peer brightly out of a ravaged, yellow and wrinkled face; they walk well and

116

uprightly, not from the knees as do most Europeans, but from the hips. There are Chinese, in trousers white, blue or black, that come to just above the ankle and they are innumerable. There are Arabs, tall and heavily bearded, with white hats and a hawklike look; they walk with assurance, leisurely, and in their bold eyes you discern contempt for the race they exploit and pride in their own astuteness. There are turbaned natives of India with dark skins and the clean, sensitive features of their Aryan blood; as in all the East outside India they seem deliberately alien and thread their way through the host as though they walked a lonely jungle path; their faces are the most inscrutable of all those inscrutable faces. The sun beats down and the road is white and the houses are white and the sky is white, there is no colour but the colour of dust and heat.

But if you turn out of the main road you will find yourself in a network of small streets, dark, shaded and squalid, and tortuous alleys paved with cobble stones. In numberless shops, open to the street, with their gay signs, the industrious Chinese ply the various crafts of an Oriental city. Here are druggists and coffin shops, money-changers and tea-houses. Along the streets, uttering the raucous cry of China, coolies lollop swiftly bearing loads and the peddling cook carries his little kitchen to sell you the hot dinner you are too busy to eat at home. You might be in Canton. Here the Chinese live their lives apart and indifferent to the Western capital that the rulers of Siam have sought to make out of this strange, flat, confused city. What they have aimed at you see in the broad avenues, straight dusty roads, sometimes running by the side of a canal, with which they have surrounded this conglomeration of sordid streets. They are handsome, spacious and stately, shaded by trees, the deliberate adornment of a great city devised by a king ambitious to have an imposing seat; but they have no reality. There is something stagy about them, so that you feel they are more apt for court pageants than for the use of every day. No one walks in them. They seem to await ceremonies and processions. They are like the deserted avenues in the park of a fallen monarch.

XXIX

It appears that there are three hundred and ninety wats in Bangkok. A wat is a collection of buildings used as a Buddhist monastery and it is surrounded by a wall, often crenellated so as to make a charming pattern, like the walled enclosure of a city. Each building has its own use. The main one is called a *bote;* it is a great and lofty hall, with a central nave generally and two aisles, and here the Buddha stands on his gilded platform. There is another building, very like the *bote,* called the *vihara* and distinguished from it by the fact that it is not surrounded by the sacred stones, which is used for feasts and ceremonies and assemblies of the common folk. The *bote,* and sometimes the *vihara,* is surrounded by a cloister. Then there are shelters, libraries, bell towers and the priests' dwellings. Round the main buildings in due order are pagodas, large and small (they have their names, Phra Prang and Phra Chedi); some contain the ashes of royal or pious persons, (it may be even of royal *and* pious persons) and some, merely decorative, serve only to acquire merit for those that built them.

But not by this list of facts (which I found in a book on the Architecture of Siam) can I hope to give an impression of the surprise, the stupefaction almost, which assailed me when I saw these incredible buildings. They are unlike anything in the world, so that you are taken aback, and you cannot fit them into the scheme of the things you know. It makes you laugh with delight to think that anything so fantastic could exist on this sombre earth. They are gorgeous; they glitter with gold and whitewash, yet are not garish; against that vivid sky, in that dazzling sunlight, they hold their own, defying the brilliancy of nature and supplementing it with the ingenuity and the playful boldness of man. The artists who developed them step by step from the buildings of the ancient Khmers had the courage to pursue their fantasy to the limit; I fancy that art meant little to them, they desired to express a symbol; they knew no reticence, they cared nothing for good taste; and if they achieved art it is as men achieve happiness, not by pursuing it, but by doing with all their heart whatever in the day's work needs doing. I do not know that in fact they achieved art; I do not know that these Siamese wats have beauty, which they say is reserved and aloof and very refined; all I know is that they are strange and gay and odd, their lines are infinitely distinguished, like the lines of a proposition in a schoolboy's Euclid, their colours are flaunting and crude, like the colours of vegetables in the greengrocer's stall at an open-air market, and, like a place where seven ways meet, they open roads down which the imagination can make many a careless and unexpected journey.

The royal wat is not a wat but a city of wats; it is a gay, coloured confusion of halls and pagodas, some of them in ruins, some with the appearance of being brand-new; there are buildings, brilliant of hue though somewhat run to seed, that look like monstrous vegetables in the kitchen-gardens of the djinn; there are structures made of tiles and encrusted with strange tile flowers, three of them enormous, but many small ones, rows of them, that look like prizes in a shooting-gallery at a village fair in the country of the gods. It is like a page of Euphues and you are tickled to death at the sesquipedalian fancy that invented so many sonorous, absurd, grandiloquent terms. It is a labyrinth in which you cannot find your way. Roof rises upon roof and the roofs in Siamese architecture are its chief glory. They are arranged in three tiers, the upper one steeply pitched, and the lower ones decreasing in angle as they descend. They are covered with glazed tiles and their red and yellow and green are a feast to the eye. The gables are framed with Narga, the sacred snake, its head at the lower eaves and its undulating body climbing up the slope of the roof to end in a horn at the apex; and the gables are decorated with reliefs in carved wood of Indra on the elephant or Vishnu on the Garuda; for the temples of Buddha extend without misgiving shelter to the gods of other faiths. It is all incredibly rich with the gilding and the glass mosaic of the architraves and door jambs and the black and gold lacquer of the doors and shutters.

It is huge, it is crowded, it dazzles the eyes and takes the breath away, it is empty, it is dead; you wander about a trifle disconsolate, for after all it means nothing to you, the 'oh' of surprise is extorted from you, but never the 'ah' of emotion wrung; it makes no sense; it is an intricacy of odd, archaic and polysyllabic words in a crossword puzzle. And when in the course of your rambles you step up to look over a tall balustrade and see a rockery it is with relief that you enter. It is made about a small piece of artificial water, with little rustic bridges built over it here and there; it looks like the stony desert in which an ancient sage in a Chinese picture has his hermitage, and on the artificial rocks by the water's edge are monkeys and wild cats in stone and little dwarfish men. A magnolia grows there and a Chinese willow and shrubs with fat, shining leaves. It is a pleasantly fantastic retreat where an oriental king might fitly meditate, in comfort and peace, on the transitoriness of compound things.

But there is another wat, Suthat by name, that gives you no such impression of pell-mell confusion. It is clean and well swept and empty and quiet, and the space and the silence make a significant decoration. In the cloisters, all round, sitting cheek by jowl are gilded Buddhas, and as night falls and they are left to undistracted meditation, they are mysterious and vaguely sinister. Here and there in the court shrubs grow and stumpy gnarled trees. There is a multitude of rooks and they caw loudly as they fly. The *bote* stands high on a double platform, and its whitewash is stained by the rain and burned by the sun to a mottled ivory. The square columns, fluted at the corners, slope slightly inwards, and their capitals are strange upspringing flowers like flowers in an enchanted garden. They give the effect of a fantastic filigree of gold and silver and precious gems, emeralds, rubies and zircons. And the carving on the gable, intricate and elaborate, droops down like maidenhair in a grotto, and the climbing snake is like the waves of the sea in a Chinese painting. The doorways, three at each end and very tall, are of wood heavily carved and dully gilt, and the windows, close together and high, have shutters of faded gilt that faintly shines. With the evening, when the blue sky turns pink, the roof, the tall steep roof with its projecting eaves, gains all kinds of opalescent hues so that you can no longer believe it was made by human craftsmen, for it seems made of passing fancies and memories and fond hopes. The silence and the solitude seem about to take shape and appear before your eyes. And now the wat is very tall and very slender and of an incredible elegance. But, alas, its spiritual significance escapes you.

XXX

It seemed to me that there was more of this in the humble little monasteries that I had passed on the road hither. With their wooden walls and thatched roofs and their small tawdry images there was a homeliness about them, but withal an austerity, that seemed to suit the homely and yet austere religion that Gautama preached. It is, to my fancy, a religion of the countryside rather than of the cities and there lingers about it always the green shade of the wild fig-tree under which the Blessed One found enlightenment. Legend has made him out to be the son of a king, so that when he renounced the world he might seem to have abandoned power and great riches and glory; but in truth he was no more than the scion of a good family of country gentlemen, and when he renounced the world I do not suppose he abandoned more than a number of buffaloes and some rice fields. His life was as simple as that of the headman of any of the villages I had passed through in the Shan States. He lived in a world that had a passion for metaphysical disquisition, but he did not take kindly to metaphysics and when he was forced by the subtle Hindu sages into argument he grew somewhat impatient. He would have nothing to do with speculations upon the origin, significance and purpose of the Universe. 'Verily,' he said, 'within this mortal body, some six feet high, but conscious and endowed with mind, is the world and its origin, and its passing away.' His followers were forced by the Brahman doctors to defend their positions with metaphysical arguments and in course of time elaborated a theory of their faith that would satisfy the keen intelligence of a philosophic people, but Gautama, like all the founders of religion, had in point of fact but one thing to say: come unto me all ye that are weary and heavy laden and I will give you rest.

Most of the gods that the world has seen have made a somewhat frantic claim that men should have faith in them, and have threatened with dreadful penalties such as could not (whatever their goodwill) believe. There is something pathetic in the violence with which they denounce those who thwart them in the bestowal of the great gifts they have to offer. They seem deep in their hearts to have felt that it was the faith of others that gave them divinity (as though their godhead standing on an insecure foundation every believer was as it were a stone to buttress it) and that the message they so

122

ardently craved to deliver could only have its efficacy if they became god. And god they could only become if men believed in them. But Gautama made only the claim of the physician that you should give him a trial and judge him by results. He was more like the artist who does his work as best he can because to produce art is his function, and having offered his gift such modifications as were rendered necessary by his disbelief in the soul. For as everyone knows the most important point of the Buddha's teaching was that there was no such thing as a soul or a self. Every person is a putting together of qualities, material and mental; there can be no putting together without a becoming different, and there can be no becoming different without a passing away. Whatever has a beginning also has an end. The thought is exhilarating like a brisk winter morning when the sun shines and the road over the Downs is springy under the feet. Karma (I venture to remind the reader) is the theory that a man's actions in one existence determine his fate in the next. At death under the influence of the desire of life the impermanent aggregation of qualities which was a man reassembles to form another aggregation as impermanent. He is merely the present and temporary link in a long chain of cause and effect. The law of Karma prescribes that every act must have its result. It is the only explanation of the evil of this world that does not outrage the heart.

On a previous page I informed the kindly reader that it was my habit to start the day with a perusal of a few pages of a metaphysical work. It is a practice as healthy to the soul as the morning bath is healthy to the body. Though I have not the kind of intelligence that moves easily among abstractions and I often do not altogether understand what I read (this does not too greatly distract me since I find that professional dialecticians often complain that they cannot understand one another) I read on and sometimes come upon a passage that has a particular meaning for me. My way is lightened now and then by a happy phrase, for the philosophers of the past often wrote more than ordinarily well, and since in the long run a philosopher only describes himself, with his prejudices, his personal hopes and his idiosyncracies, and they were for the most part men of robust character, I have often the amusement of making acquaintance with a curious personality. In this desultory way I have read most of the great philosophers that the world has seen, trying to learn a little here and there or to get some enlightenment on matters that must puzzle everyone who makes his tentative way through the labyrinthine jungle of this life: nothing has interested me more than the way they treat the problem of evil. I cannot say that I have been greatly enlightened. The best of them have no more to say than that in the long run evil will be found to be good and that we who suffer must accept our suffering with an equal mind. In my perplexity I have read what the theologians had to say on the subject. After all sin is their province and so far as they are concerned the question is simple: if God is good and all-powerful why does he permit evil? Their answers are many and confused; they satisfy neither the heart nor the head, and for my part – I speak of these things humbly because I am ignorant and it may be that though the plain man must ask the question the answer can only be understood by the expert – I cannot accept them.

Now it happened that one of the books I had brought to read on the way was Bradley's *Appearance and Reality*. I had read it before, but had found it difficult and wanted to read it again, but since it was an unwieldy volume I tore off the binding and divided it into sections that I could conveniently put in my pocket when, having read enough, I mounted my pony and rode off from the bungalow in which I had passed the night. It is good reading, and though it scarcely convinces you it is often caustic, and the author has a pleasant gift of irony. He is never pompous. He handles the abstract with a light touch. But it is like one of those cubist houses in an exhibition, very light and trim and airy, but so severe in line and furnished with such austere taste, that you cannot imagine yourself toasting your toes by the fire and lounging in an easy chair with a comfortable book. But when I came upon his treatment of the problem of evil I found myself as honestly scandalised as the Pope at the sight of a young woman's shapely calves. The Absolute, I read, is perfect, and evil, being but an appearance, cannot but subserve to the perfection of the whole. Error contributes to greater energy of life. Evil plays a part in a higher end and in this sense unknowingly is good. The absolute is the richer for every discord. And my memory brought back to me, I know not why, a scene at the beginning of the war. It was in October and our sensibilities were not yet blunted. A cold raw night. There had been what those who took part in it thought a battle, but which was so insignificant a skirmish that the papers did not so much as refer to it, and about a thousand men had been killed and wounded. They lay on straw on the floor of a country church, and the only light came from the candles on the altar. The Germans were advancing and it was necessary to evacuate them as quickly as possible. All through the night the ambulance cars, without lights, drove back and forth, and the wounded cried out to be taken, and some died as they were being lifted on to the stretchers and were thrown on the heap of dead outside the door, and they were dirty and gory, and the church stank of blood and the rankness of humanity. And there was one boy who was so shattered that it was not worth while to move him and as he lay there, seeing men on either side of him being taken out, he screamed at the top of his voice: *je ne veux pas mourir. Je suis trop jeune. Je ne veux pas mourir.* And he went on screaming that he did not want to die till he died. Of course this is no argument. It was but an inconsiderable incident the only significance of which was that I saw it with my own eyes and in my ears for days afterwards rang that despairing cry; but a greater than I, a philosopher and a mathematician into the bargain if you please, said that the heart had its reasons which the head did not know, and (in the grip of compound things, to use the Buddhist phrase, as I am) this scene is to me a sufficient refutation of the metaphysician's fine-spun theories. But my heart can accept the evils that befall me if they are the consequence of actions that I (the I that is not my soul, which perishes, but the result of my deeds in another state of existence) did in past time, and I am resigned to the evils that I see about me, the death of the young, (the most bitter of all) the grief of the mothers that bore them in anguish, poverty and sickness and frustrated hopes, if these evils are but the consequence of the sins which those that suffer them once committed. Here is an explanation that outrages neither the heart nor the head; there is only one fault that I can find in it: it is incredible.

XXXI

The hotel faced the river. My room was dark, one of a long line, with a verandah on each side of it; the breeze blew through, but it was stifling. The dining-room was large and dim, and for coolness sake the windows were shuttered. One was waited on by silent Chinese boys. I did not know why, the insipid Eastern food sickened me. The heat of Bangkok was overwhelming. The wats oppressed me by their garish magnificence, making my head ache, and their fantastic ornaments filled me with malaise. All I saw looked too bright, the crowds in the street tired me, and the incessant din jangled my nerves. I felt very unwell, but I was not sure whether my trouble was bodily or spiritual (I am suspicious of the sensibility of the artist and I have often dissipated a whole train of exquisite and sombre thoughts by administering to myself a little liver pill), so to settle the matter I took my temperature. I was startled to see that it was a hundred and five. I could not believe it, so I took it again; it was still a hundred and five. No travail of the soul can cause anything like that. I went to bed and sent for a doctor. He told me that I had probably got malaria and took some of my blood to test; then he came back to say that there was no doubt about it and to give me quinine. I remembered then that towards the end of my journey down Siam the officer in command of the post had insisted that I should stay in his own house. He gave me his best bedroom and was so anxious that I should sleep in his grand European bed, of varnished pitch-pine and all the way from Bangkok, that I had not the heart to say that I preferred my own little camp-bed, which had a mosquito net, to his which had not. The anopheles snatched at the golden opportunity.

It was apparently a bad attack, since for some days the quinine had no effect on me, my temperature soared to those vertiginous heights that are common in malaria and neither wet sheets nor ice packs brought it down. I lay there, panting and sleepless, and shapes of monstrous pagodas thronged my brain and great gilded Buddhas bore down on me. Those wooden rooms, with their verandahs, made every sound frightfully audible to my tortured ears and one morning I heard the manageress of the hotel, an amiable creature but a good woman of business, in her guttural German voice say to the doctor: 'I can't have him die here, you know. You must take him to the hospital.' And the doctor replied: 'All right. But we'll wait a day or two yet.' 'Well, don't leave it too long,' she replied.

Then the crisis came. The sweat poured from me so that soon my bed was soaking, as though I had had a bath in it, and well-being descended upon me. I could breathe easily. My head ached no longer. And then when they carried me on to a long chair and I was free from pain, I felt extraordinarily happy. My brain seemed wonderfully clear. I was as weak as a newborn child and for some days could do nothing but lie on the terrace at the back of the hotel and look at the river. Motor launches bustled to and fro. The sampans were innumerable. Large steamers and sailing vessels came up the river so that it had quite the air of a busy port; and if you have a passion for travel it is impossible to look at the smallest, shabbiest, dirtiest sea-going tramp without a thrill of emotion and a hankering to be on it and on the way to some unknown haven. In the early morning, before the heat of the day, the scene was gay and lively; and then again towards sundown it was rich with colour and vaguely sinister with the laden shadows of the approaching night. I watched the steamers plod slowly up and with a noisy rattling of chains drop their anchors and I watched the three-masted barques drop silently down with the tide.

For some reason that I forget I had not been able to see the palace, but I did not regret it since it thus retained for me the faint air of mystery which of all the emotions is that which you can least find in Bangkok. It is surrounded by a great white wall, strangely crenellated, and the crenellations have the effect of a row of lotus buds. At intervals are gateways at which stand guards in odd Napoleonic costumes, and they have a pleasantly operatic air so that you expect them at any minute to break into florid song. Towards evening the white wall becomes pink and translucent and then above it, the dusk shrouding their garishness with its own soft glamour, you see, higgledy-piggledy, the gay, fantastic and multicoloured roofs of the palace and the wats and the bright-hued tapering of the pagodas. You divine wide courtyards, with lovely gateways intricately decorated, in which officials of the court, in their sober but distinguished dress, are intent upon secret affairs;

128

and you imagine walks lined with trim, clipped trees and temples sombre and magnificent, throne-halls rich with gold and precious stones and apartments, vaguely scented, dark and cool, in which lie in careless profusion the storied treasures of the East.

And because I had nothing to do except look at the river and enjoy the weakness that held me blissfully to my chair I invented a fairy story. Here it is.

XXXII

First the King of Siam had two daughters and he called them Night and Day. Then he had two more, so he changed the names of the first ones and called the four of them after the seasons, Spring and Autumn, Winter and Summer. But in course of time he had three others and he changed their names again and called all seven by the days of the week. But when his eighth daughter was born he did not know what to do till he suddenly thought of the months of the year. The Queen said there were only twelve and it confused her to have to remember so many new names, but the King had a methodical mind and when he made it up he never could change it if he tried. He changed the names of all his daughters and called them January, February, March (though of course in Siamese) till he came to the youngest who was called August, and the next one was called September.

'That only leaves October, November, and December,' said the Queen. 'And after that we shall have to begin all over again.'

'No, we shan't,' said the King, 'because I think twelve daughters are enough for any man and after the birth of dear little December I shall be reluctantly compelled to cut off your head.'

He cried bitterly when he said this, for he was extremely fond of the Queen. Of course it made the Queen very uneasy because she knew that it would distress the King very much if he had to cut off her head. And it would not be very nice for her. But it so happened that there was no need for either of them to worry because September was the last daughter they ever had. The Queen only had sons after that and they were called by the letters of the alphabet, so there was no cause for anxiety for a long time, since she had only reached the letter J.

Now the King of Siam's daughters had had their characters permanently embittered by having to change their names in this way, and the older ones whose names of course had been changed oftener than the others had their characters more permanently embittered. But September, who had never known what it was to be called anything but September (except of course by her sisters who because their characters were embittered called her all sorts of names) had a very sweet and charming nature.

The King of Siam had a habit which I think might be usefully imitated in Europe. Instead of receiving presents on his birthday he gave them and it looks as though he liked it, for he used often to say he was sorry he had only been born on one day and so only had one birthday in the year. But in this way he managed in course of time to give away all his wedding presents and the loyal addresses which the mayors of the cities in Siam presented him with and all his old crowns which had gone out of fashion. One year on his birthday, not having anything else handy, he gave each of his daughters a beautiful green parrot in a beautiful golden cage. There were nine of them and on each cage was written the name of the month which was the name of the Princess it belonged to. The nine Princesses were very proud of their parrots and they spent an hour every day (for like their father they were of a methodical turn of mind) in teaching them to talk. Presently all the parrots could say God Save the King (in Siamese, which is very difficult) and some of them could say Pretty Polly in no less than seven oriental languages. But one day when the Princess September went to say good-morning to her parrot she found it lying dead at the bottom of its golden cage. She burst into a flood of tears, and nothing that her Maids of Honour could say comforted her. She cried so much that the Maids of Honour, not knowing what to do, told the Queen, and the Queen said it was stuff and nonsense and the child had better go to bed without any supper. The Maids of Honour wanted to go to a party, so they put the Princess September to bed as quickly as they could and left her by herself. And while she lay in her bed, crying still even though she felt rather hungry, she saw a little bird hop into her room. She took her thumb out of her mouth and sat up. Then the little bird began to sing and he sang a beautiful song all about the lake in the King's garden and the willow-trees that looked at themselves in the still water and the gold fish that glided in and out of the branches that were reflected in it. When he had finished the Princess was not crying any more and she quite forgot that she had had no supper.

'That was a very nice song,' she said.

The little bird gave her a bow, for artists have naturally good manners, and they like to be appreciated.

'Would you care to have me instead of your parrot?' said the little bird. 'It's true that I'm not so pretty to look at but on the other hand I have a much better voice.'

The Princess September clapped her hands with delight and then the little bird hopped on to the end of her bed and sang her to sleep.

When she awoke next day the little bird was still sitting there, and as she opened her eyes he said good-morning. The Maids of Honour brought in her breakfast, and he ate rice out of her hand and he had his bath in her saucer. He drank out of it too. The Maids of Honour said they didn't think it was very polite to drink one's bath water, but the Princess September said that was the artistic temperament. When he had finished his breakfast he began to sing again so beautifully that the Maids of Honour were quite surprised, for they had never heard anything like it, and the Princess September was very proud and happy.

'Now I want to show you to my eight sisters,' said the Princess.

She stretched out the first finger of her right hand so that it served as a perch and the little bird flew down and sat on it. Then, followed by her Maids of Honour, she went through the palace and called on each of the Princesses in turn, starting with January, for she was mindful of etiquette, and going all the way down to August. And for each of the Princesses the little bird sang a different song. But the parrots could only say God Save the King and Pretty Polly. At last she showed the little bird to the King and Queen. They were surprised and delighted.

'I knew I was right to send you to bed without any supper,' said the Queen.

'This bird sings much better than the parrots,' said the King.

'I should have thought you got quite tired of hearing people say God Save the King,' said the Queen. 'I can't think why those girls wanted to teach their parrots to say it too.'

'The sentiment is admirable,' said the King, 'and I never mind how often I hear it. But I do get tired of hearing those parrots say Pretty Polly.'

'They say it in seven different languages,' said the Princesses.

'I daresay they do,' said the King, 'but it reminds me too much of my councillors. They say the same thing in seven different ways and it never means anything in any way they say it.'

The Princesses, their characters as I have already said being naturally embittered, were vexed at this, and the parrots looked very glum indeed. But the Princess September ran through all the rooms of the palace, singing like a lark, while the little bird flew round and round her, singing like a nightingale, which indeed it was.

Things went on like this for several days and then the eight Princesses put their heads together. They went to September and sat down in a circle round her, hiding their feet as is proper for Siamese princesses to do.

'My poor September,' they said. 'We are sorry for the death of your beautiful parrot. It must be dreadful for you not to have a pet bird as we have. So we have all put our pocket-money together and we are going to buy you a lovely green and yellow parrot.'

'Thank you for nothing,' said September. (This was not very civil of her, but Siamese princesses are sometimes a little short with one another.) 'I have a pet bird which sings the most charming songs to me and I don't know what on earth I should do with a green and yellow parrot.'

January sniffed, then Feburary sniffed, then March sniffed; in fact all the Princesses sniffed, but in their proper order of precedence. When they had finished September asked them:

'Why do you sniff? Have you all got colds in the head?'

'Well, my dear,' they said, 'it's absurd to talk of *your* bird when the little fellow flies in and out just as he likes.' They looked round the room and raised their eyebrows so high that their foreheads entirely disappeared.

'You'll get dreadful wrinkles,' said September.

'Do you mind our asking where your bird is now?' they said.

'He's gone to pay a visit to his father-in-law,' said the Princess September.

'And what makes you think he'll come back?' asked the Princesses.

'He always does come back,' said September.

'Well, my dear,' said the eight Princesses, 'if you'll take our advice you won't run any risks like that. If he comes back, and mind you, if he does you'll be lucky, pop him into the cage and keep him there. That's the only way you can be sure of him.'

'But I like to have him fly about the room,' said the Princess September.

'Safety first,' said her sisters ominously.

They got up and walked out of the room, shaking their heads, and they left September very uneasy. It seemed to her that her little bird was away a long time and she could not think what he was doing. Something might have happened to him. What with hawks and men with snares you never knew what trouble he might get into. Besides, he might forget her, or he might take a fancy to somebody else; that would be dreadful; oh, she wished he were safely back again, and in the golden cage that stood there empty and ready. For when the Maids of Honour had buried the dead parrot they had left the cage in its old place.

Suddenly September heard a tweet-tweet just behind her ear and she saw the little bird sitting on her shoulder. He had come in so quietly and alighted so softly that she had not heard him.

'I wondered what on earth had become of you,' said the Princess.

'I thought you'd wonder that,' said the little bird. 'The fact is I very nearly didn't come back to-night at all. My father-in-law was giving a party and they all wanted me to stay, but I thought you'd be anxious.'

Under the circumstances this was a very unfortunate remark for the little bird to make.

September felt her heart go thump, thump against her chest, and she made up her mind to take no more risks. She put up her hand and took hold of the bird. This he was quite used to, she liked feeling his heart go pit-pat, so fast, in the hollow of her hand, and I think he liked the soft warmth of her little hand. So the bird suspected nothing and he was so surprised when she carried him over to the cage, popped him in, and shut the door on him that for a moment he could think of nothing to say. But in a moment or two he hopped up on the ivory perch and said:

'What is the joke?'

'There's no joke,' said September, 'but some of mamma's cats are prowling about to-night, and I think you're much safer in there.'

'I can't think why the Queen wants to have all those cats,' said the little bird, rather crossly.

'Well, you see, they're very special cats,' said the Princess, 'they have blue eyes and a kink in their tails, and they're a speciality of the royal family, if you understand what I mean.'

'Perfectly,' said the little bird, 'but why did you put me in this cage without saying anything about it? I don't think it's the sort of place I like.'

'I shouldn't have slept a wink all night if I hadn't known you were safe.'

'Well, just for this once I don't mind,' said the little bird 'so long as you let me out in the morning.'

He ate a very good supper and then began to sing. But in the middle of his song he stopped.

'I don't know what's the matter with me,' he said, 'but I don't feel like singing to-night.'

'Very well,' said September, 'go to sleep instead.'

So he put his head under his wing and in a minute was fast asleep. September went to sleep too. But when the dawn broke she was awakened by the little bird calling her at the top of his voice:

'Wake up, wake up,' he said. 'Open the door of this cage and let me out. I want to have a good fly while the dew is still on the ground.'

'You're much better off where you are,' said September. 'You have a beautiful golden cage. It was made by the best

135

workman in my papa's kingdom, and my papa was so pleased with it that he cut off his head so that he should never make another.'

'Let me out, let me out,' said the little bird.

'You'll have three meals a day served by my Maids of Honour; you'll have nothing to worry you from morning till night, and you can sing to your heart's content.'

'Let me out, let me out,' said the little bird. And he tried to slip through the bars of the cage, but of course he couldn't, and he beat against the door but of course he couldn't open it. Then the eight Princesses came in and looked at him. They told September she was very wise to take their advice. They said he would soon get used to the cage and in a few days would quite forget that he had ever been free. The little bird said nothing at all while they were there, but as soon as they were gone he began to cry again: 'Let me out, let me out.'

'Don't be such an old silly,' said September. 'I've only put you in the cage because I'm so fond of you. *I* know what's good for you much better than you do yourself. Sing me a little song and I'll give you a piece of brown sugar.'

But the little bird stood in the corner of his cage, looking out at the blue sky, and never sang a note. He never sang all day.

'What's the good of sulking?' said September. 'Why don't you sing and forget your troubles?'

'How can I sing?' answered the bird. 'I want to see the trees and the lake and the green rice growing in the fields.'

'If that's all you want I'll take you for a walk,' said September.

She picked up the cage and went out and she walked down to the lake round which grew the willow trees, and she stood at the edge of the rice fields that stretched as far as the eye could see.

136

'I'll take you out every day,' said said. 'I love you and I only want to make you happy.'

'It's not the same thing,' said the little bird. 'The rice fields and the lake and the willow trees look quite different when you see them through the bars of a cage.'

So she brought him home again and gave him his supper. But he wouldn't eat a thing. The Princess was a little anxious at this, and asked her sisters what they thought about it.

'You must be firm,' they said.

'But if he won't eat, he'll die,' she answered.

'That would be very ungrateful of him,' they said. 'He must know that you're only thinking of his own good. If he's obstinate and dies it'll serve him right and you'll be well rid of him.'

September didn't see how that was going to do *her* very much good, but they were eight to one and all older than she, so she said nothing.

'Perhaps he'll have got used to his cage by to-morrow,' she said.

And next day when she awoke she cried out good-morning in a cheerful voice. She got no answer. She jumped out of bed and ran to the cage. She gave a startled cry, for there the little bird lay, at the bottom, on his side, with his eyes closed, and he looked as if he were dead. She opened the door and putting her hand in lifted him out. She gave a sob of relief, for she felt that his little heart was beating still.

'Wake up, wake up, little bird,' she said.

She began to cry and her tears fell on the little bird. He opened his eyes and felt that the bars of the cage were no longer round him.

'I cannot sing unless I'm free and if I cannot sing, I die,' he said.

The Princess gave a great sob.

'Then take your freedom,' she said, 'I shut you in a golden cage because I loved you and wanted to have you all to myself. But I never knew it would kill you. Go. Fly away among the trees that are round the lake and fly over the green rice fields. I love you enough to let you be happy in your own way.'

She threw open the window and gently placed the little bird on the sill. He shook himself a little.

'Come and go as you will, little bird,' she said. 'I will never put you in a cage any more.'

'I will come because I love you, little Princess,' said the bird. 'And I will sing you the loveliest songs I know. I shall go far away, but I shall always come back, and I shall never forget you.' He gave himself another shake. 'Good gracious me, how stiff I am,' he said.

Then he opened his wings and flew right away into the blue. But the little Princess burst into tears, for it is very difficult to put the happiness of someone you love before your own, and with her little bird far out of sight she felt on a sudden very lonely. When her sisters knew what had happened they mocked her and said that the little bird would never return. But he did at last. And he sat on September's shoulder and ate out of her hand and sang her the beautiful songs he had learned while he was flying up and down the fair places of the world. September kept her window open day and night so that the little bird might come into her room whenever he felt inclined, and this was very good for her; so she grew extremely beautiful. And when she was old enough she married the King of Cambodia and was carried all the way to the city in which he lived on a white elephant. But her sisters never slept with their windows open, so they grew extremely ugly as well as disagreeable, and when the time came to marry them off they were given away to the King's Councillors with a pound of tea and a Siamese cat.

XXXIII

When I was strong enough a kind friend, manager of the BAT, took me in his company's launch to see the klongs, or canals, which give Bangkok its individuality. It appears that until a few years ago no one was allowed without the royal permission to build on land and the houses stood on piles driven into the mud-banks at the water's edge or were constructed on floating pontoons moored to the side. The Menam, broad and handsome, is the city's main highway. Going up it, you pass wats placed advantageously here and there along the banks; and the high wall of the palace with the crowded splendour of the buildings behind it; public buildings, very grand and new; the trim, green, old-fashioned and dignified British legation and then untidy wharves. You turn down into one of the main klongs, the Oxford Street of Bangkok, and on each side are houseboats on which are shops open to the river front, and people go about making their purchases in sampans. Some of the canals are so broad that pontoons are moored in midstream and thus make a double or a treble row of shops. Little steamers, the omnibuses of the thrifty, puff up and down quickly, crowded with passengers; and as the rich in their great cars splash the passers-by on a rainy day in London, so opulent Chinamen in motor-launches speed along with a wash that makes the tiny dug-outs rock dangerously. Great barges are rowed slowly up and down, laden with wares, and these are the horse-drawn wagons that carry goods to market or from the wholesale merchant to the shopkeeper. Then there are the pedlars, like street-hawkers with a push-cart, who go about in little boats with their fish, their meat, or their vegetables.

A woman, sitting under a yellow umbrella of oiled paper, paddles them along with a firm and easy stroke. Finally there are the pedestrians, single persons in a sampan who paddle to and fro bent on some errand or idly as one might take a stroll down Picadilly. To unaccustomed eyes it is surprising to see a decent old woman with a mop of grey hair deftly manoeuvring her canoe amid the traffic as she goes methodically about her day's shopping. And like children scampering across the road tiny boys and girls, sometimes stark naked and seldom with more than a rag round their loins, dart in and out among the steamers and motor-boats in tiny little dug-outs so that you wonder that they are not run down. On the houseboats people lounge about idly; men mostly half naked wash themselves or their children, and here and there half-a-dozen urchins scramble about in the water.

And as you pass down a klong you get a sight of little creeks running out of it, only large enough for a sampan to enter, and you have a glimpse of green trees and houses sheltering amongst them. They are like the secluded courts and alleys that you find in London leading out of a busy thoroughfare. And just as the main street of a large town winds into a suburban road the klong narrows, the traffic dwindles, and now there is but one houseboat here and there, as it might be a general store to provide for the varied wants of the neighbours; and then the trees on the banks grow thick, coconuts and fruit trees, and you come but now and then upon a little brown house, the home of some Siamese who does not fear solitude. The plantations grow more extensive and your klong, which first was a busy street, then a respectable road through the suburbs, now becomes a leafy country lane.

XXXIV

I left Bangkok on a shabby little boat of four or five hundred tons. The dingy saloon, which served also as dining-room, had two narrow tables down its length with swivel chairs on both sides of them. The cabins were in the bowels of the ship and they were extremely dirty. Cockroaches walked about on the floor and however placid your temperament it is difficult not to be startled when you go to the wash-basin to wash your hands and a huge cockroach stalks leisurely out.

We dropped down the river, broad and lazy and smiling, and its green banks were dotted with little huts on piles standing at the water's edge. We crossed the bar; and the open sea, blue and still, spread before me. The look of it and the smell of it filled me with elation.

I had gone on board early in the morning and soon discovered that I was thrown amid the oddest collection of persons I had ever encountered. There were two French traders and a Belgian colonel, an Italian tenor, the American proprietor of a circus with his wife, and a retired French official with his. The circus proprietor was what is termed a good mixer, a type which according to your mood you fly from or welcome, but I happened to be feeling much pleased with life and before I had been on board an hour we had shaken for drinks, and he had shown me his animals. He was a very short fat man and his stingah-shifter, white but none too clean, outlined the noble proportions of his abdomen, but the collar was so tight that you wondered he did not choke. He had a red, cleanshaven face, a merry blue eye and short, untidy sandy hair. He wore a battered topee well on the back of his head. His name was Wilkins and he was born in Portland, Oregon. It appears that the Oriental has a passion for the circus and Mr Wilkins for twenty years had been travelling up and down the East from Port Said to Yokohama (Aden, Bombay, Madras, Calcutta, Rangoon, Singapore, Penang, Bangkok, Saïgon, Huë, Hanoi, Hong-Kong, Shanghai, their names roll on the tongue savourily, crowding the imagination with sunshine and strange sounds and a multicoloured activity) with his menagerie and his merry-go-rounds. It was a strange life he led, unusual and one that, one would have thought, must offer the occasion for all sorts of curious experiences, but the odd thing about him was that he was a perfectly commonplace little man and you would have been prepared to find him running a garage or keeping a third-rate hotel in a second-rate town in California. The fact is, and I have noticed it so often that I do not know why it should always surprise me, that the extraordinariness of a man's life does not make him extraordinary, but contrariwise if a man is extraordinary he will make extraordinariness out of a life as humdrum as that of a country curate. I wish I could feel it reasonable to tell here the story of the hermit I went to see on an island in the Torres Straits, a shipwrecked mariner who had lived there alone for thirty years, but when you are writing a book you are imprisoned by the four walls of your subject and though for the entertainment of my own digressing mind I set it down now I should be forced in the end by my sense of what is fit to go between two covers and what is not, to cut it out. Anyhow, the long and short of it is that notwithstanding this long and intimate communion with nature and his thoughts the man was as dull, insensitive and vulgar an oaf at the end of this experience as he must have been at the beginning.

The Italian singer passed us and Mr Wilkins told me that he was a Neapolitan who was on his way to Hong-Kong to rejoin his company which he had been forced to leave owing to an attack of malaria in Bangkok.

He was an enormous fellow, and very fat, and when he flung himself into a chair it creaked with dismay. He took off his topee, displaying a great head of long, curly, greasy hair, and ran podgy and beringed fingers through it.

'He ain't very sociable,' said Mr Wilkins. 'He took the cigar I gave him, but he wouldn't have a drink. I shouldn't wonder if there wasn't somethin' rather queer about him. Nasty lookin' guy, ain't he?'

Then a little fat woman in white came on deck holding by the hand a Wa-Wa monkey. It walked solemnly by her side.

'This is Mrs Wilkins,' said the circus proprietor, 'and our youngest son. Draw up a chair, Mrs Wilkins, and meet this gentleman. I don't know his name, but he's already paid for two drinks for me and if he can't shake any better than he has yet he'll pay for one for you too.'

Mrs Wilkins sat down with an abstracted, serious look, and with her eyes on the blue sea suggested that she did not see why she shouldn't have a lemonade.

'My, it's hot,' she murmured, fanning herself with the topee which she took off.

'Mrs Wilkins feels the heat,' said her husband. 'She's had twenty years of it now.'

'Twenty-two and a half,' said Mrs Wilkins, still looking at the sea.

'And she's never got used to it yet.'

'Nor never shall and you know it,' said Mrs Wilkins.

She was just the same size as her husband and just as fat, and she had a round red face like his and the same sandy, untidy hair. I wondered if they had married because they were so exactly alike, or if in the course of years they had acquired this astonishing resemblance. She did not turn her head but continued to look absently at the sea.

'Have you shown him the animals?' she asked.

'You bet your life I have.'

'What did he think of Percy?'

'Thought him fine.'

I could not but feel that I was being unduly left out of a conversation of which I was at all events partly the subject, so I asked:

'Who's Percy?'

'Percy's our eldest son. There's a flyin'-fish, Elmer. He's the oran-utan. Did he eat his food well this morning?'

'Fine. He's the biggest oran-utan in captivity. I wouldn't take a thousand dollars for him.'

'And what relation is the elephant?' I asked.

Mrs Wilkins did not look at me, but with her blue eyes still gazed indifferently at the sea.

'He's no relation,' she answered. 'Only a friend.'

The boy brought lemonade for Mrs Wilkins, a whisky and soda for her husband and a gin and tonic for me. We shook dice and I signed the chit.

'It must come expensive if he always loses when he shakes,' Mrs Wilkins murmured to the coastline.

'I guess Egbert would like a sip of your lemonade, my dear,' said Mr Wilkins.

Mrs Wilkins slightly turned her head and looked at the monkey sitting on her lap.

'Would you like a sip of mother's lemonade, Egbert?'

The monkey gave a little squeak and putting her arm round him she handed him a straw. The monkey sucked up a little lemonade and having drunk enough sank back against Mrs Wilkins' ample bosom.

'Mrs Wilkins thinks the world of Egbert,' said her husband. 'You can't wonder at it, he's her youngest.'

Mrs Wilkins took another straw and thoughtfully drank her lemonade.

'Egbert's all right,' she remarked. 'There's nothin' wrong with Egbert.'

Just then the French official who had been sitting down got up and began walking up and down. He had been accompanied on board by the French minister at

144

Bangkok, one or two secretaries and a prince of the Royal Family. There had been a great deal of bowing and shaking of hands and as the boat slipped away from the quay much waving of hats and handkerchiefs. He was evidently a person of consequence. I had heard the captain address him as Monsieur le Gouverneur.

'That's the big noise on this boat,' said Mr Wilkins. 'He was governor of one of the French colonies and now he's makin' a tour of the world. He came to see my circus at Bangkok. I guess I'll ask him what he'll have. What shall I call him, my dear?'

Mrs Wilkins slowly turned her head and looked at the Frenchman, with the rosette of the legion of honour in his button hole, pacing up and down.

'Don't call him anything,' she said. 'Show him a hoop and he'll jump right through it.'

I could not but laugh. Monsieur le Gouverneur was a little man, well below the average height, and smally made, with a very ugly little face and thick, almost negroid features; and he had a bushy grey head, bushy grey eyebrows and a bushy grey moustache. He did look a little like a poodle and he had the poodle's soft, intelligent and shining eyes. Next time he passed us Mr Wilkins called out:

'*Monsoo. Qu'est ce que vous prenez?*' I cannot reproduce the eccentricities of his accent. '*Une petite verre de porto.*' He turned to me. 'Foreigners, they all drink porto. You're always safe with that.'

'Not the Dutch,' said Mrs Wilkins, with a look at the sea. 'They won't touch nothin' but Schnaps.'

The distinguished Frenchman stopped and looked at Mr Wilkins with some bewilderment. Whereupon Mr Wilkins tapped his breast and said:

'*Moa, proprietarre Cirque. Vous avez visite.*'

Then, for a reason that escaped me, Mr Wilkins made his arms into a hoop and outlined the gestures that represented a poodle jumping through it. Then he pointed at the Wa-Wa that Mrs Wilkins was still holding on her lap.

'*La petit fils de mon femme,*' he said.

Light broke upon the governor and he burst into a peculiarly musical and infectious laugh. Mr Wilkins began laughing too.

'*Oui, oui,*' he cried. '*Moa,* circus proprietor. *Une petite verre de porto. Oui. Oui. N'est ce pas?*'

'Mr Wilkins talks French like a Frenchman,' Mrs Wilkins informed the passing sea.

'*Mais très volontiers,*' said the governor, still smiling. I drew him up a chair and he sat down with a bow to Mrs Wilkins.

'Tell poodle-face his name's Egbert,' she said, looking at the sea.

I called the boy and we ordered a round of drinks.

'You sign the chit, Elmer,' she said. 'It's not a bit of good Mr What's-his-name shakin' if he can't shake nothin' better than a pair of treys.'

'*Vous comprenez le français, madame?*' asked the governor politely.

'He wants to know if you speak French, my dear.'

'Where does he think I was raised? Naples?'

Then the governor, with exuberant gesticulations, burst into a torrent of English so fantastic that it required all my knowledge of French to understand what he was talking about.

Presently Mr Wilkins took him down to look at his animals and a little later we assembled in the stuffy saloon for luncheon. The governor's wife appeared and was put on the captain's right. The governor explained to her who we all were and she gave us a gracious bow. She was a large woman, tall and of a robust build, of fifty-five perhaps, and she was dressed somewhat severely in black silk. On her head she wore a huge round topee. Her features were so large and regular, her form so statuesque, that you were reminded of the massive females who take part in processions. She would have admirably suited the role of Columbia or Britannia in a patriotic demonstration. She towered over her diminutive husband like a skyscraper over a shack. He talked incessantly, with vivacity and wit, and when he said anything amusing her heavy features relaxed into a large, fond smile.

'Que tu es bête, mon ami,' she said. She turned to the captain. 'You must not pay any attention to him. He is always like that.'

We had indeed a very amusing meal and when it was over we separated to our various cabins to sleep away the heat of the afternoon. On such a small boat having once made the acquaintance of my fellow passengers, it would have been impossible, even had I wished it, not to pass with them every moment of the day that I was not in my cabin. The only person who held himself aloof was the Italian tenor. He spoke to no one, but sat by himself as far forward as he could get, twanging a guitar in an undertone so that you had to strain your ears to catch the notes. We remained in sight of land and the sea was like a pail of milk. Talking of one thing and another we watched the day decline, we dined, and then we sat out again on deck under the stars. The two traders played piquet in the hot saloon, but the Belgian colonel joined our little group. He was shy and fat and opened his mouth only to utter a civility. Soon, influenced perhaps by the night and encouraged by the darkness that gave him, up there in the bows, the sensation of being alone with the sea, the Italian tenor, accompanying himself on his guitar, began to sing, first in a low tone, and then a little louder, till presently, his music captivating him, he sang with all his might. He had the real Italian voice, all macaroni, olive oil and sunshine, and he sang the Neapolitan songs that I had heard in my youth in the Piazza San Ferdinando, and fragments from *La Bohème*, and *Traviata* and *Rigoletto*. He sang with emotion and false emphasis and his tremolo reminded you of every third-rate Italian tenor you had ever heard, but there in the openness of that lovely night his exaggerations only made you smile and you could not but feel in your heart a lazy sensual pleasure. He sang for an hour, perhaps, and we all fell silent; then he was still, but he did not move and we saw his huge bulk dimly outlined against the luminous sky.

I saw that the little French governor had been holding the hand of his large wife and the sight was absurd and touching.

'Do you know that this is the anniversary of the day on which I first saw my wife,' he said, suddenly breaking the silence which had certainly weighed on him, for I had never met a more loquacious creature. 'It is also the anniversary of the day on which she promised to be my wife. And, which will surprise you, they were one and the same.'

'Voyons, mon ami,' said the lady, 'you are not going to bore our friends with that old story. You are really quite insupportable.'

But she spoke with a smile on her large, firm face, and in a tone that suggested that she was quite willing to hear it again.

'But it will interest them, mon petit chou.' It was in this way that he always addressed his wife and it was funny to hear this imposing and even majestic lady thus addressed by her small husband. 'Will it not, monsieur?' he asked me. 'It is a romance and who does not like romance, especially on such a night as this?'

I assured the governor that we were all anxious to hear and the Belgian colonel took the opportunity once more to be polite.

'You see, ours was a marriage of convenience pure and simple.'

'C'est vrai,' said the lady. 'It would be stupid to deny it. But sometimes love comes after marriage and not before, and then it is better. It lasts longer.'

I could not but notice that the governor gave her hand

148

an affectionate little squeeze.

'You see, I had been in the navy, and when I retired I was forty-nine. I was strong and active and I was very anxious to find an occupation. I looked about: I pulled all the strings I could. Fortunately I had a cousin who had some political importance. It is one of the advantages of democratic government that if you have sufficient influence merit, which otherwise might pass unnoticed, generally receives its due reward.'

'You are modesty itself, *mon pauvre ami,*' said she.

'And presently I was sent for by the Minister to the Colonies and offered the post of governor in a certain colony. It was a very distant spot that they wished to send me to and a lonely one, but I had spent my life wandering from port to port, and that was not a matter that troubled me. I accepted with joy. The minister told me that I must be ready to start in a month. I told him that would be easy for an old bachelor who had nothing much in the world but a few clothes and a few books.'

'"*Comment, mon lieutenant,*" he cried, "You are a bachelor?"

'"Certainly," I answered. "And I have every intention of remaining one."

'"In that case I am afraid I must withdraw my offer. For this position it is essential that you should be married."

'It is too long a story to tell you, but the gist of it was that owing to the scandal my predecessor, a bachelor, had caused by having native girls to live in the Residency and the consequent complaints of the white people, planters and the wives of functionaries, it had been decided that the next governor must be a model of respectability. I expostulated. I argued. I recapitulated my services to the country and the services my cousin could render at the next elections.

'"But what can I do?" I cried with dismay.

'"You can marry," said the minister.

'"*Mais voyons, monsieur le ministre,* I do not know

any women. I am not a lady's man and I am forty-nine. How do you expect me to find a wife?"

'"Nothing is more simple. Put an advertisement in the paper."

'I was confounded. I did not know what to say.

'"Well, think it over," said the minister. "If you can find a wife in a month you can go, but no wife no job. That is my last word." He smiled a little, to him the situation was not without humour. "And if you think of advertising I recommend the *Figaro*."

'I walked away from the ministry with death in my heart. I knew the place to which they desired to appoint me and I knew it would suit me very well to live there; the climate was tolerable and the Residency was spacious and comfortable. The notion of being a governor was far from displeasing me and, having nothing but my pension as a naval officer, the salary was not to be despised. Suddenly I made up my mind. I walked to the offices of the *Figaro*, composed an advertisement and handed it in for insertion. But I can tell you, when I walked up the Champs Elysées afterwards my heart was beating much more furiously than it had ever done when my ship was stripped for action.'

The governor leaned forward and put his hand impressively on my knee.

'*Mon cher monsieur*, you will never believe it, but I had four thousand three hundred and seventy-two replies. It was an avalanche. I had expected half-a-dozen; I had to take a cab to take the letters to my hotel. My room was swamped with them. There were four thousand three hundred and seventy-two women who were willing to share my solitude and be a governor's lady. It was staggering. They were of all ages from seventeen to seventy. There were maidens of irreproachable ancestry and the highest culture, there were unmarried ladies who had made a little slip at one period of their career and now desired to regularise their situation; there were widows whose husbands had died in the most harrowing circumstances; and there were widows whose children would be a solace to my old age. They were blonde and dark, tall and short, fat and thin; some could speak five languages and others could play the piano. Some offered me love and some craved for it; some could only give me a solid friendship but mingled with esteem; some had a fortune and others golden prospects. I was overwhelmed. I was bewildered. At last I lost my temper, for I am a passionate man, and I got up and I stamped on all those letters and all those photographs and I cried: I will marry none of them. It was hopeless, I had less than a month now and I could not see over four thousand aspirants to my hand in that time. I felt that if I did not see them all, I should be tortured for the rest of my life by the thought that I had missed the one woman the fates had destined to make me happy. I gave it up as a bad job.

'I went out of my room hideous with all those photographs and littered papers and to drive care away went on the boulevard and sat down at the Café de la Paix. After a time I saw a friend passing and he nodded to me and smiled. I tried to smile but my heart was sore. I realised that I must spend the years that remained to me in a cheap pension at Toulon or Brest as an *officier de marine en retraite. Zut!* My friend stopped and coming up to me sat down.

'"What is making you look so glum, *mon cher!*" he asked me. "You who are the gayest of mortals."

'I was glad to have someone in whom I could confide my troubles and told him the whole story. He laughed consumedly. I have thought since that perhaps the incident had its comic side, but at the time, I assure you, I could see in it nothing to laugh at. I mentioned the fact to my friend not without asperity and then, controlling his mirth as best he could, he said to me: "But, my dear fellow, do you really want to marry?" At this I entirely lost my temper.

'"You are completely idiotic," I said. "If I did not want to marry, and what is more marry at once, within the next fortnight, do you imagine that I should have spent three days reading love letters from women I have never set eyes on?"

'"Calm yourself and listen to me," he replied. "I have a cousin who lives in Geneva. She is Swiss, *du reste*, and she belongs to a family of the greatest respectability in the republic. Her morals are without reproach, she is of a suitable age, a spinster for she has spent the last fifteen years nursing an invalid mother who has lately died, she is well educated and *pardessus le marché* she is not ugly."

'"It sounds as though she were a paragon," I said.

'"I do not say that, but she has been well brought-up and would become the position you have to offer her."

'"There is one thing you forget. What inducement would there be for her to give up her friends and her accustomed life to accompany in exile a man of forty-nine who is by no means a beauty?"'

Monsieur le Gouverneur broke off his narrative and shrugging his shoulders so emphatically that his head almost sank between them, turned to us.

'I am ugly. I admit it. I am of an ugliness that does not inspire terror or respect, but only ridicule, and that is the worst ugliness of all. When people see me for the first time they do not shrink with horror, there would evidently be something flattering in that, they burst out laughing. Listen, when the admirable Mr Wilkins showed me his animals this morning Percy, the oran-utan, held out his arms and but for the bars of the cage would have clasped me to his bosom as a long lost brother. Once indeed when I was at the Jardin des Plantes in Paris and was told that one of the anthropoid apes had escaped I made my way to the exit as quickly as I could in fear that, mistaking me for the refugee, they would seize me and, notwithstanding my expostulations, shut me up in the monkey house.'

'*Voyons, mon ami,*' said Madame his wife, in her deep slow voice, 'you are talking even greater nonsense than usual. I do not say that you are an Apollo, in your position it is unnecessary that you should be, but you have dignity, you have poise, you are what any woman would call a fine man.'

'I will resume my story. When I made this remark to my friend he replied: "One can never tell with women. There is something about marriage that wonderfully attracts them. There would be no harm in asking her. After all it is regarded as a compliment by a woman to be asked in marriage. She can but refuse."

'"But I do not know your cousin and I do not see how I am to make her acquaintance. I cannot go to her house, ask to see her and when I am shown into the drawing-room say: *Voila*, I have come to ask you to marry me. She would think I was a lunatic and scream for help. Besides, I am a man of an extreme timidity, and I could never take such a step."

'"I will tell you what to do," said my friend. "Go to Geneva and take her a box of chocolates from me. She will be glad to have news of me and will receive you with pleasure. You can have a little talk and then if you do not like the look of her you take your leave and no harm is done. If on the other hand you do, we can go into the matter and you can make a formal demand for her hand."

'I was desperate. It seemed the only thing to do. We went to a shop at once and bought an enormous box of chocolates and that night I took the train to Geneva. No sooner had I arrived than I sent her a letter to say that I was the bearer of a gift from her cousin and much wished to give myself the pleasure of delivering it in person. Within an hour I received her reply to the effect that she would be pleased to receive me at four o'clock in the afternoon. I spent the interval before my mirror and seventeen times I tied and retied my tie. As the clock struck four I presented myself at the door of her house and was immediately ushered into the drawing-room. She was waiting for me. Her cousin said she was not ugly. Imagine my surprise to see a young woman, *enfin* a woman still young, of a noble presence, with the dignity of Juno, the features of Venus, and in her expression the intelligence of Minerva.'

'You are too absurd,' said Madame. 'But by now these gentlemen know that one cannot believe all you say.'

'I swear to you that I do not exaggerate. I was so taken aback that I nearly dropped the box of chocolates. But I said to myself: *la garde meurt mais ne se rend pas.* I presented the box of chocolates. I gave her news of her cousin. I found her amiable. We talked for quarter of an hour. And then I said to myself: *Allons-y.* I said to her:

'"Mademoiselle, I must tell you that I did not come here merely to give you a box of chocolates."

'She smiled and remarked that evidently I must have had reasons to come to Geneva of more importance than that.

'"I came to ask you to do me the honour of marrying me." She gave a start.

'"But, monsieur, you are mad," she said.

'"I beseech you not to answer till you have heard the facts," I interrupted, and before she could say another word I told her the whole story. I told her about my advertisement in the *Figaro* and she laughed till the tears ran down her face. Then I repeated my offer.

'"You are serious?" she asked.

'"I have never been more serious in my life."

'"I will not deny that your offer has come as a surprise. I had not thought of marrying, I have passed the age; but evidently your offer is not one that a woman should refuse without consideration. I am flattered. Will you give me a few days to reflect?"

'"Mademoiselle, I am absolutely desolated," I replied.

"But I have not time. If you will not marry me I must go back to Paris and resume my perusal of the fifteen to eighteen hundred letters that still await my attention."

'"It is quite evident that I cannot possibly give you an answer at once. I had not set eyes on you a quarter of an hour ago. I must consult my friends and my family."

'"What have they got to do with it? You are of full age. The matter is pressing. I cannot wait. I have told you everything. You are an intelligent woman. What can prolonged reflection add to the impulse of the moment?"

'"You are not asking me to say yes or no this very minute? This is outrageous."

'"That is exactly what I am asking. My train goes back to Paris in a couple of hours."

'She looked at me reflectively.

'"You are quite evidently a lunatic. You ought to be shut up both for your own safety and that of the public."

'"Well, which is it to be?" I said. "Yes or no?"

'She shrugged her shoulders.

'"*Mon dieu.*" She waited a minute and I was on tenterhooks. "Yes."

The Governor waved his hand towards his wife.

'And there she is. We were married in a fortnight and I became governor of a colony. I married a jewel, my dear Sirs, a woman of the most charming character, one in a thousand, a woman of a masculine intelligence and a feminine sensibility, an admirable woman.'

'But hold your tongue, *mon ami,*' his wife said. 'You are making me as ridiculous as yourself.'

He turned to the Belgian colonel.

'Are you a bachelor, *mon colonel?* If so I strongly recommend you to go to Geneva. It is a nest (*une pépinière* was the word he used) of the most adorable young women. You will find a wife there as nowhere else. Geneva is besides a charming city. Do not waste a minute, but go there and I will give you a letter to my wife's nieces.'

It was she who summed up the story.

'The fact is that in a marriage of convenience you expect less and so you are less likely to be disappointed. As you do not make senseless claims on one another there is no reason for exasperation. You do not look for perfection and so you are tolerant to one another's faults. Passion is all very well, but it is not a proper foundation for marriage. *Voyez-vous*, for two people to be happy in marriage they must be able to respect one another, they must be of the same condition and their interests must be alike; then if they are decent people and are willing to give and take, to live and let live, there is no reason why their union should not be as happy as ours.' She paused. 'But, of course, my husband is a very, very remarkable man.'

XXXV

It was but a run of thirty-six hours from Bangkok to Kep, on the Cambodian coast, to which I was bound so that I could get to Phnom-Penh and so to Angkor. Kep, a strip of land in front of the sea backed by green hills, is a health station established by the French for the officials of their government, and there is a large bungalow filled with them and their wives. It is in charge of a retired sea-captain and through him I was able to get a car to take me to Phnom-Penh. This is the ancient capital of Cambodia, but nothing remains of its antiquity; it is a hybrid town built by the French and inhabited by the Chinese; it has broad streets with arcades in which are Chinese shops, formal gardens and, facing the river, a quay neatly planted with trees like the quay in a French riverside town. The hotel is large, dirty and pretentious, and there is a terrace outside it where the merchants and the innumerable functionaries may take an *apéritif* and for a moment forget that they are not in France.

Here the enthusiastic traveller may visit a palace, built

156

within thirty years or so, where the descendant of so long a line of kings keeps up a semblance of royalty; and he will be shown his jewels, gold head-dresses pyramidal and tinselly, a sacred sword, a sacred lance, and odd, old-fashioned ornaments presented to him by European potentates in the sixties; he may see a throne-room with a gorgeous gaudy throne surmounted by a huge white nine-tiered umbrella; he may see a wat, very spick and span and new, with a great deal of gilt about it and a silver floor; and should he have a well-furnished memory and an alert imagination he may amuse himself with sundry reflections upon the trappings of royalty, the passing of empire, and the deplorable taste in art of crowned heads.

But if rather than a serious traveller he is a silly flippant person he may amuse himself with a little story.

Once upon a time at the palace of Phnom-Penh there was a great function for the reception of the new French governor and his wife, and the king and all his court were dressed in their grandest clothes. The governor's wife was shy and new to the country and for something to say admired a beautiful and jewelled belt that the monarch wore. Etiquette and oriental politeness forced him immediately to take it off and offer it to her; but the belt was the only thing that kept up his royal trousers, so he turned to the prime minister and asked him to give him the belt, a trifle less grand, that he himself was wearing. The prime minister undid it and gave it to his master, but turned to the minister of war who stood next to him and asked him to give him his. The minister of war turned to the grand chamberlain and made the same request, and so it went on down the line from minister to minister, from one official to another, till at last a small page-boy was seen hurrying from the palace holding up his trousers with both hands. For he, the most insignificant of all that gathering, had found no one to give him a belt.

But the traveller before he leaves Phnom-Penh will be well advised to visit the museum, since here, probably for the first time in his life, he will see, among much that is dull and commonplace, examples of a school of sculpture that will give him a good deal to think about. He will see at least one statue that is as beautiful as anything that the Mayans or the archaic Greeks ever wrought from stone. But if, like me, he is a person of slow perceptions, it will not for some time occur to him that here, unexpectedly, he has come upon something that will for the rest of his life enrich his soul. So might a man buy a plot of land to build himself a little house and then discover that there was a gold mine underneath it.

XXXVI

One thing that makes a visit to Angkor an event of unusual significance – preparing you to enter into the state of mind proper to such an experience – is the immense difficulty of getting there. For once you have reached Phnom-Penh – itself a place sufficiently off the beaten track – you must take a steamer and go a long way up a dull and sluggish river, a tributary of the Mehkong, till you reach a wide lake; you change into another steamer, flat-bottomed, for there is no great depth, and in this you travel all night; then you pass through a narrow defile and come to another great stretch of placid water. It is night again when you reach the end of it. Then you get into a sampan and are rowed among clumps of mangroves up a tortuous channel. The moon is full and the trees on the banks are sharply outlined against the night and you seem to traverse not a real country but the fantastic land of the silhouettist. At last you come to a bedraggled little village of watermen, whose dwellings are houseboats, and landing you drive down by the river side through plantations of coconut, betel and plantain, and the river is now a shallow little stream (like the country stream in which on Sundays in your childhood you used to catch minnows and put them in a jam-pot) till at length, looming gigantic and black in the moonshine, you see the great towers of Angkor Wat.

But now that I come to this part of my book I am seized with dismay. I have never seen anything in the world more wonderful than the temples of Angkor, but I do not know how on earth I am going to set down in black and white such an account of them as will give even the most sensitive reader more than a confused and shadowy impression of their grandeur. Of course to the artist in words, who takes pleasure in the sound of them and their look on the page, it would be an opportunity in a thousand. What a chance for prose pompous and sensual, varied, solemn and harmonious; and what a delight to such a one it would be to reproduce in his long phrases the long lines of the buildings, in the balance of his paragraphs to express their symmetry, and in the opulence of his vocabulary their rich decoration! It would be enchanting to find the apt word and by putting it in its right place give the same rhythm to the sentence as he had seen in the massed grey stones; and it would be a triumph to hit upon the unusual, the revealing epithet that translated into another beauty the colour, the form and the strangeness of what he alone had had the gift to see.

Alas, I have not the smallest talent for this sort of thing, and – doubtless because I cannot do it myself – I do not very much like it in others. A little of it goes a long way with me. I can read a page of Ruskin with enjoyment, but ten only with weariness; and when I have finished an essay by Walter Pater I know how a trout feels when you have taken him off the hook and he lies on the bank flapping his tail in the grass. I admire the ingenuity with which, little piece of glass by little piece of glass, Pater fitted together the mosaic of his style, but it bores me. His prose is like one of those period houses, all Genoese velvet and carved wood, that they used to have in America twenty years ago, and you looked round desperately for a corner on which to put down your empty glass. I can bear it better when this kind of stately writing is done by our forefathers. The grand style became them. I am awed by the magnificence of Sir Thomas Browne; it is like staying in a great Palladian palace with frescoes by Veronese on the ceilings and tapestries on the walls. It is impressive rather than homely. You cannot see yourself doing your daily dozen in those august surroundings.

When I was young I took much trouble to acquire a style; I used to go to the British Museum and note down the names of rare jewels so that I might give my prose magnificence, and I used to go to the Zoo and observe the way an eagle looked or linger on a cab-rank to see how a horse champed so that I might on occasion use a nice metaphor; I made lists of unusual adjectives so that I might put them in unexpected places. But it was not a bit of good. I found I had no bent for anything of the kind; we do not write as we want to but as we can, and though I have the greatest respect for those authors who are blessed with a happy gift of phrase I have long resigned myself to writing as plainly as I can. I have a very small vocabulary and I manage to make do with it, I am afraid, only because I see things with no great subtlety. I think perhaps I see them with a certain passion and it interests me to translate into words not the look of them, but the emotion they have given me. But I am content if I can put this down as briefly and baldly as if I were writing a telegram.

XXXVII

On my journey up the river and across the lake I read
the *Travels in Indo-China* of Henri Mouhot, a French
naturalist, who was the first European to give a detailed
description of the ruins of Angkor. His book is pleasant
to read. It is a painstaking and straightforward account
very characteristic of the period when the traveller had
still the ingenuous belief that people who did not dress,
eat, talk and think as he did were very odd, and not
quite human; and M Mouhot narrated many things that
would scarcely excite the astonishment of the more
sophisticated and also more modest traveller of our day.
But apparently he was not always accurate and my copy
of his book had been at some time annotated in pencil
by a later pilgrim. The corrections were neatly written
in a hand that looked determined, but whether this *not
so*, this *far from it*, this *quite wrong*, this *a palpable
error* were due to a disinterested desire for truth, a wish
to guide future readers, or merely to a sense of superiority,
I had no means of telling. Perhaps, however, poor Mouhot
may justly claim a certain indulgence, for, dying before
he completed his journey, he had no opportunity to
correct and explain his notes. Here are the last two
entries in his diary:

19th – Attacked by fever.

29th – Have pity on me, oh my God . . . !

And here is the beginning of a letter he wrote a little
while before he died:

Louang Prabang (Laos),
23rd July, 1861.
Now, my dear Jenny, let us converse together.

Do you know of what I often think when every one around me is asleep, and I, lying wrapped in my mosquito-curtains, let my thoughts wander back to all the members of my family? Then I seem to hear again the charming voice of my little Jenny, and to be listening once more to 'La Traviata', 'The Death of Nelson', or some other of the airs that I loved so much to hear you sing. I then feel regret, mingled with joy, at the souvenir of the happy – oh, how happy! – past. Then I open the gauze curtains, light my pipe, and gaze out upon the stars, humming softly the 'Patre' of Béranger, or the 'Old Sergeant' . . .

By the portraits of him he was a man of an open countenance, with a full curly beard and a long moustache, and his thinning curly hair gave him a noble brow. In a frock coat he looked a respectable rather than a romantic figure, but in a *beret* with a long tassel there was in his mien something dashing and naïvely ferocious. He might then very well have passed for a corsair in a drama of the sixties.

But it was a very different Angkor Wat that met the intrepid gaze of Henri Mouhot from that which the tourist now can so conveniently visit. If indeed you are curious to know what this stupendous monument looked like before the restorer set to work upon it (it must be admitted unobtrusively), you can get a very good impression by taking a narrow path through the forest when you will come presently upon a huge grey gateway covered with lichen and moss. On the upper part of it, on the four sides, dimly emerging from ruined masonry is, four times repeated, the impassive head of Siva. On each side of the gateway, half hidden by jungle, are the remains of a massive wall and in front of it, choked with weeds and water-plants, a broad moat. Entering you find yourself in a vast courtyard, strewn with fragments of statues and green stones on which you vaguely discern sculpture; you walk softly on dead brown leaves and they squelch ever so faintly under your tread. Here grow enormous trees, towering above you, shrubs of all kinds and dank weeds; they grow among the crumbling masonry, forcing it apart, and their roots writhe like snakes upon the surface of the stony soil. The courtyard is surrounded by ruined corridors and you climb hazardously up steep, slippery and broken stairs, threading your way through passages and vaulted chambers dripping with wet and heavy with the stink of bats; the pedestals on which stood the gods are overturned, the gods are gone. And in the corridors and on the terraces the tropical vegetation grows fiercely. Here and there the great pieces of carved stone hang perilously. Here and there on a bas-relief still miraculously in place stand the dancing-girls veiled with lichen, mockingly, in their everlasting gestures of abandonment.

For centuries nature has waged its battle with the handiwork of man; it has covered, disfigured and transformed it, and now all these buildings that a multitude of slaves built with so much labour lie a confused tangle among the trees. Here lurk the cobras whose broken images you see on the stones around you. Hawks fly high overhead and the gibbons leap from branch to branch; but it is green and dark and you seem beneath that wanton leafage to wander at the bottom of the sea.

It chanced that one day towards dusk, when I was wandering about this temple, for in its ruin it offered peculiar sensations that I found it curious to expose myself to, I was overtaken by a storm. I had seen the great dark clouds massed in the North-West and it had seemed to me that never again could the temple in the jungle be seen by me more mysteriously; but after a while I felt something strange in the air and looking up saw that the dark clouds were on a sudden charging down upon the forest. The rain came suddenly and then the thunder, not a single peal but roll upon roll reverberating down the sky, and lightning that blinded me, darting and slashing fiercely. I was deafened and confused by the noise, and the lightning startled me. The rain fell not as in our temperate zone, but with an angry vehemence, in sheets, storming down as though the heavens were emptying themselves of flooded lakes. It seemed to fall with no blind unconscious force, but with a purpose and a malignancy which were, alas, but too human. I stood in a doorway, not a little frightened, and as the lightning tore the darkness like a veil I saw the jungle stretching endlessly before me, and it seemed to me that these great temples and their gods were insignificant before the fierce might of nature. Its power there was so manifest, spoke with so stern and insistent a voice, that it was easy to understand how man had devised his gods and built great temples to house them to serve as a screen between himself and the force that terrified and crushed him. For nature is the most powerful of all the gods.

XXXVIII

In case the reader is a trifle perplexed by all this commotion of the elements I will set down now for his edification a few facts of general interest. Angkor was a city of great extent, the capital of a powerful empire, and for ten miles around the jungle is dotted with the remains of the temples that adorned it. Angkor Wat is but one of these and has claimed more than the rest the attentions of the archaeologist, the restorer and the traveller, only because when discovered by the West it was in a less ruined state. No one knows why the city was abandoned so suddenly that they have found blocks of stones in the quarries ready to take their place in an unfinished temple, and the experts have in vain sought for a plausible explanation.

Some of the temples look as though they had been in

great part wantonly destroyed; and the notion has been hazarded that when the rulers after some unfortunate battle fled the country, the wretched slaves who had spent their lives through so many generations to erect these massive buildings in vengeance overthrew what they had been obliged with blood and sweat to construct. This is conjecture. The only thing certain is that here was a city thriving and populous and now there remains nothing but a few ruined temples and the teeming forest. The houses were of wood, surrounded by their little compounds, like the houses I had so lately seen at Keng Tung, and it would not have taken long for them to decay; the jungle, held in check for a while by the business of man, flowed back, an irresistible green sea, upon the scene of his futile activity. At the end of the thirteenth century it was one of the great cities of the East; two hundred years later it was the resort of wild beasts.

Angkor Wat is placed due east and west and the sun rises directly behind the five towers that surmount it. It is surrounded by a broad moat, which you cross by a great causeway paved with flagstones, and the trees are delicately reflected in the still water.

It is an impressive rather than a beautiful building and it needs the glow of sunset or the white brilliance of the moon to give it a loveliness that touches the heart. It is grey veiled by a faint green, which is the colour of the moss and the mould of all the rainy seasons it has seen, but at sunset it is buff, pale and warm. At dawn when the country is bathed in a silver mist the towers have an aspect that is strangely unsubstantial; they have then an airy lightness which they lack in the hard white light of noon. Twice a day, when the sun rises and when it sets, a miracle is performed and they gain a beauty not their own. They are the mystic towers of the spirit's high citadel. The temple and its dependencies are built on a strictly formal plan. This part balances that and one side repeats the other. The architects exercised no great power of invention, but built on the pattern dictated to them by the rites of their religion. They had neither wanton fancy nor vivid imagination. They yielded to no sudden inspiration. They were deliberate. They gained their effects by regularity and by vastness. The modern eye, of course, has been distorted by the huge buildings that are now so easily constructed, mammoth hotel and enormous apartment house, so that the great size of Angkor Wat must be realised by an effort of the imagination; but to those for whom it was built it must have seemed stupendous. The very steep steps that lead from one storey to another give it a singular effect of height. They are not the broad and noble stairs of the West, fit for the pageantry of processions, but an arduous and hurried means of ascent to the presence of a secret and mysterious god. They render the divinity remote and enigmatic. On each storey, four to each, are large sunken basins in which was water for purification, and the water at those strange heights must have added strangely to the silence and the awe. It is a religion of which the temples are empty and the god lives alone except at stated periods when the devout bring gifts to appease him. It is the house now of innumerable bats and the air is fetid with them; in each dark passage and sombre chamber you hear their twitterings.

This plainness of construction gave the sculptors ample occasion for decoration. Capitals, pilasters, pediments, doorways, windows are enriched with carving of an unimaginable variety. The themes are few, but on them they embroidered many beautiful inventions. Here they had a free hand and with a fury of creation crammed into these narrow limits all the adventures of their impetuous souls. It is interesting to note, as you go from temple to temple, how in the course of centuries these unknown craftsmen passed from rude strength to consummate grace; and how at first, regardless of the whole they made their decoration an end in itself, but at long last learnt to submit themselves to the general plan. What they lost in power they gained in taste; it is for each one to say which he prefers.

The galleries are adorned with bas-reliefs; they are interminable; they are world-famous; but to attempt to describe them would be as foolish as to attempt to describe the jungle. Here you have princes on elephants with the state umbrellas open over their heads making a progress among graceful trees; they form a pleasing pattern which is repeated along the length of a wall like the pattern of a paper. There you have long lines of soldiers marching into battle, and the gestures of their arms and the movements of their legs follow the same formal design as that of the dancers in a Cambodian dance. But they join battle and break into frenzied movement; even the dying and the dead are contorted into violent attitudes. Above them the chieftains advance on their elephants and in their chariots, brandishing swords and lances. And you get a feeling of unbridled action, of the turmoil and stress of battle, a breathlessness, an agitation and a disorder, which is infinitely curious. Every inch of the space is covered with figures, horses, elephants and chariots, you can discern neither plan nor pattern, and only the chariot-wheels rest the eye in this chaos. You cannot discover a rhythm. For it was not beauty that the artists sought, but action; they cared little for elegance of gesture or purity of line; theirs was no emotion recollected in tranquillity, but a living passion that brooked no limits. Here is nothing of the harmony of the Greeks, but the rush of a torrential stream and the terrible, vehement life of the jungle. Yet there are not a few that are withal as lovely as the Elgin Marbles and when you look at them you would be dull indeed if you were not caught by the rapture that pure beauty affords. But alas, this excellence was produced only for a brief period; for the rest the drawing for the most part is poor and the patterns tedious. The sculptors seem to have been content to go on from generation to generation slavishly copying one another and you wonder that sheer boredom did not induce them now and again to break into a new design. The draughtsmen who make laborious drawings of them discern in the sameness many differences, but they are only such as you might find in a piece of prose copied by a hundred hands. The writing is different, but the sense remains the same. And as I wandered about looking disconsolately at so much that was dull I wished that I had by my side a philosopher who could explain to me why it is that man can never remain in one stay. Why is it, I wanted to ask him, that having known the best he should content himself so comfortably with the mediocre? Is it that circumstances – or is it genius, the genius of the individual? – raise him for a while to heights at which he cannot breathe easily so that he is content to make his way down again to the homely plain? Is man like water that can be forced to an artificial altitude, but that reverts as soon as the force is removed to its own level? It looks as though his normal condition were the lowest state of civilisation compatible with his environment and in this he can remain unchanged from age to age. Perhaps my philosopher would have told me that only a few races are capable of raising themselves above the dust, and then only for a little while; and even they are conscious that their state is extraordinary, and they fall back with relief to the condition that is only a little better than the beasts. But if he had, then I would have asked him if man were not perfectible. But I should have accepted it with humility if he had said: come along, don't stay there talking a lot of nonsense, let's go and have tiffin. I should have said to myself that perhaps he had varicose veins and to stand so long made his legs ache.

XXXIX

I came to the last day I could spend at Angkor. I was
leaving it with a wrench, but I knew by now that it
was the sort of place that, however long one stayed,
it would always be a wrench to leave. I saw things
that day that I had seen a dozen times, but never with
such poignancy; and as I sauntered down those long
grey passages and now and then caught sight of the
forest through a doorway all I saw had a new beauty.
The still courtyards had a mystery that made me wish
to linger in them a little longer, for I had a notion that I
was on the verge of discovering some strange and subtle
secret; it was as though a melody trembled in the air,
but so low that the ears could just not catch it. Silence
seemed to dwell in these courts like a presence that you
could see if you turned round and my last impression of
Angkor was like my first, that of a great silence. And
it gave me I know not what strange feeling to look at
the living forest that surrounded this great grey pile so
closely, the jungle luxuriant and gay in the sunlight, a
sea of different greens; and to know that there all round
me had once stood a multitudinous city.

That night a troupe of Cambodian dancers were dancing on the terrace of the temple. We were escorted along
the causeway by boys carrying a hundred lighted torches.
The resin of which they were made charged the air with
an acrid, pleasant perfume. They formed a great circle
of flame, flickering and uncertain on the terrace and in
the middle of it the dancers trod their strange measure.
Musicians, hidden by the darkness, played on pipes and
drums and gongs, a vague and rhythmical music that
troubled the nerves. My ears awaited with a sort of

tremor the resolution of harmonies strange to me, but never attained it. The dancers wore tight-fitting dresses of richly glowing colours and on their heads high golden crowns. By day no doubt they would have looked trumpery, but in that unexpected light they had a gorgeousness and a mystery that you find with difficulty in the East. Their impassive faces were dead white with powder so that they looked like masks. No emotion, no fleeting thought was permitted to disturb the immobility of their expression. Their hands were beautiful, with small and tapering fingers, and in the progress of the dance their gestures, elaborate and complicated, pointed their elegance and emphasised their grace. Their hands were like rare and fantastic orchids. There was no abandon in their dance. Their attitudes were hieratic and their movements formal. They were like idols that had come to life, but still were impregnated with divinity.

And those gestures, those attitudes, were the same as of those of the bayadères that the old sculptors had graven on the stone walls of the temples. They had not changed in a thousand years. Repeated endlessly on every wall in every temple, you will see the self-same elegant writhing of the delicate fingers, the self-same arching of the slender body, as delights your eye in the living dancer before you. No wonder they are grave under their gold crowns when they bear the weight of so long an ancestry.

The dance ended, the torches were extinguished, and the little crowd shuffled away pell-mell into the night. I sat on a parapet taking a last look at the five towers of Angkor Wat.

My thoughts went back to a temple that I had visited a day or two before. It is called Bayon. It surprised me because it had not the uniformity of the other temples I had seen. It consists of a multitude of towers one above the other, symmetrically arranged, and each tower is a four-faced, gigantic head of Siva the Destroyer. They stand in circles one within the other and the four faces of the god are surmounted by a decorated crown. In the middle is a great tower with face rising above face till the apex is reached. It is all battered by time and weather, creepers and parasitic shrubs grow all about, so that at a first glance you see only a shapeless mass and it is only when you look a little more closely that these silent, heavy, impassive faces loom out at you from the rugged stone. Then they are all round you. They face you, they are at your side, they are behind you, and you are watched by a thousand unseeing eyes. They seem to look at you from the remote distance of primeval time and all about you the jungle grows fiercely. You cannot wonder that the peasants when they pass should break into loud song in order to frighten away the spirits; for towards evening the silence is unearthly and the effect of all those serene and yet malevolent faces is eerie. When the night falls the faces sink away into the stones and you have nothing but a strange, shrouded collection of oddly shaped turrets.

But it is not on account of the temple itself that I have described it – I have, albeit with a halting pen, already described more than enough – it is for the sake of the bas-reliefs that line one of its corridors. They are not very well done, and the sculptors had but too obviously little sense of form or line, but they have notwithstanding an interest which at this moment called them up vividly to my memory. For they represent scenes in the common life of the day in which they were done, the preparation of rice for the pot, the cooking of food, the catching of fish and the snaring of birds, the buying and selling at the village shop, the visit to the doctor, and in short the various activities of a simple people. It was startling to discover how little in a thousand years this life of theirs had changed. They still do the same things with the same utensils. The rice is pounded or husked in the self-same way and the village shopkeeper on the same tray offers for sale the same bananas and the same sugar cane. These patient industrious folk carry the same burdens on the same yokes as their ancestors carried so many generations back. The centuries have passed leaving no trace upon them, and some sleeper of the tenth century awakening now in one of these Cambodian villages would find himself at home in the artless round of daily life.

Then it seemed to me that in these countries of the East the most impressive, the most awe-inspiring monument of antiquity is neither temple, nor citadel, nor great wall, but man. The peasant with his immemorial usages belongs to an age far more ancient than Angkor Wat, the great wall of China, or the Pyramids of Egypt.

XL

At the mouth of the little river I got once more into the flat-bottomed steamer and crossed the wide, shallow lake, changed into another boat and went down another river. Finally I reached Saïgon.

Notwithstanding the Chinese city that has grown up since the French occupied the country, and notwithstanding the natives who saunter along the pavements or, in wide straw hats like extinguishers, pull rickshaws, Saïgon has all the air of a little provincial town in the South of France. It is laid out with broad streets, shaded with handsome trees, and there is a bustle in them that is quite unlike the bustle of an Eastern town in an English colony. It is a blithe and smiling little place. It has an opera house white and shining, built in the flamboyant style of the Third Republic, which faces a broad avenue; and it has a Hotel de Ville which is very grand, new and ornate. Outside the hotels are terraces and at the hour of the *apéritif* they are crowded with bearded, gesticulating Frenchmen, drinking the sweet and sickly beverages,

Vermouth Cassis, Byrrh and Quinquina Dubonnet which they drink in France, and they talk nineteen to the dozen in the rolling accent of the Midi. Gay little ladies who have something to do with the local theatre are dressed in smart clothes and with their pencilled eyebrows and rouged cheeks bring a cheerful air of sophistication to this far-distant spot. In the shops you will find Paris dresses from Marseilles and London hats from Lille. Victorias drawn by two little ponies gallop past and motor cars toot their horns. The sun beats down from a cloudless sky and the shade is heavy with the heat and solid.

Saïgon is a pleasant enough place to idle in for a few days; life is made easy for the casual traveller; and it is very agreeable to sit under the awning on the terrace of the Hotel Continental, an electric fan just above your head, and with an innocent drink before you to read in the local paper heated controversies upon the affairs of the Colony and the *faits divers* of the neighbourhood. It is charming to be able to read steadily through the advertisements without an uneasy feeling that you are wasting your time and it must be a dull mind that in such a perusal does not find here and there occasion for a pleasant gallop on a hobby-horse through the realms of time and space. But I only stayed long enough to catch my boat for Huë.

Huë is the capital of Annam and I was bound there in order to see the festivities for the Chinese New Year which were to be held at the Emperor's court. But Huë is situated on a river and the port for it is Tourane. It was there then that the Messageries boat – a clean white comfortable craft properly arranged for travel in hot latitudes with plenty of space and plenty of air and cold drinks – set me down at two one morning. She anchored in the bay, seven to eight kilometres from the wharf, and I got into a sampan. The crew consisted of two women, a man and a small boy. The bay was calm and the stars were shining thick overhead. We rowed out into the night and the lights on the quay seemed immensely far away. The boat was heavy with water and every now and then one of the women stopped rowing and baled it out with an empty kerosene tin. There was the shadow of a breeze and presently they put up a great square sail of bamboo matting, but it was too light a wind to help us much and the journey looked as though it would last till day-break. So far as I was concerned it might have lasted for ever; I lay on bamboo mats, smoking a pipe and now and then falling into a light doze, and when I awoke and relit my pipe the match showed me for a moment the brown fat faces of the two women squatting by the mast. The man at the tiller made a short remark and one of the women answered him. Then again the silence was complete but for the faint swish of the water under the boards on which I lay. The night was so warm that with nothing on but a shirt and a pair of khaki trousers I did not feel cold and the air was as soft as the feel of flowers. We made a long tack into the night and then going about found our slow way to the mouth of the river. We passed fishing-boats lying at anchor and others silently creeping out into the stream. The banks of the river were dark and mysterious. On a word from the man the two women lowered the clumsy sail and began once more to row. We came to the quay and the water was so shallow that I had to be carried ashore on the back of a coolie. It is a proceeding that has always seemed to me both terrifying and undignified and I clung to the coolie's neck in a manner that I well knew ill became me. The hotel was just across the road and coolies shouldered my luggage. But it was barely five and still very dark and no one was awake in the hotel. The coolies hammered on the door and at last a sleepy servant opened it. The rest of them were lying about fast asleep on the billiard table and on the floor. I asked for a room and coffee. The fresh bread was just ready and my *café au lait* with rolls hot from the oven very welcome after that long journey across the bay, made a meal such as I have not often had the good luck to eat. I was shown a dirty, sordid little room, with a mosquito net grimy and torn, and I do not know how many commercial travellers and officials of the French government had passed through the sheets on the bed since last they were washed. I did not care. It seemed to me that I had never arrived anywhere in such romantic style and I could not but think that this must be the preface to an experience that would be memorable.

But there are places of which the only point is the arrival; they promise the most fantastic adventures of the spirit and give you no more than three meals a day and last year's films. They are like a face, full of character that intrigues and excites you, but that on closer acquaintance you discover is merely the mask of a vulgar soul. Such is Tourane.

I spent one morning there in order to visit the museum in which there is a collection of Khmer sculpture. The reader may possibly remember that when I wrote of Phnom-Penh I became strangely eloquent (for a person who does not much like others to gush and is shy of superlatives) about a statue to be seen there. This was a Khmer work and now I may remind him (or tell him if like me till I went to Indo-China he never knew that Khmers or their sculpture existed) that this was a mighty nation, the offspring of the aboriginal tribes of Indo-China and an invading race from the plateaux of Central Asia, who founded a far-flung and powerful empire. Immigrants from Eastern India brought them the Sanskrit language, Brahmanism and the culture of their native land; but the Khmers were vigorous people and they had a creative instinct that enabled them to make their own use of the knowledge the strangers brought them. They built magnificent temples and adorned them with sculptures, founded it is true on the art of India, but which have at their best an energy, a boldness of execution, a fertility and a brilliant fancy to be found nowhere else in the East. The statue of Harihara* at Phnom-Penh testifies to the greatness of their genius. It is a miracle of grace. It calls to mind the archaic statuary of Greece and the Mayan sculpture of Mexico; but it has a character all its own. Those early Greek works have the dewy freshness of the morning, but their beauty is a trifle vacant; the Mayan statues have something primeval in them, they excite awe rather than admiration, for they have in them still the touch of early man who drew in the dark recesses of his caverns magic pictures to cast a spell on the beasts he feared or hunted; but in the Harihara you have a singular and enigmatic union of the archaic and the sophisticated. It has the candour of the primitive quickened by the complexity of the civilised. The Khmer brought a long inheritance of thought to the craft which had so suddenly captivated his fancy. It is as though to the England of the Elizabethan age had come, a bolt from the blue, the art of painting in oil; and the artists, their souls charged with the plays of Shakespeare, the conflict of religions at the Reformation, and the Armada, had begun to paint with the hand of Cimabue. Something like this must have been the state of mind of the sculptor who made the statue in Phnom-Penh. It has power and simplicity and an exquisite line, but it has also a spiritual quality that is infinitely moving. It has not only beauty, but intelligence.

These great works of the Khmers gain a peculiar poignancy when you reflect that a few ruined temples strewn about the jungle and a few mutilated statues scattered

* I am somewhat puzzled by the name given by the French authorities to the deity represented in this statue. I always thought that Hari and Hara were the names under which were commonly known Siva and Vishnu, and to call a god Harihara looks very much like calling a single respectable person Crosseandblackwell. But since I suppose the experts know better than I, I have referred to this statue throughout by the name they give it.

here and there in museums are all that remains of this mighty empire and this restless people. Their power was broken, they were dispersed, becoming drawers of water and hewers of wood, they died out; and now, the rest of them assimilated by their conquerors, their name endures only in the art they so lavishly produced.

XLI

Huë is a pleasant little town with something of the leisurely air of a cathedral city in the West of England and though the capital of an empire it is not imposing. It is built on both sides of a wide river, crossed by a bridge, and the hotel is one of the worst in the world. It is extremely dirty and the food is dreadful; but it is also a general store in which everything is provided that the colonist may want from camp-equipment and guns, women's hats and men's reach-me-downs to sardines, *pâté de foie gras* and Worcester sauce; so that the hungry traveller can make up with tinned goods for the inadequacy of the bill of fare. Here the inhabitants of the town come to drink their coffee and *fine* in the evening and the soldiers of the garrison to play billiards. The French have built themselves solid, rather showy houses without much regard for the climate or the environment; they look like the villas of retired grocers in the suburbs of Paris.

The French carry France to their colonies just as the English carry England to theirs; and the English, reproached for their insularity, can justly reply that in this matter they are no more singular than their neighbours. But not even the most superficial observer can fail to notice that there is a great difference in the manner in which these two nations behave towards the natives of the countries of which they have gained possession. The Frenchman has deep down in him a persuasion that all men are equal and that mankind is a brotherhood. He is slightly ashamed of it and in case you should laugh at him makes haste to laugh at himself; but there it is, he cannot help it; he cannot prevent himself from feeling that the native, black, brown or yellow, is of the same clay as himself, with the same loves, hates, pleasures and pains, and he cannot bring himself to treat him as though he belonged to a different species. Though he will brook no encroachment on his authority and deals firmly with any attempt the native may make to lighten his yoke, in the ordinary affairs of life he is friendly with him without condescension and benevolent without superiority. He inculcates in him his peculiar prejudices; Paris is the centre of the world, and the ambition of every young Annamite is to see it at least once in his life; you will hardly meet one who is not convinced that outside France there is neither art, literature nor science. But the Frenchman will sit with the Annamite, eat with him, drink with him and play with him. In the market-place you will see the thrifty Frenchwoman with her basket on her arm jostling the Annamite housekeeper and bargaining just as fiercely. No one likes having another take possession of his house, even though he conducts it more efficiently and keeps it in better repair than ever he could himself; he does not want to live in the attics even though his master has installed a lift for him to reach them; and I do not suppose that Annamites like it any more than the Burmese that strangers hold their country. But I should say that whereas the Burmese only respect the English, the Annamites admire the French. When in course of time these peoples inevitably regain their freedom it will be curious to see which of these emotions has borne the better fruit.

The Annamites are a pleasant people to look at, very small, with yellow fat faces and bright dark eyes, and they look very spruce in their clothes. The poor wear brown of the colour of rich earth, a long tunic slit up the sides and trousers, with a girdle of apple green or orange round their waists; and on their heads a large flat straw hat or a small black turban with very regular folds. The well-to-do wear the same neat turban, with white trousers, a black silk tunic and over this sometimes a black lace coat. It is a costume of great elegance.

But though in all these lands the clothes the people wear attract our eyes because they are peculiar, in each everyone is dressed very much alike; it is a uniform they wear, picturesque often and always suitable to the climate, but it allows little opportunity for individual taste; and I could not but think it must amaze the native of an Eastern country visiting Europe to observe the bewildering and vivid variety of costume that surrounds him. An oriental crowd is like a bed of daffodils at a market gardener's, brilliant but monotonous; but an English crowd, for instance that which you see through a faint veil of smoke when you look down from above on the floor of a Promenade Concert, is like a nosegay of every kind of flower. Nowhere in the East will you see costumes so gay and multifarious as on a fine day in Piccadilly. The diversity is prodigious. Soldiers, sailors, policemen, postmen, messenger boys; men in tail coats and top hats, in lounge suits and bowlers, men in plus four and caps, women in silk and cloth and velvet, in all the colours, and in hats of this shape and that. And besides this there are the clothes worn on different occasions and to pursue different sports, the clothes servants wear, and workmen, jockeys, huntsmen, and courtiers. I fancy the Annamite will return to Huë and think his fellow-countrymen dress very dully.

XLII

Annam was for long centuries under the suzerainty of China and its Emperor sent tribute to the Son of Heaven. Its civilisation was Chinese and its temples were erected in honour of Confucius rather than of Gautama. The palace, surrounded by a moat and a wall, covers a vast extent. It is Chinese, but in a shoddy and second-hand way; it is tired and a trifle depressing. You pass down a trim road planted with little trees and on each side of this are gardens and pavilions. But in the gardens the grass grows ragged and rank; there are untidy bushes that look like ill-cared for children, and stunted trees. They are so deserted that you find it hard to believe that somewhere in the background, unseen by you, dwells surrounded by his women and eunuchs and mandarins an emperor ruling shadowy under the power of France. You feel that it is a pretence that he can hardly be at pains to keep up. You pass through throne rooms gaudily painted and decorated with gold, long dimly lit halls in which are the ancestral tablets of the Emperor, and apartments in which are displayed the gifts that from time to time have been presented to him, French clocks and Sèvres porcelain, Chinese pottery and ornaments of jade; but just as at the marriage of your friends you give them a more costly present if they are rich and do not need it than if they are poor and do, so here the donors have measured their generosity with acumen.

But the ceremonies of the Tet were conducted with pomp. This is the celebration of the Chinese New Year when the Emperor, in imitation again of the Son of Heaven, receives the homage of his mandarins. I had received an invitation and at seven in the morning, feeling embarrassed in a dinner jacket and a stiff shirt, I found at the Palace gate a group of French civilians similarly dressed and a number of officers in uniform. The Résident Supérieur drove up and we followed him into the courtyard. In the large open space soldiers in bright and fantastic uniforms were lined up and in front of them two lines of mandarins according to their rank, the civil on the right and the military on the left. A little below were the eunuchs and the imperial orchestras and on each side was a royal elephant in state caparison with a man holding a state umbrella over the howdah. The mandarins were dressed in the Manchu fashion in high boots with thick white soles, silk robes splendidly embroidered, with voluminous sleeves, and black hats decorated with gold. Bugles blew and we, the Europeans, crowded into the throne room. It was rather dark. The Emperor sat on the dais. In his gold robes he sank into the gold of the throne and the gold backcloth of the canopy over it so that at first you were hardly conscious that a living person was there. He stood up. At each corner of the dais stood a man in blue holding a state fan and behind the throne a row of servants in darker blue bore the royal utensils, the betel nut tray, the spittoon and I know not what. A little in front two soldiers magnificently dressed in orange held before them upright golden swords; they stood like images and looked neither to the right nor to the left. The Emperor too looked like an image as he stood motionless with no expression on his sallow long thin face.

The Résident Supérieur read an address and the Emperor read his reply. He read in a high-pitched voice in a sort of sing-song that made it sound like a litany. The Europeans retired to the side of the hall and the Emperor sat down. In front of the throne was a low altar and on this the Emperor's uncle, a little old man with a sparse grey beard, now placed what looked like two books wrapped in red silk. Then the two brothers of the Emperor took up their positions in front of the altar, not facing the Emperor but each other, and at the same moment the mandarins in the courtyard, who had been standing quite still during the reading of the speeches, came forward on to bamboo mats that had been set for them, but in order according to their rank and class. They also faced not the Emperor but each other. A band began to play and singers burst into song. This was the signal for the two princes of the blood and for the mandarins in the courtyard to turn and face the Emperor. The chorus was silent and the princes and the mandarins knelt down and touched the ground with their foreheads. They moved as one. A huge gong sounded from the tower over the palace gateway and the chorus again began to sing. Then with one impressive movement like well-drilled soldiers the mandarins prostrated themselves. This was repeated five times. The emperor sat impassive and made no acknowledgement of the obeisances. He might have been a golden idol. The throne-room, which had looked so tawdry the day before, now, set off by the gorgeous clothes and smart uniforms, had if not magnificence at least a barbaric splendour. Then all the mandarins bowed three times and unceremoniously shuffled out of their ranks, the princes of the blood smiled, shook hands with their French friends and complained of the heat of their robes, the Emperor, without much dignity, stepped off his throne. He walked quickly into a sort of ante-chamber and the officials of the court and the foreigners followed him. Here in two rows stood soldiers holding the royal umbrellas and various staffs, and a band of page boys in green played drums and fifes and with vigour struck gongs. Sweet champagne was handed round with biscuits and sweetmeats and cigars. In a little while the Emperor was borne away on his palanquin, a low round gilt chair, by twelve men in red. The ceremony was over.

In the evening I went to a party at the palace. The Emperor and the Résident Supérieur sat on large gilt armchairs in the central doorway of the throne-room and the guests were gathered round about. The courtyard was lit with unnumerable little oil lamps and a native orchestra played lustily. Three fantastic figures, like those of the Chinese drama, in splendid Chinese dresses came upon the scene and trod a grotesque measure. Then the Imperial ballet, a large number of boys and youths in beautiful old-fashioned costumes that reminded one of the eighteenth century pictures of the Far East, danced and sang. They had lanterns on their shoulders, with lighted candles in them, and they moved about in complicated patterns that formed Chinese characters wishing the Emperor good luck and prosperity. It was more like a drill than dance, but the effect was strange and pretty. They gave place to other dancers, men dressed up as huge cocks, emitting fire from their beaks, or as buffaloes and fearful dragons and they cut fantastic capers; then came fireworks and the courtyard was filled with smoke and the noisiness of crackers.

This ended the native part of the entertainment and the foreigners gathered round the buffet. The court pages, on European instruments, began to play a one-step. The foreigners danced.

The Emperor wore a tunic of yellow silk richly embroidered and on his head a yellow turban. He was a man of thirty-five, rather taller than most of the Annamites, and very thin. His face was strangely smooth. He looked very frail but incredibly distinguished. My last impression of the party was of him leaning in a careless attitude against a table, smoking a cigarette and chatting with a young Frenchman. Every now and then his eyes rested for a moment incuriously on the conquerors clumsily dancing.

It was late now and I was setting out at dawn by car for Hanoi. It seemed hardly worth while to go to bed and as I drove in my rickshaw to the hotel I asked myself why I should not spend the rest of the night on the river. It would do if I got back in time to change, bathe myself and have a cup of coffee before starting. I explained to my rickshaw boy what I wanted and he took me down to the river. There was a landing-stage just below the bridge and here we found half-a-dozen sampans moored to the side. Their owners were sleeping in them, but at least one of them was sleeping lightly, for he awoke as he heard me walk down the stone steps and put his head out of the blanket in which he was wrapped. The rickshaw boy spoke to him and he got up. He called to a woman asleep in the boat. I stepped in. The woman untied and we slipped out into the stream. These boats have a low round awning of bamboo matting, just high enough to sit upright under, and bamboo matting on the boards. You can shut them up with shutters, but I told the man to leave the front open so that I could look at the night. In the heights of heaven the stars shone very bright as though up there too there were a party. The man brought me a pot of Chinese tea and a cup. I poured some out and lit my pipe. We went along very slowly and the sound of the paddle in the water was the only sound that broke the silence. It was delightful to think that I had all those hours before me to enjoy that sense of well-being and I thought to myself how when I was once more in Europe, imprisoned in stony cities, I would remember that perfect night and the enchanting solitude. It would be the most imperishable of my memories. It was a unique occasion and I said to myself that I must hoard the moments as they passed. I could not afford to waste one of them. I was laying up treasure for myself. And I thought of all the things I would reflect upon, and of the melancholy that I would subtly savour as you savour the first scented strawberries of the year; and I would think of love, and invent stories and meditate upon beautiful things like art and death. The paddle hit the water very gently and I could just feel the boat glide on. I made up my mind to watch and cherish every exquisite sensation that came to me.

Suddenly I felt a bump. What was it? I looked out and it was broad day. The bump was the bump of the boat against the landing-stage, and there was the bridge just above me.

'Good God,' I cried, 'I've been asleep.'

I had slept right through the night and there was my cup of tea cold by my side. My pipe had fallen out of my mouth. I had lost all those priceless moments and had slept solidly through the hours. I was furious. I might never have the opportunity again to spend a night in a sampan on an Eastern river and now I should never have those wonderful thoughts and matchless emotions that I had promised myself. I paid for the boat and still in evening clothes ran up the steps and went to the hotel. My hired car was waiting for me at the door.

XLIII

Here I had the intention of finishing this book for at Hanoi I found nothing much to interest me. It is the capital of Tonkin and the French tell you it is the most attractive town in the East, but when you ask them why, answer that it is exactly like a town, Montpellier or Grenoble, in France. And Haiphong to which I went in order to get a boat to Hong-Kong is a commercial town and dull. It is true that from it you can visit the Bay of Along, which is one of the *sehenswürdigkeiten* of Indo-China, but I was tired of sights. I contented myself with sitting in the café, for here it was none too warm and I was glad to get out of tropical clothes, and reading back numbers of *l'Illustration*, or for the sake of exercise taking a brisk walk along straight, wide streets. Haiphong is traversed by canals and sometimes I got a glimpse of a scene which in its varied life, with all the native craft on the water, was multicoloured and charming. There was one canal, with tall Chinese houses on each side of it, that had a pleasant curve. The houses were whitewashed, but the whitewash was discoloured and stained; with their grey roofs they made an agreeable composition against the pale sky. The picture had the faded elegance of an old water-colour. There was nowhere an emphatic note. It was soft and a little weary and inspired one with a faint melancholy. I was reminded I scarcely know why, of an old maid I knew in my youth, a relic of the Victorian age, who wore black silk mittens and made crochet shawls for the poor, black for widows and white for married women. She had suffered in her youth, but whether from ill-health or unrequited love, no one exactly knew.

But there was a local paper at Haiphong, a small dingy sheet with stubby type the ink of which came off on your fingers, and it gave you a political article, the wireless news, advertisements and local intelligence. The editor doubtless hard pressed for matter, printed the names of the persons, Europeans, natives of the country and Chinese, who had arrived at Haiphong or left it, and mine was put in with the rest. On the morning of the day before that on which my boat was to sail for Hong-Kong I was sitting in the café of the hotel drinking a Dubonnet before luncheon when the boy came in and said that a gentleman wished to see me. I did not know a soul in Haiphong and asked who it was. The boy said he was an Englishman and lived there, but he could not tell me his name. The boy spoke very little French and it was hard for me to understand what he said. I was mystified, but told him to show the visitor in. A moment later he came back followed by a white man and pointed me out to him. The man gave me a look and walked towards me. He was a very tall fellow, well over six feet high, rather fat and bloated, with a red, clean-shaven face and extremely pale blue eyes. He wore very shabby khaki shorts, and a stingah-shifter unbuttoned at the neck, and a battered helmet. I concluded at once that he was a stranded beachcomber who was going to touch me for a loan and wondered how little I could hope to get off for.

He came up to me and held out a large red hand with broken, dirty nails.

'I don't suppose you remember me,' he said. 'My name's Grosely. I was at St Thomas's Hospital with you. I recognised your name as soon as I saw it in the paper and I thought I'd look you up.'

186

I had not the smallest recollection of him, but I asked him to sit down and offered him a drink. By his appearance I had first thought he would ask me for ten piastres and I might have given him five, but now it looked more likely that he would ask for a hundred and I should have to think myself lucky if I could content him with fifty. The habitual borrower always asks twice what he expects to get and it only dissatisfies him to give him what he has asked since then he is vexed with himself for not having asked for more. He feels you have cheated him.

'Are you a doctor?' I asked.

'No, I was only at the bloody place a year.'

He took off his sun-helmet and showed me a mop of grey hair, which much needed a brush. His face was curiously mottled and he did not look healthy. His teeth were badly decayed and at the corners of his mouth were empty spaces. When the boy came to take the orders he asked for brandy.

'Bring the bottle,' he said. *'La bouteille.* Savvy?' He turned to me. 'I've been living here for the last five years, but I can't get along with French somehow. I talk Tonkinese.' He leaned his chair back and looked at me. 'I remember you, you know. You used to go about with those twins. What was their name? I expect I've changed more than you have. I've spent the best part of my life in China. Rotten climate, you know. It plays hell with a man.'

I still had not the smallest recollection of him. I thought it best to say so.

'Were you the same year as I was?' I asked.

'Yes. '92.'

'It's a devil of a long time ago.'

About sixty boys and young men entered the hospital every year; they were most of them shy and confused by the new life they were entering upon; many had never been in London before; and to me at least they were shadows that passed without any particular rhyme or reason across a white sheet. During the first year a certain number for one reason or another dropped out, and in the second year those that remained gained by degrees the beginnings of a personality. They were not only themselves, but the lectures one had attended with them, the scone and coffee one had eaten at the same table for luncheon, the dissection one had done at the same board in the same dissecting room, and *The Belle of New York*, one had seen together from the pit of the Shaftesbury Theatre.

The boy brought the bottle of brandy and Grosely, if that was really his name, pouring himself out a generous helping drank it down at a gulp without water or soda.

'I couldn't stand doctoring,' he said, 'I chucked it. My people got fed up with me and I went out to China. They gave me a hundred pounds and told me to shift for myself. I was damned glad to get out, I can tell you. I guess I was just about as much fed up with them as they were with me. I haven't troubled them much since.'

Then from somewhere in the depths of my memory a faint hint crept into the rim, as it were, of consciousness, as on a rising tide the water slides up the sand and then withdraws to advance with the next wave in a fuller volume. I had first an inkling of some shabby little scandal that had got into the papers. Then I saw a boy's face, and so gradually the facts recurred to me; I remembered him now. I didn't believe he was called Grosely then, I think he had a one syllabled name, but that I was uncertain of. He was a very tall lad (I began to see him quite well) thin, with a slight stoop, he was only eighteen and had grown too fast for his strength, he had curly, shining brown hair, rather large features (they did not look so large now, perhaps because his face was fat and puffy) and a peculiarly fresh complexion, very pink and white, like a girl's. I imagine people, women especially, would have thought him a very handsome boy, but to us he was only a clumsy, shuffling lout. Then I remembered that he did not often come to lectures, no, it wasn't that I remembered, there were too many students in the theatre to recollect who was there and who wasn't. I remembered the dissecting room. He had a leg at the next table to the one I was working at and he hardly ever touched it; I forget why the men who had other parts of the body complained of his neglecting the work, I suppose somehow it interfered with them. In those days a good deal of gossip went on over the dissection of a 'part' and out of the distance of thirty years some of it came back to me. Someone started the story that Grosely was a very gay dog. He drank like a fish and was an awful womaniser. Most of those boys were very simple, and they had brought to the hospital the notions they had acquired at home and at school. Some were prudish and they were shocked; others, those who worked hard, sneered at him and asked how he could hope to pass his exams; but a good many were excited and impressed, he was doing what they would have liked to do if they had had the courage. Grosely had his admirers and you could often see him surrounded by a little band listening open-mouthed to stories of his adventures. Recollections now were crowding upon me. In a very little while he lost his shyness and assumed the airs of a man of the world. They must have looked absurd on this smooth-cheeked boy with his pink and white skin. Men (so they called themselves) used to tell one another of his escapades. He became quite a hero. He would make caustic remarks as he passed the museum and saw a pair of earnest students going over their anatomy together. He was at home in the public-houses of the neighbourhood and was on familiar terms with the barmaids. Looking back, I imagine that, newly arrived from the country and the tutelage of parents and schoolmasters, he was captivated by his freedom and the thrill of London. His dissipations were harmless enough. They were due only to the urge of youth. He lost his head.

But we were all very poor and we did not know how Grosely managed to pay for his garish amusements. We knew his father was a country doctor and I think we knew exactly how much he gave his son a month. It was not enough to pay for the harlots he picked up on the promenade at the Pavilion and for the drinks he stood his friends in the Criterion Bar. We told one another in awe-struck tones that he must be getting fearfully into debt. Of course he could pawn things, but we knew by experience that you could not get more than three pounds for a microscope and thirty shillings for a skeleton. We said he must be spending at least ten pounds a week. Our ideas were not very grand and this seemed to us the wildest pitch of extravagance. At last one of his friends disclosed the mystery: Grosely had discovered a wonderful system for making money. It amused and impressed us. None of us would have thought of anything so ingenious or have had the nerve to attempt it if he had. Grosely went to auctions, not Christie's, of course, but auctions in the Strand and Oxford Street, and in private houses, and bought anything portable that was going cheap. Then he took his purchase to a pawnbroker's and pawned it for ten shillings or a pound more than he had paid. He was making money, four or five pounds a week, and he said he was going to give up medicine and make a regular business of it. Not one of us had ever made a penny in his life and we regarded Grosely with admiration.

'By Jove, he's clever,' we said.

'He's just about as sharp as they make them.'

'That's the sort that ends up as a millionaire.'

We were all very worldly-wise and what we didn't know about life at eighteen we were pretty sure wasn't worth knowing. It was a pity that when an examiner asked us a question we were so nervous that the answer often flew straight out of our head and when a nurse asked us to post a letter we blushed scarlet. It became known that the Dean had sent for Grosely and hauled him over the coals. He had threatened him with sundry penalties if he continued systematically to neglect his work. Grosely was indignant. He'd had enough of that sort of thing at school, he said, he wasn't going to let a horse-faced eunuch treat him like a boy. Damn it all, he was getting on for nineteen and there wasn't much you could teach him. The Dean had said he heard he was drinking more than was good for him. Damned cheek. He could carry his liquor as well as any man of his age, he'd been blind last Saturday and he meant to get blind next Saturday, and if anyone didn't like it he could do the other thing. Grosely's friends quite agreed with him that a man couldn't let himself be insulted like that.

But the blow fell at last and now I remembered quite well the shock it gave us all. I suppose we had not seen Grosely for two or three days, but he had been in the habit of coming to the hospital more and more irregularly, so if we thought anything about it, I imagine we merely said that he was off on one of his bats. He would turn up again in a day or so, rather pale, but with a wonderful story of some girl he had picked up and the time he had had with her. The anatomy lecture was at nine in the morning and it was a rush to get there in time. On this particular day little attention was paid to the lecturer who, with a visible pleasure in his limpid English and admirable elocution, was describing I know not what part of the human skeleton, for there was much excited whispering along the benches and a newspaper was surreptitiously passed from hand to hand. Suddenly the lecturer stopped. He had a pedagogic sarcasm. He affected not to know the names of his students.

'I am afraid I am disturbing the gentleman who is reading the paper. Anatomy is a very tedious science and I regret that the regulations of the Royal College of Surgeons oblige me to ask you to give it enough of your attention to pass an examination in it. Any gentleman, however, who finds this impossible is at liberty to continue his perusal of the paper outside.'

The wretched boy to whom this reproof was addressed reddened to the roots of his hair and in his embarrassment tried to stuff the newspaper in his pocket. The professor of anatomy observed him coldly.

'I am afraid, sir, that the paper is a little too large to go into your pocket,' he remarked. 'Perhaps you would be good enough to hand it down to me?'

The newspaper was passed from row to row to the well of the theatre, and, not content with the confusion to which he had put the poor lad, the eminent surgeon, taking it, asked:

'May I enquire what it is in the paper that the gentleman in question found of such absorbing interest?'

The student who gave it to him without a word pointed out the paragraph that we had all been reading. The professor read it and we watched him in silence. He put the paper down and went on with his lecture. The headline ran *Arrest of a Medical Student*. Grosely had been brought before the police-court magistrate for getting goods on credit and pawning them. It appears that this is an indictable offence and the magistrate had remanded him for a week. Bail was refused. It looked as though his method of making money by buying things at auctions and pawning them had not in the long run proved as steady a source of income as he expected and he had found it more profitable to pawn things that he was not at the expense of paying for. We talked the matter over excitedly as soon as the lecture was over and I am bound to say that, having no property ourselves, so deficient was our sense of its sanctity we could none of us look upon his crime as a very serious one; but with the natural love of the young for the terrible there were few who did not think he would get anything from two years hard labour to seven years penal servitude.

I do not know why, but I did not seem to have any recollection of what happened to Grosely. I think he may have been arrested towards the end of a session and his case may have come on again when we had all separated for holidays. I did not know if it was disposed of by the police-court magistrate or whether it went up for trial. I had a sort of feeling that he was sentenced to a short term of imprisonment, six weeks perhaps, for his operations had been pretty extensive; but I knew that he had vanished from our midst and in a little while was thought of no more. It was strange to me that after all these years I should recollect so much of the incident so clearly. It was as though, turning over an album of old snapshots, I saw all at once the photographs of a scene I had quite forgotten.

But of course in that gross elderly man with grey hair and mottled red face I should never have recognised the lanky pink-cheeked boy. He looked sixty, but I knew he must be much less than that. I wondered what he had done with himself in the intervening time. It did not look as though he had excessively prospered.

'What were you doing in China?' I asked him.

'I was a tide-waiter.'

'Oh, were you?'

It is not a position of great importance and I took care to keep out of my tone any note of surprise. The tide-waiters are employees of the Chinese customs whose duty it is to board the ships and junks at the various treaty ports and I think their chief business is to prevent opium-smuggling. They are mostly retired ABs from the Royal Navy and non-commissioned officers who have finished their time. I have seen them come on board at various places up the Yangtze. They hobnob with the pilot and the engineer, but the skipper is a trifle curt with them. They learn to speak Chinese more fluently than most Europeans and often marry Chinese women.

'When I left England I swore I wouldn't go back till I'd made my pile. And I never did. They were glad enough to get anyone to be a tide-waiter in those days, any white man I mean, and they didn't ask any questions. They didn't care who you were. I was damned glad to get the job, I can tell you, I was about broke to the wide when they took me on. I only took it till I could get something better, but I stayed on, it suited me, I wanted to make money and I found out that a tide-waiter could make a packet if he knew the right way to go about. I was with the Chinese customs for the best part of twenty-five years and when I came away I wouldn't mind betting that lots of commissioners would have been glad to have the money I had.'

He gave me a sly, mean look. I had an inkling of what he meant. But there was a point on which I was willing to be reassured; if he was going to ask me for a hundred piastres (I was resigned to that sum now) I thought I might just as well take the blow at once.

'I hope you kept it,' I said.

'You bet I did. I invested all my money in Shanghai and when I left China I put it all in American railway bonds. Safety first is my motto. I know too much about crooks to take any risks myself.'

I liked that remark, so I asked him if he wouldn't stay and have luncheon with me.

'No, I don't think I will. I don't eat much tiffin and anyway my chow's waiting for me at home. I think I'll be getting along.' He got up and he towered over me. 'But look here, why don't you come along this evening and see my place? I've married a Haiphong girl. Got a baby too. It's not often I get a chance of talking to anyone about London. You'd better not come to dinner. We only eat native food and I don't suppose you'd care for that. Come along about nine, will you?'

'All right,' I said.

I had already told him that I was leaving Haiphong next day. He asked the boy to bring him a piece of paper so that he might write down his address. He wrote laboriously in the hand of a boy of fourteen.

'Tell the porter to explain to your rickshaw boy where it is. I'm on the second floor. There's no bell. Just knock. Well, see you later.'

He walked out and I went in to luncheon.

After dinner I called a rickshaw and with the porter's help made the boy understand where I wanted to go. I found presently that he was taking me along the curved canal the houses of which had looked to me so like a faded Victorian water-colour; he stopped at one of them and pointed to the door. It looked so shabby and the neighbourhood was so squalid that I hesitated, thinking he had made a mistake. It seemed unlikely that Grosely could live so far in the native quarter and in a house so bedraggled. I told the rickshaw boy to wait and pushing open the door saw a dark staircase in front me. There was no one about and the street was empty. It might have been the small hours of the morning. I struck a match and fumbled my way upstairs; on the second floor I struck another match and saw a large brown door in front of me. I knocked and in a moment it was opened by a little Tonkinese woman holding a candle. She was dressed in the earth-brown of the poorer classes, with a tight little black turban on her head; her lips and the skin round them were stained red with betel and when she opened her mouth to speak I saw that she had the black teeth and black gums that so disfigure these people. She said something in her native language and then I heard Grosely's voice:

'Come along in. I was beginning to think you weren't going to turn up.'

I passed through a little dark ante-chamber and entered a large room that evidently looked on the canal. Grosely was lying on a long chair and he raised his length from

195

it as I came in. He was reading the Hong-Kong papers by the light of a paraffin lamp that stood on a table by his side.

'Sit down', he said, 'and put your feet up.'

'There's no reaon I should take your chair.'

'Go on. I'll sit on this.'

He took a kitchen chair and sitting on it put his feet on the end of mine.

'That's my wife,' he said pointing with his thumb at the Tonkinese woman who had followed me into the room. 'And over there in the corner's the kid.'

I followed his eyes and against the wall, lying on bamboo mats and covered with a blanket, I saw a child sleeping.

'Lively little beggar when he's awake. I wish you could have seen him. She's going to have another soon.'

I glanced at her and the truth of what he said was apparent. She was very small, with tiny hands and feet, but her face was flat and the skin muddy. She looked sullen, but may only have been shy. She went out of the room and presently came back with a bottle of whisky, two glasses and a syphon. I looked round. There was a partition at the back of dark unpainted wood, which I suppose shut off another room, and pinned against the middle of this was a portrait cut out of an illustrated paper of John Galsworthy. He looked austere, mild and gentlemanly, and I wondered what he did there. The other walls were whitewashed, but the whitewash was dingy and stained. Pinned on to them were pages of pictures from *The Graphic* or *The Illustrated London News*.

'I put them up,' said Grosely, 'I thought they made the place look homelike.'

'What made you put up Galsworthy? Do you read his books?'

'No, I didn't know he wrote books. I liked his face.'

There were one or two torn and shabby rattan mats on the floor and in a corner a great pile of *The Hong-Kong*

Times. The only furniture consisted of a wash-hand stand, two or three kitchen chairs, a table or two and a large teak native bed. It was cheerless and sordid.

'Not a bad little place, is it?' said Grosely. 'Suits me all right. Sometimes I've thought of moving, but I don't suppose I ever shall now.' He gave a little chuckle. 'I came to Haiphong for forty-eight hours and I've been here five years. I was on my way to Shanghai really.'

He was silent. Having nothing to say I said nothing. Then the little Tonkinese woman made a remark to him, which I could not of course understand, and he answered her. He was silent again for a minute or two, but I thought he looked at me as though he wanted to ask me something. I did not know why he hesitated.

'Have you ever tried smoking opium on your travels in the East?' he enquired at last, casually.

'Yes, I did once, at Singapore. I thought I'd like to see what it was like.'

'What happened?'

'Nothing very thrilling to tell you the truth. I thought I was going to have the most exquisite emotions. I expected visions, like de Quincey's, you know. The only thing I felt was a kind of physical well-being, the same sort of feeling that you get when you've had a Turkish bath and are lying in the cooling room, and then a peculiar activity of mind so that everything I thought of seemed extremely clear.'

'I know.'

'I really felt that two and two are four and there could not be the smallest doubt about that. But next morning – oh God! My head reeled. I was as sick as a dog, I was sick all day, I vomited my soul out, and as I vomited I said to myself miserably: And there are people who call this fun.'

Grosely leaned back in his chair and gave a low mirthless laugh.

'I expect it was bad stuff. Or you went at it too hard.

197

They saw you were a mug and gave you dregs that had been smoked already. They're enough to turn anybody up. Would you like to have another try now? I've some stuff here that I know's good.'

'No, I think once was enough for me.'

'D'you mind if I have a pipe or two? You want it in a climate like this. It keeps you from getting dysentery. And I generally have a bit of a smoke about this time.'

'Go ahead,' I said.

He spoke again to the woman and she, raising her voice, called out something in a raucous tone. An answer came from the room behind the wooden partition and after a minute or two an old woman came out carrying a little round tray. She was shrivelled and old and when she entered gave me an ingratiating smile of her stained mouth. Grosely got up and crossed over to the bed and lay on it. The old woman set the tray down on the bed; on it was a spirit lamp, a pipe, a long needle and a little round box of opium. She squatted on the bed and Grosely's wife got on it too and sat, her feet tucked up under her, with her back against the wall. Grosely watched the old woman while she put a little pellet of the drug on the needle, held it over the flame till it sizzled and then plugged it into the pipe. She handed it to him and with a great breath he inhaled it, he held the smoke for a little while and then blew it out in a thick grey cloud. He handed her back the pipe and she started to make another. Nobody spoke. He smoked three pipes in succession and then sank back.

'By George, I feel better now. I was feeling all in. She makes a wonderful pipe, this old hag. Are you sure you won't have one?'

'Quite.'

'Please yourself. Have some tea then.'

He spoke to his wife who scrambled off the bed and went out of the room. Presently she came back with a little china pot of tea and a couple of Chinese bowls.

198

'A lot of people smoke here, you know. It does you no harm if you don't do it to excess. I never smoke more than twenty to twenty-five pipes a day. You can go on for years if you limit yourself to that. Some of the Frenchmen smoke as many as forty or fifty a day. That's too much. I never do that, except now and then when I feel I want a binge. I'm bound to say it's never done me any harm.'

We drank our tea, pale and vaguely scented and clean on the palate. Then the old woman made him another pipe and then another. His wife had got back on to the bed and soon curling herself up at his feet went to sleep. Grosely smoked two or three pipes at a time, and while he was smoking seemed intent upon nothing else, but in the intervals he was loquacious. Several times I suggested going, but he would not let me. The hours wore on. Once or twice while he smoked I dozed. He told me all about himself. He went on and on. I spoke only to give him a cue. I cannot relate what he told me in his own words. He repeated himself. He was very long-winded and he told me his story confusedly, first a late bit, then an early bit, so that I had to arrange the sequence for myself; sometimes I saw that, afraid he had said too much, he held something back; sometimes he lied and I had to make a guess at the truth from the smile he gave me or the look in his eyes. He had not the words to describe what he had felt, and I had to conjecture his meaning from slangy metaphors and hackneyed, vulgar phrases. I kept on asking myself what his real name was, it was on the tip of my tongue and it irritated me not to be able to recall it, though why it should in the least matter to me I did not know. He was somewhat suspicious of me at first and I saw this escapade of his in London and his imprisonment had been all these years a tormenting secret. He had always been haunted by the fear that sooner or later someone would find out.

'It's funny that even now you shouldn't remember me

at the hospital,' he said, looking at me shrewdly. 'You must have a rotten memory.'

'Hang it all, it's nearly thirty years ago. Think of the thousands of people I've met since then. There's no reason why I should remember you any more than you remember me.'

'That's right. I don't suppose there is.'

It seemed to reassure him. At last he had smoked enough and the old woman made herself a pipe and smoked it. Then she went over to the mat on which the child was lying and huddled down beside it. She lay so still that I supposed she had fallen directly asleep. When at last I went I found my boy curled up on the foot-board of the rickshaw in so deep a slumber that I had to shake him. I knew where I was and I wanted air and exercise, so I gave him a couple of piastres and told him I would walk.

It was a strange story I carried away with me.

It was with a sort of horror that I had listened to Grosely, telling me of those twenty years he had spent in China. He had made money, I do not know how much, but from the way he talked I should think something between fifteen and twenty thousand pounds, and for a tide-waiter it was a fortune. He could not have come by it honestly, and little as I knew of the details of his trade, by his sudden reticences, by his leers and hints I guessed that there was no base transaction that, if it was made worth his while, he jibbed at. I suppose that nothing paid him better than smuggling opium, and his position gave him the opportunity to do this with safety and profit. I understood that his superior officers had often had their suspicions of him, but had never been able to get such proof of his malpractices as to justify them in taking any steps. They contented themselves with moving him from one port to another, but that did not disturb him; they watched him, but he was too clever for them. I saw that he was divided between the fear of telling me too much to his discredit and the desire to boast of his own astuteness. He prided himself on the confidence the Chinese had placed in him.

'They knew they could trust me,' he said, 'and it gave me a pull. I never double-crossed a Chinaman once.'

The thought filled him with the complacency of the honest man. The Chinese discovered that he was keen on curios and they got in the habit of giving him bits or bringing him things to buy; he never made enquiries how they had come by them and he bought them cheap. When he had got a good lot he sent them to Peking and sold them at a handsome profit. I remembered how he had started his commercial career by buying things at auctions and pawning them. For twenty years by shabby shift and petty dishonesty he added pound to pound, and everything he made he invested in Shanghai. He lived penuriously, saving half his pay; he never went on leave because he did not want to waste his money, he would not have anything to do with the Chinese women, he wanted to keep himself free from entanglement; he did not drink. He was consumed by one ambition, to save enough to be able to go back to England and live the life from which he had been snatched as a boy. That was the only thing he wanted. He lived in China as though in a dream; he paid no attention to the life around him; its colour and strangeness, its possibilities of pleasure, meant nothing to him. There was always before him the mirage of London, the Criterion Bar, himself standing with his foot on the rail, the promenade at the Empire and the Pavilion, the picked-up harlot, the serio-comic at the music hall and the musical comedy at the Gaiety. This was life and love and adventure. This was romance. This was what he yearned for with all his heart. There was surely something impressive in the way in which during all those years he had lived like an anchorite with that one end in view of leading again a life that was so vulgar. It showed character.

'You see,' he said to me, 'even if I'd been able to get back to England on leave I wouldn't have gone. I didn't want to go till I could go for good. And then I wanted to do the thing in style.'

He saw himself putting on evening clothes every night and going out with a gardenia in his buttonhole, and he saw himself going to the Derby in a long coat and a brown hat and a pair of opera glasses slung over his shoulder. He saw himself giving the girls a look over and picking out the one he fancied. He made up his mind that on the night he arrived in London he would get blind, he hadn't been drunk for twenty years; he couldn't afford to in his job, you had to keep your wits about you. He'd take care not to get drunk on the ship on the way home. He'd wait till he got to London. What a night he'd have! He thought of it for twenty years.

I do not know why Grosely left the Chinese customs, whether the place was getting too hot for him, whether he had reached the end of his service or whether he had amassed the sum he had fixed. But at last he sailed. He went second class; he did not intend to start spending money till he reached London. He took rooms in Jermyn Street, he had always wanted to live there, and he went straight to a tailor's and ordered himself an outfit. Slap up. Then he had a look round the town. It was different from how he remembered it, there was much more traffic and he felt confused and a little at sea. He went to the Criterion and found there was no longer a bar where he had been used to lounge and drink. There was a restaurant in Leicester Square where he had been in the habit of dining when he was in funds, but he could not find it; he supposed it had been torn down. He went to the Pavilion, but there were no women there; he was rather disgusted and went on to the Empire, he found they had done away with the Promenade. It was rather a blow. He could not quite make it out. Well, anyhow, he must be prepared for changes in twenty years, and if he couldn't do anything else he could get drunk. He had had fever several times in China and the change of climate had brought it on again, he wasn't feeling any too well, and after four or five drinks he was glad to go to bed.

That first day was only a sample of many that followed it. Everything went wrong. Grosely's voice grew peevish and bitter as he told me how one thing and another had failed him. The old places were gone, the people were different, he found it hard to make friends, he was strangely lonely; he had never expected that in a great city like London. That's what was wrong with it, London had become too big, it wasn't the jolly, intimate place it had been in the early nineties. It had gone to pieces. He picked up a few girls, but they weren't as nice as the girls he had known before, they weren't the fun they used to be, and he grew dimly conscious that they thought him a rum sort of cove. He was only just over forty and they looked upon him as an old man. When he tried to cotton on to a lot of young fellows standing round a bar they gave him the cold shoulder. Anyway, these young fellows didn't know how to drink. He'd show them. He got soused every night, it was the only thing to do in that damned place, but, by Jove, it made him feel rotten next day. He supposed it was the climate of China. When he was a medical student he could drink a bottle of whisky every night and be as fresh as a daisy in the morning. He began to think more about China. All sorts of things that he never knew he had noticed came back to him. It wasn't a bad life he'd led there. Perhaps he'd been a fool to keep away from those Chinese girls, they were pretty little things some of them, and they didn't put on the airs these English girls did. One could have a damned good time in China if one had the money he had. One could keep a Chinese girl and get into the club, and there'd be a lot of nice fellows to drink with and play bridge with and billiards. He remembered the Chinese shops and all the row in the streets and the coolies carrying loads and the ports with the junks in them and the rivers with pagodas on the banks. It was funny, he never thought much of China while he was there and now – well, he couldn't get it out of his mind. It obsessed him. He began to think that London was no place for a white man. It had just gone to the dogs, that was the long and short of it, and one day the thought came to him that perhaps it would be a good thing if he went back to China. Of course it was silly, he'd worked like a slave for twenty years to be able to have a good time in London, and it was absurd to go and live in China. With his money he ought to be able to have a good time anywhere. But somehow he couldn't think of anything else but China. One day he went to the pictures and saw a scene at Shanghai. That settled it. He was fed up with London. He hated it. He was going to get out and this time he'd get out for good. He had been home a year and a half, and it seemed longer to him than all his twenty years in the East. He took a passge on a French boat sailing from Marseilles, and when he saw the coast of Europe sink into the sea he heaved a great sigh of relief. When they got to Suez and he felt the first touch of the East he knew he had done the right thing. Europe was finished. The East was the only place.

He went ashore at Djibouti and again at Colombo and Singapore, but though the ship stopped for two days at Saïgon he remained on board there. He'd been drinking a good deal and he was feeling a bit under the weather. But when they reached Haiphong, where they were staying for forty-eight hours, he thought he might just as well have a look at it. That was the last stopping-place before they got to China. He was bound for Shanghai. When he got there he meant to go to a hotel and look around a bit and then get hold of a girl and a place of his own. He would buy a pony or two and race. He'd soon make friends. In the East they weren't so stiff and standoffish as they were in London. Going ashore, he dined at the hotel and after dinner got into a rickshaw and told the boy he wanted a woman. The boy took him to the shabby tenement in which I had sat for so many hours and there were the old woman and the girl who was now the mother of his child. After a while the old woman asked him if he wouldn't like to smoke. He had never tried opium, he had always been frightened of it, but now he didn't see why he shouldn't have a go. He was feeling good that night and the girl was a jolly cuddlesome little thing; she was rather like a Chinese girl, small and pretty, like an idol. Well, he had a pipe or two, and he began to feel very happy and comfortable. He stayed all night. He didn't sleep. He just lay, feeling very restful, and thought about things.

'I stopped there till my ship went on to Hong-Kong,' he said. 'And when she left I just stopped on.'

'How about your luggage?' I asked.

For I am perhaps unworthily interested in the manner people combine practical details with the ideal aspects of life. When in a novel penniless lovers drive in a long, swift racing car over the distant hills I have always a desire to know how they managed to pay for it; and I have often asked myself how the characters of Henry James in the intervals of subtly examining their situation coped with the physiological necessities of their bodies.

'I only had a trunk full of clothes, I was never one to want much more than I stood up in, and I went down with the girl in a rickshaw to fetch it. I only meant to stay on till the next boat came through. You see, I was so near China here I thought I'd wait a bit and get used to things if you understand what I mean, before I went on.'

I did. Those last words of his revealed him to me. I knew that on the threshold of China his courage had failed him. England had been such a terrible disappointment that now he was afraid to put China to the test too.

If that failed him he had nothing. For years England had been like a mirage in the desert, but when he had yielded to the attraction, those shining pools and the palm-trees and the green grass were nothing but the rolling sandy dunes. He had China, and so long as he never saw it again he kept it.

'Somehow I stayed on. You know, you'd be surprised how quickly the days pass. I don't seem to have time to do half the things I want to. After all I'm comfortable here. The old woman makes a damned good pipe, and she's a jolly little girl, my girl, and then there's the kid. A lively young beggar. If you're happy somewhere what's the good of going somewhere else?'

'And are you happy here?' I asked him.

I looked round that large bare sordid room. There was no comfort in it and not one of the little personal things that one would have thought might have given him the feeling of home. Grosely had taken on this equivocal little apartment, which served as a house of assignation and as a place for Europeans to smoke opium in, with the old woman who kept it, just as it was, and he camped, rather than lived, there still as though next day he would pack his traps and go. After a little while he answered my question.

'I've never been so happy in my life. I often think I'll go on to Shanghai some day, but I don't suppose I ever shall. And God knows, I never want to see England again.'

'Aren't you awfully lonely sometimes for people to talk to?'

'No. Sometimes a Chinese tramp comes in with an English skipper or a Scotch engineer, and then I go on board and we have a talk about old times. There's an old fellow here, a Frenchman who was in the customs, and he speaks English; I go and see him sometimes. But the fact is I don't want anybody very much. I think a lot. It gets on my nerves when people come between me and my thoughts. I'm not a big smoker, you know, I just have a pipe or two in the morning to settle my stomach, but I don't really smoke till night. Then I think.'

'What d'you think about?'

'Oh, all sorts of things. Sometimes about London and what it was like when I was a boy. But mostly about China. I think of the good times I had and the way I made my money, and I remember the fellows I used to know, and the Chinese. I had some narrow squeaks now and then, but I always came through all right. And I wonder what the girls would have been like that I might have had. Pretty little things. I'm sorry now I didn't keep one or two. It's a great country, China; I love those shops, with an old fellow sitting on his heels smoking a water-pipe, and all the shop-signs. And the temples. By George, that's the place for a man to live in. There's life.'

The mirage shone before his eyes. The illusion held him. He was happy. I wondered what would be his end. Well, that was not yet. For the first time in his life perhaps he held the present in his hand.

XLIV

I took a shabby little steamer from Haiphong to Hong-Kong, which ran along the coast stopping at various French ports on the way to take on and discharge cargo. It was very old and dirty. There were but three passengers beside myself. Two were French missionaries bound for the island of Hainan. One was an elderly man with a large square grey beard and the other was young, with a round red face on which his beard grew in little black patches. They spent most of the day reading their breviaries and the younger one studied Chinese. Then there was an American Jew called Elfenbein who was travelling in hosiery. He was a tall fellow, powerfully built and strong, clumsy of gesture, with a long sallow face, a big straight nose and dark eyes. His voice was loud and strident. He was aggressive and irascible. He abused the ship, he abused the steward, he abused the boys, he abused the food. Nothing satisfied him. All the time you heard his voice raised in anger because his boxes of show goods were not placed as they should be, because he couldn't get a hot bath, because the soda water wasn't cold enough. He was a man with a chip on his shoulder. Everyone seemed in a conspiracy to slight or injure him and he kept threatening to give the captain or the steward a hit on the nose. Because I was the only person on board who spoke English he attached himself to me and I could not settle down on deck for five minutes without his coming to sit by me and telling me his latest grievance. He forced drinks on me which I did not want, and when I refused, cried: Oh, come on, be a sport, and ordered them notwithstanding. To my confusion he addressed me constantly as brother. He was odious, but I must admit that he was often amusing; he would tell damaging stories about his fellow Jews in a racy idiom that made them very entertaining. He talked interminably. He hated to be alone for a minute and it never occurred to him that you might not want his company; but when he was with you he was perpetually on the look out for affronts. He trod heavily on your corns and if you tucked your feet out of the way thought you insulted him. It made his society excessively fatiguing. He was the kind of Jew who made you understand the pogrom. I told him a little story about the peace conference. It appears that on one occasion Monsieur Paderewski was pressing upon Mr Wilson, Mr Lloyd George and Monsieur Clemenceau the Polish claims on Danzig.

'If the Poles do not get it,' he said, 'I warn you that their disappointment will be so great, there will be an outbreak and they will assassinate the Jews.'

Mr Wilson looked grave, Mr Lloyd George shook his head and M. Clemenceau frowned.

'But what will happen if the Poles get Danzig?' asked Mr Wilson.

M Paderweski brightened. He shook his leonine mane.

'Ah, that will be quite another thing,' he replied. 'Their enthusiasm will be so great there will be an outbreak and they will assassinate the Jews.'

Elfenbein saw nothing funny in it.

'Europe's no good,' he said. 'If I had my way I'd sink the whole of Europe under the sea.'

Then I told him about Henri Deplis. He was by birth a native of the Grand Duchy of Luxemburg. On maturer reflection he became a commercial traveller. This did not amuse him either, so with a sigh for Saki's sake I desisted. We must accept with resignation the opinion of the hundred per cent American that the English have no sense of humour.

At meal times the captain sat at the head of the table, and two priests on one side of him and Elfenbein and I on the other.

The captain, a jovial little grey-headed man from Bordeaux, was retiring at the end of the year to make his own wine in his own vineyard.

'*Je vous enverrai un fût, mon père,*' he promised the elderly priest.

Elfenbein spoke fluent and bad French. He seized the conversation and held it. Pep, that's what he'd got. The Frenchmen were polite to him, but it was not hard to see that they heartily disliked him. Many of his remarks were singularly tactless, and when he used obscene language in addressing the boy who was serving us, the priests looked down their noses and pretended not to hear. But Elfenbein was argumentative, and at one luncheon began to talk of religion. He made a number of observations upon the Catholic faith which were certainly not in good taste. The younger priest flushed and was about to make some observation, when the elder said something to him in an undertone and he held his tongue. But when Elfenbein addressed a direct question to him the old man answered him mildly.

'There is no compulsion in these matters. Everyone is at liberty to believe what he pleases.'

Elfenbein made a long tirade, but it was received in silence. He was not abashed. He told me afterwards that they couldn't answer his arguments.

'I don't think they chose to,' I said. 'I imagine they merely thought you a very rude, vulgar and ill-mannered fellow.'

'Me?' he cried in astonishment.

'They are perfectly inoffensive and they have devoted their lives to what they think is the service of God, why should you gratuitously insult them?'

'I wasn't insultin' them. I was only puttin' my point of view as a rational man. I wanted to start an argument. D'you think I've hurt their feelings? Why, I wouldn't do that for the world, brother.'

His surprise was so ingenuous that I laughed.

'You've sneered at what they look upon as most holy. They probably think you're a very ignorant and uneducated man; otherwise I fancy they'd think you were trying deliberately to insult them.'

His face fell. I really think he was under the impression that he had been pleasantly facetious. He looked at the old priest who was sitting in a corner reading his breviary and went up to him.

'Father, my friend here says I hurt your feelings by what I said. I hadn't any wish to do no such thing. I beg you to pardon me if I said anythin' to offend you.'

The priest looked up and smiled.

'Do not mention it, monsieur, it was of no consequence.'

'I guess I must make up somehow, father, and if you'll allow me I'd like to make a contribution to your fund for the poor. I've got a lot of piastres that I didn't have time to change at Haiphong and if you'll accept them you'll be doin' me a favour.'

Before the priest could answer he had pulled out of his trouser pocket a wad of notes and a handful of silver and put them down on the table.

'But that is very kind of you,' said the priest. 'This is a large sum.'

'Take it, it's no good to me, I should only lose on the exchange if I turned it into real money at Hong-Kong. You'll do me a favour by takin' it.'

It was really a considerable amount and the priest looked at it with some embarrassment.

'Our mission is very poor. We shall be extremely grateful. I hardly know how to thank you. I don't know what I can do.'

'Well, I'm an atheist, father, but if you like to remember me in your prayers next time you say them I guess it won't harm me any an' if you'd add the name of my mother Rachel Obermeyer Kahanski I reckon we'd be about even-stephen.'

Elfenbein lumbered back to the table at the end of which I was sitting, drinking a glass of brandy with my coffee.

'I made it all right with him. Least I could do, wasn't it? Listen, brother, I've got quite an assortment of men's garters in one of my trunks. You come along down to my stateroom and I'll give you a dozen pairs.'

His round took him from Batavia to Yokohama and he had been travelling now for one firm now for another for twenty years.

'Tell me,' I said now, 'you must have known an awful lot of people, what opinion have you formed of the human race?'

'Sure I'll tell you. I think they're bully. You'd be surprised at the kindness I've received from everybody. If you're ill or anythin' like that, perfect strangers will nurse you like your own mother. White, yellow, or brown they're all alike. It's surprisin' what they'll do for you. But they're stupid, they're terribly stupid. They've got no more brains than a turnip. They can't even tell you the way in their own home town. I'll give you my opinion of the human race in a nutshell, brother; their heart's in the right place, but their head's a thoroughly inefficient organ.'

This really is the end of this book.

penguin.co.uk/vintage